Rain of Scorpions
and Other Stories

Bilingual Press/Editorial Bilingüe

General Editor
    Gary D. Keller

Managing Editor
    Karen S. Van Hooft

Associate Editor
    Ann Waggoner Aken

Assistant Editor
    Linda St. George Thurston

Editorial Consultants
    Jennifer Hartfield Lawrence
    Janet Woolum

Editorial Board
    Juan Goytisolo
    Francisco Jiménez
    Eduardo Rivera
    Severo Sarduy
    Mario Vargas Llosa

Address:
Bilingual Review/Press
Hispanic Research Center
Arizona State University
Tempe, Arizona 85287
(602) 965-3867

Rain of Scorpions and Other Stories

Clásicos Chicanos/Chicano Classics 9

Estela Portillo Trambley

Bilingual Press/Editorial Bilingüe
TEMPE, ARIZONA

An earlier collection, *Rain of Scorpions and Other Writings,* the contents of which are substantially different from this volume, was published in 1975 by Tonatiuh-Quinto Sol. It contains earlier versions of the title novella and four of the stories included here.

ISBN 0-927534-28-2 (cloth)
ISBN 0-927534-29-0 (paper)

Library of Congress Cataloging-in-Publication Data

Trambley, Estela Portillo, 1936-
    Rain of scorpions and other stories / by Estela Portillo Trambley.
       p.   cm. — (Clásicos chicanos/Chicano classics ; 9)
    Includes bibliographical references.
    ISBN 0-927534-28-2 (cloth) : $24.00. — ISBN 0-927534-29-0 (paper)
: $14.00
    1. Mexican Americans—Fiction. I. Title. II. Series: Clásicos
chicanos ; 9.
PS3570.R3342R29   1992
813'.54—dc20   92-25450
                                                  CIP

Cover design by Kerry Curtis

Back cover photo by Achilles Studio

Acknowledgments
Partial funding provided by the Arizona Commission on the Arts through appropriations from the Arizona State Legislature; additional funding provided by a grant from the National Endowment for the Arts in Washington, D.C., a Federal agency.

About Clásicos Chicanos/Chicano Classics

The Clásicos Chicanos/Chicano Classics series is intended to ensure the long-term accessibility of deserving works of Chicano literature and culture that have become unavailable over the years or that are in imminent danger of becoming inaccessible. Each of the volumes in the series carries with it a scholarly apparatus that includes an extended introduction contextualizing the work within Chicano literature and a bibliography of the existent works by and about the author. The series is designed to be a vehicle that will help in the recuperation of Raza literary history, maintain the instruments of our culture in our own hands, and permit the continued experience and enjoyment of our literature by both present and future generations of readers and scholars.

Estela Portillo Trambley's *Rain of Scorpions and Other Writings* originally appeared in 1975; it was the first published book of short stories by a Chicana. Her fiction has been described as reflecting an uncompromising concern for the equality of women and their liberation from the antiquated social norms of present-day society. But Portillo Trambley does not stop with mere social protest. Several of her stories, including "Rain of Scorpions," cultivate the theme of the healing power of love between women and men and the ability of Chicano culture to serve as a bridge between the traditional and the new.

The collection was first published in Berkeley, California, by the venerable Tonatiuh International, the mother of nearly all Chicano literature of the period. However, it has been out of print for many years despite its overriding importance in American letters and, of course, to the Chicana/Chicano community.

The collection of stories published here differs significantly from the original book. All of the changes are the result of the author's revisions of the texts. The title novella and four of the stories have been substantially reworked, adding depth and subtlety to the plots and the characters alike. A few selections from the original book could not withstand Portillo Trambley's critical eye as it has developed since 1975 and therefore have been eliminated. In their place, four new stories are included. This new edition of *Rain of Scorpions and Other Stories* not only invites comparison with the original edition, it renews, replenishes, and expands the prose fiction of one of our most valuable and recognized writers.

G. D. Keller

To Bethany, my daughter,
and to my grandchildren:
Jonas, Simon, Arielle, Megan,
Tessa, Whitney, and Ashley

Contents

Crafting Other Visions: Estela Portillo Trambley's New *Rain of Scorpions*

Vernon E. Lattin
Brooklyn College
Patricia Hopkins
Arizona State University West

Estela Portillo Trambley is a fiction writer, playwright, poet, and essayist. Generally recognized as the first book of fiction published by a Chicana, *Rain of Scorpions and Other Writings* originally appeared in 1975. This revised version, published more than fifteen years later with a slightly altered title, attests to the author's growing importance in Chicano literature. This new edition also presents readers and literary critics a gold mine of special material in that it revises five of the 1975 stories and therefore invites comparisons.

Portillo Trambley's writing career began seriously after a reading spree in philosophy: Bergson, Jung, Jaspers, Nietzsche, and others. As she describes it,

> An idea for a book came to mind. It was about the creation of a new kind of utopia mating Eastern philosophy to Western pragmatism. I wrote 340 pages of a book that I titled *After Hierarchy*. When I finished it, I sent it to Eastern publishers. It was rightfully refused; it was a bad, bad book. I call it my "getting rid of the measles" book.[1]

This reading/writing spree was her escape from the pain of the death of her nine-month-old son, and it reflects a pattern in Portillo Trambley's writings: a mixture of pragmatism, idealism, and life's realities.

Estela Portillo was born in El Paso, Texas, on January 16, 1936. She was raised by her grandparents until the age of twelve, when she returned to live with her parents until she was married just after high school. Her stories assert the importance of grandparents and of family love. They also reflect her somewhat traditional early married

1

life. She describes this period as one where she "played a woman's role with great timidity and the usual illusions; always wanting much more . . . life always becomes a matter of priorities. Raising my family and working took most of my time."[2] Not surprisingly, several of her stories, such as "The Paris Gown" in this collection, deal with escape from oppressive relationships or male hierarchies.

Portillo Trambley earned a B.A. in English in 1956 from the University of Texas at El Paso; in 1978 she received an M.A. in English from the same university. She has earned her living in a variety of jobs with the El Paso public schools and the El Paso Technical Institute; she hosted *Cumbres*, a television cultural program, and worked as a drama instructor and producer at El Paso Community College.

During all this time, she has been writing and accumulating awards for her publications. Besides this collection, she has been recognized for her drama *The Day of the Swallows* (1971), her collection of plays *Sor Juana and Other Plays* (1983), and her novel *Trini* (1986). In 1972 Quinto Sol Publications awarded her the annual Quinto Sol Prize for literature, and her drama *Blacklight* was a second-place winner in the 1985 New York Shakespeare Festival's Hispanic American Playwrights' competition. Throughout the United States she is sought after to read from her works.

Estela Portillo Trambley's place within contemporary Chicano literature is well established. If we date the beginning of contemporary Chicano fiction with the novel *Pocho* (1959) and the great 1970s flowering of the novel with Rivera's ". . . y no se lo tragó la tierra" (1971), Anaya's *Bless Me, Ultima* (1972), Hinojosa-Smith's *Estampas del Valle y otras obras* (1973), and Candelaria's *Memories of the Alhambra* (1977), then Portillo Trambley's *Rain of Scorpions* (1975) should be seen as part of the flowering.

However, there are major distinctions between Portillo Trambley's work and the other early Chicano fiction. Pocho and the other early novels are dominated by the subjective quest for a new Chicano identity. They deal with young men seeking their identity as they mature. Richard Rubio, for example, is a Stephen Dedalus trying to free and find himself in order to become a writer. This quest for artistic freedom is part of the larger quest for self within a world that, especially for Chicanos, is often hostile. These early novels systematically expose the difference between a Chicano youth and the surrounding Anglo society. Antonio Márez in *Bless Me, Ultima* experiences the sadness of life when he is laughed at for eating his beans, while the unnamed protagonist of Rivera's novel has only unpleasant memories of being singled out as different. Oscar in *The Autobiography of a Brown Buffalo* is ridiculed when a schoolmate complains of his body odor; Oscar also sees himself as inferior to the blue-eyed girl who has rejected him. In these and other early works the authors capture the profound sense of alienation a Chicano feels in the United States. Some of the novels, such as *Macho!* (1973), *Peregrinos de Aztlán* (1974), and *El diablo en Texas* (1976), reflect more directly the constant physical and spiritual threat Chicanos face in a hostile Anglo world. The protagonist is generally male; the alienation, threats to identity, and violence most often come from a racist, dominant society.

Rain of Scorpions and Other Writings introduced a new dimension to Chicano fiction. It added not only the female voice and the feminist theme but also a different view of Chicano reality. Take the title story as an example. Portillo Trambley has rightly complained that most critics have ignored the novella "Rain of Scorpions":

> There have been many studies of *Rain of Scorpions*, but they all deal with the stories about women, and ignore the novella "Rain of Scorpions" because it is not about women's liberation. Most male teachers of Chicano literature will look at all the men before they'll tackle me. After all, I am just a woman. I hate to say that, especially about Chicano men, but we still have our closed doors and our own way of polarizing everything between men and women.[3]

"Rain of Scorpions" is more about bridges and healing than it is about alienation and a hostile world. This is true both of the 1975 original and this revised version. Portillo Trambley has said that Chicano literature is "a bridge between the old and the new, between the primitive and technological. The Chicano can cement tradition to changing trends; a restructuring toward universality; the new American, the cosmic man."[4] She is actually talking about "Rain of Scorpions."[5]

Although the novella is set in Smeltertown, a hellhole created by an industrial, Anglo society, it is more than a protest work. It tells of the healing of love between Fito and Lupe, of Papá At and his vision of the "green valley," and of the young boys who, seeking an ideal home for themselves and the other barrio dwellers, find that the green valley is not outside but rather inside themselves.

Portillo Trambley has revised the story significantly for the new edition. In the early version Fito develops his quixotic, abortive plan for the people to leave Smeltertown en masse to cause negative publicity that will force the city fathers to clean up the air and make Smeltertown a better place to live. In the new edition Portillo Trambley gives Fito's plan a more practical motivation: the company itself plans to evacuate the barrio residents to "offset lawsuits" and "scatter the evidence" of the longtime poisoning of the air; the people will be relocated "wherever," therefore breaking up the community. In urging the people to leave town on their own, Fito wants to embarrass the bosses and pressure them into providing one place where the whole community can be relocated. In this version Fito is seeking not only health but also wholeness for the community.

In the revised edition of the novella Portillo Trambley has also enhanced the stature of several characters. For example, in the early edition the old man Champurrado is a pathetic figure grieving for his lost wife as he drinks and waits for his body to die, his friends taking up collections to pay for his drinks. The narrator does not assign any special value to the old drunk. In the new version a more vital Champurrado appears, known for the gorditas and champurrados he makes and sells and for the miztamal he prepares for holy days at the church. He is an important part of the community: women push and shove around his cart, trying to buy his gorditas before they are gone. Fortified by drink and his shotgun, he vows to fight against the planned evacuation by ASARCO.

Portillo Trambley's most significant revisions in this new edition, however, relate to the women of the novella. In the 1975 story Lupe is a strange, eccentric young woman obsessed with Fito to the point that the reader is somewhat embarrassed for her. Although she has a high school education, reads a lot, and goes to concerts, libraries, and museums alone, she has made herself a servant to Fito, going to his house on the weekends to clean and cook for him. In a characteristic scene, she strokes Fito's head while he sits in his favorite chair. Lupe in the revised version is a stronger, more confident character. She has "made it to the university," where she excels in chemistry and plans to become a teacher. Although she loves Fito, she does not serve him; he comes over to breakfast, but the only time we see food going from her house to his, it is the grandmother, not Lupe, who takes it. In the 1975 novella, after being rescued from the mud, Lupe is delivered to Fito's house, where she agrees to stay. In the revised version, she returns to her grandmother's house, helps her grandmother clean out all the mud and scorpions, and gets the place back to normal. It is only then that, significantly, she herself decides that the time is right, "all things . . . in accord," and she goes to Fito's house of her own will.

In both editions Lupe, like Aeneas with his father, carries her abuelita on her back to escape the mud. However, like her granddaughter, the old woman gains stature in the new version of "Rain of Scorpions." In the earlier edition the narrator tells us little about the grandmother except that she spends most of her time in church or praying. She is a weak, helpless figure who draws energy from Lupe without seeming to contribute anything in return. However, in her longest addition to the story, Portillo Trambley has elaborated on the old woman's character, making her a nurturing, loving presence in Lupe's life—a woman who has found her salvation in hard work. Drawing a contrast between herself and her foremothers, this strong woman says, "I know my great-grandmother and my grandmother and my mother believed women were made to suffer. I do not believe it, my Lord!" (1992, p. 152). The ties between the two women assume depth and richness in the new edition, with Lupe deciding that she wants to be like her abuelita someday. As Lupe, the new generation of Chicana, moves forward, one step at a time, carrying the person who has taught her how to love, Portillo Trambley enunciates an evolutionary change: a mixture of the pragmatic and the idealistic, the old and the new. The new reality is internal, a vision of the self that transcends the hostile world. It is also a vision of a strong woman carrying a strong woman forward.

At the end of the novella not much has changed externally. The Chicanos will still be forced to leave, and most do not even believe that the boys have found the green valley. Yet, as Portillo Trambley says, "Gods play in full circle." The lives of the young boys and of Fito and Lupe have changed; they have found themselves, and there will be time to understand this inner change more fully in other journeys. Balance has been attained for the moment.

Portillo Trambley has been criticized for asserting this optimistic view of the Chicano world, some saying that her writings tend to ignore the conflicts of Chicano existence. Her response is that she does not "cop out," but that she sees a larger world view. Life is not limited to the hostilities that exist between Chicanos and Anglos or workers and bosses; life goes beyond these external conflicts. Nor is the quest of this novella the traditional quest of a young man to find himself: it is the larger human quest for peace, balance, an understanding and acceptance of the yin and yang of existence. The answer for the people of Smeltertown—find within yourself the peaceful place where you will belong—remains the central theme of the novella and is central to understanding Portillo Trambley's view of existence. Miguel understands this as "the wisdom beyond years to feel whole, to be a part of the earth, to believe in mysteries—for human beings could not know everything—to understand that every breathing being was a miracle, a green valley" (1992, p. 169).

This new edition of *Rain of Scorpions and Other Stories* includes eight short stories besides the title novella. Four of the eight stories have been rewritten from the first edition ("Pay the Criers," "The Paris Gown," "If It Weren't for the Honeysuckle," and "The Burning"). Four new stories ("Leaves," "Looking for God," "Village," and "La Yonfantayn") replace the remaining five original stories ("The Trees," "Pilgrimage," "Duende," "Recast," and "The Secret Room"). "The Paris Gown," the opening story of the 1975 edition, has been moved to the second spot, with "Pay the Criers" now opening the collection.

The four original stories all have feminist themes in that the main characters are strong, brave women with special gifts. "Pay the Criers" tells of a young wife who spends her life waiting on a lazy husband, Chucho. Juana seems to accept her role among the vanquished, while Chucho claims he has made a conscious choice to be free by avoiding work and responsibility. The main character of the story, however, is Refugio, Juana's mother, who lies dead in her bed at the beginning of the story. An earthy, vigorous woman with a voracious appetite for life, Refugio supported herself, Juana, and Chucho, but also managed to put aside a little money so she could have a grand funeral; these savings were often a source of contention between her and her son-in-law. Now Chucho connives to get the savings from Juana under the pretense that he will arrange for the funeral; of course, he spends everything on drink and women. However, the story does not end here. Chucho, returning home and regretting his dishonest deed, tries to compensate by burying the decaying body in the bitter winter cold and planting a cross to mark the grave. Before the burial he holds the old woman's body so that she can "see" the sunrise one more time, and he kisses her on the lips, declaring, "I love you, Refugio, for having lived" (1975, p. 40).

The basic outline of the plot is the same in both versions of the story, but Portillo Trambley has strengthened Chucho's motivation, character, and humanity in the new edition. The first part of the original story is dominated by Chucho's antipathy toward "the old dead bitch" and only hints that his hate was always mixed with love; therefore, when he returns home and remembers that her stinking body is still in the house, his remorse and grief surprise the reader. In the new version, however, the reader learns early in the story that Chucho and Refugio spent a lot of time together, drinking, talking, and laughing, to the point that Juana felt like an outsider. Chucho's subsequent contrition and outpouring of emotion toward his dead mother-in-law ring much truer in the revised story.

One of the new details the author has added to the Chucho-Refugio relationship is the clown that appears several times in the story. The early version contains only one reference to a clown: "Clowns must be because the world sometimes does not see" (1975, p. 40). In the later edition, however, this seed of an idea turns into a life-size, straw-filled man that Chucho gives to Refugio; after a night of drinking, Juana finds her husband and mother asleep with their arms around the clown. Chucho later tells his friend Chapo that he gave the clown to his mother-in-law so she would have "something to hug at night, after a few drinks" (1992, p. 33). He also admits to Chapo that, although he had never acted on his feelings, he did have "desires" toward his mother-in-law. That the straw-filled man is where Refugio has concealed her life's savings enhances the sexual/monetary aura surrounding the old woman throughout the new version of the story.

This Chucho is a more sympathetic character than the Chucho of the original story. The early Chucho strikes Juana when she tries to get the money from him, but the later story has no such violence. In the early story Chucho and Chapo spend part of Refugio's money in a bordello not long after Chucho has made love to Juana; the narrator tells us that the women were "most splendid and companionable." In the revision, Chucho insists to the madam that when he and his friend visited her establishment, they spent money only to see the show. In a significant addition to the plot, which enhances the characters of both Refugio and Chucho, the narrator reveals that Chucho helped Refugio carry out a godlike plan when she filled in a large hole near the junkyard, built an adobe house on the land she had created, and planted and tended the trees in this "Garden of Eden." When, in the second version, the landlord gives the land to Refugio posthumously, Chucho hints that he is a changed person by insisting that he does not plan to use the property for monetary gain. "The deed belongs to Refugio. It is her land now" (1992, p. 26). The more sensitive Chucho of the revised story is also capable of understanding how special women are: ". . . she understood how precious life was. We men are a bad lot, Chapo. Women are much better creatures" (1992, p. 33).

This sentiment about the relative value of men and women appears also in the other revised stories of the new edition. "The Paris Gown" has been modified extensively, but the strong feminist presentation of a woman's escape from male hierarchies remains. The story has one of Portillo Trambley's most exciting heroines, Clotilde, a "liberated" woman who was raised in Mexico at a time when women had few possibilities and who seized her freedom by daring to come down the stairs naked during the party given to announce her arranged marriage to a repulsive elderly man. The idea for the plan to escape the marriage had come to Clo while she was watching a child playing in her father's symmetrical, manicured garden. In this patterned world the child spontaneously removed his clothes and waded into the pond, prompting a spanking from his nurse. Clo saw in this event a model for her escape. After she comes down the stairs naked, her father sends her to Paris, where she becomes a sophisticated woman of the world in control of her life and with a strong hope that others can know a similar freedom. Knowing that "For thousands of years men have believed themselves superior to women" (1992, p. 40), she has created a world beyond tradition, a world that allows for freedom. She has created a romantic garden where "flowers grew like surprises" and where there are stone paths leading to nowhere in particular.

Although both versions of "The Paris Gown" have the same theme, the revision offers some riches not found in the original. The new version introduces the striking observation that "Each generation has its dead ends for women" (1992, pp. 39-40), a statement binding Clotilde to her granddaughter, Teresa, who is trying to understand her own need to escape from tradition and male domination. The new version also introduces the concept of the "solitary journey," Clotilde's lonely, difficult trip to freedom. A reader familiar with the original story will be pleased to discover a new character mentioned in the revised version. Although she does not know where he is at the moment, Clotilde sometimes shares her Paris life with a man who "knows the pricelessness of our aloneness" (1992, p. 41), who knows that a solitary journey is necessary "to find the heights of oneself." Relating to this emphasis on separateness is a new reference to Kahlil Gibran and his admonition to "let there be spaces in your togetherness" (1992, p. 41). Clotilde's last statement in the story is that the solitary journey is "all that matters."

Adding a good man to Clotilde's present life is only one of the ways Portillo Trambley has softened her indictment of men, although not of the patriarchal system, in "The Paris Gown." While in the new version Clotilde minces no words in attacking Don Ignacio, the old man who thought he could buy her ("What makes old, rich, doddering fools think they deserve a young wife?" 1992, p. 45), Clotilde treats her father more gently than in the original story. Whereas in the early version she says that she came to hate her father because he never recognized her accomplishments, in the revised story she simply says, "I did all things well, but I never heard a word of praise from my father" (1992, p. 42). In the new story Clo refers twice to "my poor darling father," and, looking back two generations, she compassionately says of him, "I will really never know the full extent of his distress, his shame" (1992, p. 46). Much of the rhetoric of Clotilde's comments about men in the early version ("blind to the equality of all life," "violence of men against women," "gross injustice"), has been muted; for example, in the original version her Paris gown is her "final revenge against the injustice of men" (1975, p. 7), while in the revised story she states, "I knew that what I intended to do would assure my freedom" (1992, p. 45). Although the total story testifies to Portillo Trambley's continued outrage that men often deny equality and freedom to women, careful readers will note that in the revised version the author has chosen the more artistic route of minimizing the explicit rhetoric and letting the story tell itself.

In "If It Weren't for the Honeysuckle" Portillo Trambley creates another woman who, like Clotilde, seizes her freedom through a daring act. Victimized since age fourteen by the dirty, abusive Robles, the peasant woman Beatriz is so disgusted by his plan to rape another young waif and so afraid that he will take from her the home she has built block by block with her own hands, that she knows she must act. She has suffered for many years, but, like the deep-rooted cottonwood trees that continue to live even though the river has dried up, Beatriz reaches deep down to a primitive, subterranean river within herself and finds strength to do what she has to do. The garden that she cultivates bears a deadly fruit, a mushroom that she uses to poison Robles, freeing herself and a younger "wife" Sofía, and sparing the fourteen-year-old Lucretia.

Beatriz does not feel that the murder is a sin but rather simply a way of ridding the world of weeds or dragons. When Beatriz was a child, her job was to take care of babies born while their mothers worked in the fields. So that the mother could continue working and the newborn baby would not die, it would be partially buried in cool sand under a shade tree. Beatriz would kill any scorpions that came near the baby. In a striking metaphor that reverberates all the way back through Beatriz's difficult life, she sees killing Robles to be like killing those scorpions. It is a natural response to the old injustices of the world where it had been "decreed that women should be posses-sions, slaves, pawns, in the hands of men with ways of beasts" (1975, p. 106). To Beatriz, Robles's death brings balance between growth and pruning and brings to chaos an order, even a sacred order. The women wrap Robles in sheets and place him gently in the earth under the honeysuckle where Beatriz found the mushrooms, "where a fairy ring had once grown," and his grave is described as an offering to a "god dressed in honeysuckle vines" (1975, p. 109). After the burial, Beatriz and Sofía go to church to meet Lucretia for rosary services. As in "Rain of Scorpions," balance has been re-stored, and the pagan and Christian exist side by side.

Like the other stories, "If It Weren't for the Honeysuckle" has been extensively revised for the new edition. It is now much longer, and most of the narration of the early version has been turned into dialogue. A more significant change is that an added subplot gives Beatriz a new dimension. She is not just a simple peasant woman but is someone who, even though she never went to school, has "read more books than all the people in the village, including the doctor" (1992, p. 56). Her house is full of books, and as Beatriz tells how she got the books, the reader learns that she has killed before. An old man who she had thought would help her had instead tricked and victimized her; when the old lecher had a heart attack while he was "playing like an idiot with [her] naked body" (1992, p. 63), she with-held his medicine from him. This earlier experience has strengthened Beatriz and for the reader makes it more believable that she could free herself and the other women from Robles. That the old Don Carlos was known as a "wise and learned man," very different from the ignorant, brutish Robles, is also significant: in the original story the oppression that Beatriz has to fight is confined to her own social class, but the new story makes it clear that uneducated peasant men do not have a monopoly on cruelty toward women.

At the same time, however, that Portillo Trambley has broadened the range of villainy, she has, as in "The Paris Gown," added to the new story a note of hope that good women will find good men to love. When Sofía questions whether there can be any good men in the world, Beatriz responds, "Oh, Sofía, there must be—somewhere" (1992, p. 69).

The main character of the fourth revised story, "The Burning," is another strong, unusual woman: Lela is an Indian healer, a curandera, who has lived a lonely existence in a Christian village that has been willing to accept her help but, because of her pagan beliefs, has never accepted her. The ironic plot presents two simultaneously unfolding events: as the women of the village decide to burn Lela as a witch, they do not know that she is dying inside her little hut, still full of love for the villagers she has served. While the women collect the wood for the fire, Lela, eager to go home to the goddess Ta Te, breathes her final, pagan wish: "Oh, find me a clean burning, a dying by fire, give my ashes to the wind, the destiny of all my fathers . . ." (1992, p. 79). The reader knows that the perverted Christian actions of the women will allow Lela's pagan wish to be fulfilled.

"The Burning" has been revised less extensively than the other stories. The plot has been somewhat simplified and clarified, the narrator now making clear why the women finally turn on Lela so ferociously: as an "act of love," she shaped a "little god" for each family and "reverently placed one on each doorstep." The early version only hints at this transgression. Both versions are, however, dominated by Lela's "little gods," which she seeks in the "glint of the sun," sees in the "crystal shine of rocks," and feels in the "breath of the wind" (1992, p. 74). When she gives them colorful clay forms, they are like humans: laughing, dancing, singing, and making love, unlike the Christian saints, "whose eyes saw only heaven." Reflecting their maker, their eyes have a "fierceness for life, a wonder for having life" (1992, p. 78), in contrast to the barrio women, whose minds are "a dark, narrow tunnel that had long ago withered their souls" (1992, p. 71).

The four new stories prepared for this edition of *Rain of Scorpions and Other Stories* replace five original stories. These new stories, which do not share the feminist motif of the other stories in the present collection, cluster around themes dealing with the loss of innocence, the reality of a cruel world, and the inner strength of human beings. Because all the stories have characters who have appeared in other works, the stories also introduce a new element of intertextuality into Portillo Trambley's writings.

"Looking for God," for example, a brief story about innocence and experience, features a young girl, Josefa, who as an older woman is the lesbian protagonist of Portillo Trambley's 1971 play, *The Day of the Swallows*. Before the action of the play begins, Doña Josefa has already committed the violent crime of cutting the tongue of a young boy who saw her and her young lover Alysea together. Trying to convince Alysea to stay with her rather than go out into the world with a man, Doña Josefa tells of the time she was initiated into evil as a child: when she tried to keep some boys from catching and killing swallows, the boys held her down, and one boy used a knife to cut a bird right over her, the blood spilling on her face and running into her mouth. Portillo Trambley has taken that brief sketch and turned it into a story. In the play Doña Josefa, who likens Alysea to the injured swallow she is taking care of, contrasts the protected life she can offer the young woman with the threats of life in the outside world; the story contrasts the protected innocence reigning inside the church, where the young girl's grandmother works, with the dusty outside world from which her grandmother wants to protect her, a world with rough barrio children "running, shouting, and spitting on the desert ground" (1992, p. 86). Josefa's escape from the church and into life destroys her innocence, the miracle of swallows dissolving into a nightmare of jeering boys, dead birds, spilled intestines, blood, and terror. After this experience Josefa feels alone in "the vastness of trees and lake"; the warm sun has changed to the cool moon; her alive body has become numb; she doubts that God is there.

The story adds to the reader's understanding of Doña Josefa's cruel act of cutting the tongue of the young boy, David: in trying to protect her haven with Alysea from the outside world, Doña Josefa is repeating the pattern of her grandmother's unsuccessful attempt to protect her in the story. Ironically, Doña Josefa's "protection" results in an act more cruel than that committed by the boys in the story.

The story helps us more fully to understand how her innocence has been perverted and her protection become destruction. In both works, hope and beauty are lost in fear and terror, which are enlarged by the interplay between texts.

"Leaves" is also about the cruel world. Like "Pay the Criers," this story begins with a daughter trying to face the reality of her mother's dead body in the house. Unlike Refugio, however, Isabel's mother was not a strong woman but a heroin addict who often left her thirteen-year-old daughter alone for days at a time before finally dying with a needle in her arm. In her grief, young Isabel wants to live with her friend Rico the way her mother had lived with Pepe—to become her mother, an unrealistic dream that Rico quickly dismisses. There seems no way out of her despair. However, the story is also about miracles, the miracles of nature, of leaves that fall from their mother tree, huddle in the wind, but then rise to dance and live. Isabel comes to accept this cycle as she sits by her mother's grave in the cemetery, a spot filled with sounds coming in "brazenly" from the living world. Life and death cannot be separated, and Isabel takes strength from this natural truth.

A similarly optimistic world view emerges from the story "Village," which is connected to "Leaves" by the presence of Rico, also the son of the title character of Portillo Trambley's 1986 novel, *Trini*. With a male as the main character, this is Portillo Trambley's only story set in war—the Vietnam War. The son of a Tarahumara chieftain, Rico is like the author's strong women characters in having special insights: he comes from "a world of instinct and intuitive decisions" (1992, p. 93). Unlike the other soldiers, he feels a kinship with the "enemy" villagers; they are like his mother's people from Mexico, and the village reminds him of the barrio where he grew up in Texas. People are "all the same everywhere." With his respect for the oneness of humankind and the sanctity of life, Rico naturally cannot participate in destroying the village. When he refuses to follow orders, injures his sergeant, and prevents the destruction, he becomes a savior; like other saviors, however, he is not understood. The story leaves him under arrest, with steel rings around his ankles, externally imprisoned but internally free.

The final story, "La Yonfantayn," first published in 1982, is a lighthearted satire about Alicia, a rich woman who lives more in the movies than in life. Her yard boy is the Rico of the other stories, and her lover is Rico's uncle, Buti. Alicia sees herself as Joan Fontaine and her lover as Clark Gable, and that's all right. It works. Life imitates the films.

Portillo Trambley's use of repeating characters and places from story to story is a technique that deserves more critical attention in the future, particularly as the stories relate to *Trini*. This technique in the new stories creates a richness and density not previously seen in the author's fiction, and one hopes that future stories will tell us more about Rico, his sister Linda, Uncle Buti, and Trini.

This new collection is also superior to the early edition because of the careful revision of the stories that have been retained. As we have seen, the plots are tighter, the language more condensed, the characters better developed, and the stories freer of the thematic insistence that in the 1975 version sometimes came close to preaching. Most significantly, Portillo Trambley has strengthened her characters, giving them a depth and stature that attest to the author's continuing growth and respect for humans and the human condition.

Notes

[1] Juan D. Bruce-Novoa, "Estela Portillo," *Chicano Authors: Inquiry by Interview* (Austin: University of Texas Press, 1980) p. 168.

[2] *Ibid.*, p. 165.

[3] *Ibid.*, p. 171.

[4] *Ibid.*, p. 176.

[5] Estela Portillo Trambley, *Rain of Scorpions and Other Writings* (Berkeley: Tonatiuh International, 1975). In this introduction all references to *Rain of Scorpions* will be indicated by page numbers in the text; 1975 will indicate the original edition, while 1992 will indicate the new edition.

Pay the Criers

Chucho had gotten home before the storm broke. The act of apologizing to Juana for staying away for three days was heavy on his mind. When he went into the house, he found his wife crying over the body of her dead mother. She had rushed into Chucho's arms from the back room where Refugio lay dead in her own bed. She had left her work as a maid in El Paso because she was feeling bad, only to die of a heart attack in her daughter's arms. Chucho thought of Juana grieving in loneliness; he thought of his mother-in-law who had died like a warrior in the midst of the daily battle for bread. The old woman's life had been nothing but work. Sure, she had had her share of good times and had enjoyed them fully, but the duty of the daily struggle had always been foremost in her life. That's why she had been a tiger, wearing a shawl, carrying a rosary in her hand, ready to pounce on him for being what she called "shiftless."

The old woman had disliked him because he couldn't keep a job, because it had been up to her to support the household. The fifteen dollars a week she earned in the American city were enough when she crossed to Juárez on the Mexican side. It was enough to feed them and pay the rent on the lot where their house stood. More important, Refugio was able to save a dollar a week for a grand funeral. She had been saving for seventeen years, and the more she added to her little nest egg, the more she planned for the festivities that were to take place at her wake. Chucho was thinking of the money at this moment as Juana broke out tormentedly in sobs. She had loved and depended on her mother all her life. Now the security was gone.

Refugio had always resented giving Chucho even a nickel. Once in a while she had opened up her purse strings to send him out for beer, and she had graciously not asked for the change. When his mother-in-law came home for weekends, they locked horns like

15

bulls. Well not all the time, for they had shared some good times together. The money . . . He tried to put the thought out of his mind,
but the thought would not leave. All that funeral money somewhere
in the house! Or else, she had given it to Juana before she died. Certainly Juana would know where it was. While he held his weeping
wife, he imagined the money in his pocket. He could coax Juana to
give it to him. Money was never meant to be wasted on the dead. He
knew he was planning something low and underhanded, and he
fought the idea within himself for a minute or so, only to give way
again to his unprincipled ways. His life had been lived so far without
creed or rules. Juana and Chucho looked at each other, a look that
held them together. It was time to comfort.

He led his pretty little wife to their bed in the front room and held
her close as he stroked her hair. Suddenly there was a burst of
thunder and a flash of lightning nearby. It frightened her, and she
nestled in the haven of his arms. He kissed her in sympathy at first,
but then the rain began to fall hard, fierce and exciting. His kisses became passionate and she did not resist. She was the hungry earth
after a dry spell, wanting rain. And like the parched earth welcoming
rain, Juana welcomed love. Temporarily the thoughts of her dead
mother were forgotten.

Afterwards Chucho felt the warmth of her happiness. Juana lay
on the bed, breathing softly, her eyes closed; she had loosened her
neat braids until they were undone to please him, for he loved her
hair soft and wild. Chucho stood by the bed looking down at Juana
with great fondness, then he went to the door to watch the falling
rain; the jarros outside the house were already half full with rain-
water. There was a newness in the world outside. Death could wait
for a little while.

He felt Juana's small hands caressing his back, then she pressed
her lips on his bareness as if to claim him. He felt the warmth of her
tears. "She's dead in the other room, Chucho. What am I going to
do without her?"

He turned and gathered her in his arms. "I'm here, querida."

"For how long?" It was asked in anticipated fear; it was not a condemnation.

"I'm just the way I am, Juana." He said it with a certain guilt, but
the rainbow lights of rain were beckoning.

"What about her? The burial, the arrangements . . . Oh, Chucho,

I can't." She was yielding to timidity, to indecision, to the inability of accepting that her mother would no longer be.

"I'll take care of everything," Chucho offered accommodatingly. It was a craving now, wanting that money. "First to Domínguez's Funeral Home, then the plot, and of course, the criers. She wanted criers."

"No! I can't let you take care of the funeral. She made me promise—"

"—Not to give me the money," Chucho interrupted. He concluded matter-of-factly, "Then you'll have to do it. There's no one else."

"She said you would just steal it, get drunk and go whoring." She was sobbing in abject desolation. "But I can't—I can't go to the funeral home. I can't . . ."

"If I can't be of help, I'll just go," he insisted perversely, then he paused and waited for her to give in.

She grasped his arm in desperation. "You do it." He could feel her distress over giving him the money, but he paid no heed. He tried to be kind. "You don't have to give it to me. That way you've kept your promise. I'll look for it myself. It's in the house isn't it?" She nodded, helpless as a child.

Now that the rain had stopped, the jolt of life sounds from the barrio made his blood race. He left the door, looking around for his clothes. As he dressed he started opening drawers. With one hand he zipped his pants while with the other he rummaged through paper bags and boxes piled in a corner. Juana watched him, her face a conflict of loyalties. The only place the money could be, he decided as he put on his shoes, was in the room where Refugio lay. Juana seemed to sense what he was going to do. "Don't go in there, Chucho."

"Why not? It's my house."

"It's her room."

"Does that make sense, woman? In that room, Refugio and me, we'd drink ourselves to sleep in there, we planned our destinies in there, she cured me of the fever in there with her incantations, her curandera ways. It's really—our room."

Juana began to cry, remembering her own jealousy watching her husband and her mother—sharing drink, talking crazy, or beating each other half to death; then, the joking—the laughing at them-

selves after all the havoc. She never understood how two people
who hated each other so much could have spent so much time together, in that little room no bigger than a chicken coup. She hated
those times because she was always the outsider. Juana offered resignedly, "I'll get you the money."

She went into the room where her mother lay. The money was in
the rag clown. Many years before, when Chucho and Refugio had
had good feelings, he had come home one weekend with a life-size
clown; he wore all the colors of the world. Chucho had given it to her
mother as a gift. He had joked, "Now you have a man. You don't
have to sleep alone." Juana had been embarrassed by his crassness,
and her mother had cursed him at first; then she had laughed, ob-
viously delighted with the rag man. Chucho and her mother had
gone out for wine to celebrate. They had drunk half a dozen bottles
that night, joking and singing to the clown until the wee hours of the
morning. Juana had found them the next morning with their arms
around the clown, fast asleep. The daughter had learned to accept
all their craziness because they were the only two people she had in
the world. Refugio, in time, had slit the back of the clown's suit,
taken out some of the rags, and hidden the shoe box with the funeral
money. Every time Refugio added money to the box, she opened up
the slit, then sewed it back.

The rag man hung on a hook in the corner by her bed. As she
reached for it, she glanced at her mother's face. How peaceful death
was! She did not look like a woman who had battled a lifetime. The
tumult of living had been erased. Juana felt the brightness of her love
for the woman in whose womb she had been cradled thirty-two years
before. Now her mother was gone; the womb was gone . . . Juana
felt an inquietude as she took the clown from the hook, ripped
opened the now-worn seam, and found the box. She used a large
safety pin to close the rag man's wound, to keep the stuffing safe.
She sat the clown on the bed at her mother's feet, as if to give her the
company of an old friend.

Juana found Chucho drinking his mother's beer, memories in his
eyes. She handed Chucho the box and reminded him, "You must
pay the criers." Chucho took the money. Juana shivered with dread,
apprehension growing. She was still warm with love, but the money
was now in Chucho's hands. "You must keep your promise,
Chucho."

He kept quiet, averting his eyes, as he put on his only coat and took the box under his arm. Then he was gone.

The money was gone; her mother was gone. Juana's sobs began again, slowly at first; soon they were hard and painful. Instinct flared. The lost child from the womb went to her mother. She dropped by the side of Refugio, flinging one arm around the body as if cradling a nonexisting safeness, a nipple of security with no nourishment for her. She remained thus for a long, long time, the clown smiling at her with a special kind of sympathy.

*   *   *

Chucho walked out of the two rooms he had built with Refugio. The old coyote was dead. He touched the box under his arm as he went down the hill. The small adobe house was surrounded by fruit trees, flowers, and all kinds of plants. The land belonged to Don Tiburcio, the junk man, who had refused to sell it to Refugio. It had been a huge hole next to the junkyard. That's why the owner rented it cheap. But Refugio had seen the possibilities. It was close to a canal (water for trees!) and to the bus stop where she caught the bus that took her to the bridge between Mexico and the United States. Refugio decided to fill the hole and make a level surface on which to build a house. For three years Chucho and Refugio had worked filling in the hole with discarded tires which they begged, stole, or paid for until the land was level. The top was filled with soil from the canal and with horse manure. "I want rich soil," Refugio would say, "for around my house I shall bring to life the Garden of Eden." She sure did, Chucho thought, looking up at the only patch of green in the whole barrio.

He quickened his step, smelling the aroma of cooking food mixed with the fragrance of wet earth. Yes, the first thing he would do with the money would be to buy a good supper for his best friend, Chapo, and himself. The most expensive on the menu: he could afford it now. He felt rather lightheaded and a shout of gladness escaped from his throat. Whoever heard him slammed an open door. The whole world would be his for the next few hours. He imagined that the lighted lamps were happy eyes belonging to the houses; they too, anticipated the good times he was going to have. He would treat everybody tonight. What a beautiful thought. His friends would not believe it, for he was always broke.

As soon as he could he'd fill Chapo's old car with gas. After supper they'd go to the poker game behind Chen's Laundry and gamble the way he liked to gamble, with money in his pocket. He would then go to the Red Chapulín, and he and Chapo would drink with all their friends. He had to break the news of Refugio's death to Don Tiburcio, owner of the bar and of Refugio's land. After all, Don Tiburcio was his landlord and his friend. After that, a visit to Adela's girls.

He was not far from Chapo's house. Chapo washed cars all day long with a trancelike vigor. This was the pattern of his day: soap, rag, mop, water—soap, rag, mop, water—car after car. Poor Chapo! He was a machine. His soul had been numbed. His life was a desperation, working for a few pesos to feed his family. Chucho knew he would never give up his own life for a few pesos. The whole world looked upon him as shiftless, worthless, no-account; that was the price of freedom.

The old dead witch had been the worst one. He remembered her wild roars and accusations. Why tell him what he already knew? He had made that choice in life and was well satisfied with it. The old woman's venom had been the fuel for many battles, but she was well aware of why she hated his ways. She had been jealous, jealous of his freedom. "You pay for that freedom with my money, desgraciado!" she would scream at him. True, true, she was tired of the money responsibilities, but she had chosen her life, just like he had chosen his. What could he do? Beneath it all, he respected her sense of respectability, her honesty, and most of all her generosity, especially after a few drinks.

Some time back he had gone to watch some ice skaters at the coliseum across the border. Chapo had a job cleaning up the place after the Ice Capades, and Chucho had gone along to help. He had been overwhelmed by the skill of the skaters. Their skill was freedom, making something hard seem so easy, so effortless. He had decided with a happy sigh, *that* was beauty. For some reason his brain could not make a clear connection, but he kept thinking their skating had something to do with the way he wanted to live. He knew those skaters had worked very hard to achieve that beauty, the easy, swift, graceful gliding on the ice. Chucho wanted to work like that at living—to make an art of enjoying life, a constant celebrating, to be a spectator to the freedom of others, to share the openness of that freedom. Every man in life must know his part well in that life, develop the skill in what he could do best, then skate through life enjoying, spreading beauty like confetti, or the joy of circus balloons. He had remarked to Chapo while watching the skaters, "I want a skill like that, Chapo."

"You want to be a skater, eh?" Chapo was never surprised by anything Chucho said.

"I want a skill for living, so I can skate smoothly into freedom, so my friends can see that I can see." Chucho was well pleased with that thought.

"Oh, you have a skill in life, Chucho. You drink more, fight harder than anyone I know. You've been in jail more times than anyone I know."

"Oh, shut up." Sometimes it was useless trying to explain anything to Chapo.

"You can afford the freedom. You have a mother-in-law to support you. Look at me. The bastard without balls that I work for, the thief pays me slave wages, but I need the money to feed my little ones. I would like to spit in his face, but I don't think about it. I just wash cars until they shine, then I get my centavos and I go home to my family. We eat one more day."

"I want to skate through life like a god," Chucho had wished.

"You're full of beans."

He reached Chapo's house. Next to it stood Chapo's bright green car like a sentinel against total decay. The lamps were lit. His friend must be sitting down to an early supper. Chucho whistled, loud and shrill, calling, "Hey, Chapo!"

Chapo stuck his head out of the door, then came out hurriedly closing the door behind him. Chucho was not welcomed at Chapo's house.

"Ese, Chapo, let's go buy some new tires for your car and fill it with gas." Chucho grinned, moving about, jabbing right and left, in a dance of delight.

"Hey, paisano, you won the lottery?" Chapo scratched his head.

"The old lady died today. I got the funeral money!" Chucho informed his friend with some gravity.

Chapo crossed himself. "May her soul rest in peace . . . all the money?"

"All the money . . ." Chucho relished the thought.

"Jaaaaaaaa!" Chapo grabbed Chucho and they began to wrestle like bears. They fell to the ground laughing, rolling about on the grass. When their play was done, they lay face up, feeling good, and watched the first stars of the evening. Chucho broke the silence. "What a night we're going to have!"

Chapo jumped to his feet and kicked Chucho who was still looking at the stars. "You see anything special, you old dog?"

"It's all so big, isn't it?" Chucho was awed by a thousand stars. "Let's go!"

A short time later the old green car was rattling off toward town where city lights spoke of temporary lightning dreams.

*   *   *

Juana sat in her neighbor's kitchen. Her voice was tired. "I'm waiting for Chucho." She had waited for Chucho for one whole day. Now it was another day, and in her house there was the growing stench of death.

She blamed herself. "Why do I wait for him? I should do something about my poor mother, but I don't know what."

The neighbor looked at her skeptically. "You really think he's coming back when he has all that money? Ha!"

"But he has a responsibility to me, to my mother. He promised to make all the funeral arrangements."

"Poor child. God sure made you pretty, but decided to hold back on brains. He's not coming back. You should get the police after him before he spends all of your mother's hard-earned money. Pobrecita!"

"What am I going to do?"

"Well, you better do something. Someone told the authorities about your mother. You know what they're going to do if you don't bury her soon."

"I won't let them." Juana began to cry painfully.

"That's all you know how to do, Juana—cry. That crematory was built by the city at great expense. According to the municipal president, it is the clean, efficient way to get rid of the dead, of the ones who can't pay."

"The church says it's a sin to burn a body. Father Vallejo will not allow them to take her." Juana felt her betrayal.

"What can he do? He's just a poor priest. If she can't afford a funeral, she'll go into the ovens."

Juana's crying became hysterical. "Chucho has to come! He has to!"

"I wouldn't put my hopes on that. He's probably passed out somewhere."

"If he spent all my mother's money, he's feeling guilty. He always comes back when he's feeling guilty."

"The devil he does!"

"He's always full of remorse when he drinks." Juana remembered the many times Refugio and Chucho had cried with a bottle between them.

"If I were you I'd just accept that your mother will be ashes in the wind." The neighbor was a realist.

Juana put her head down on the table. "Mamacita, forgive me. Why did I give him the money?"

"Why do you think? Because you're putty in that man's hands, because you love it when he gets into your pants. Animal."

"I was talking to my mother."

"I know, I know. You poor little thing." She smoothed out Juana's disheveled hair in sympathy.

They heard Chapo's car. Juana rushed out of the house. She saw Chapo following Chucho, and all she could do was stand at her neighbor's door and cry. Chucho and Chapo were now making their way to the house. She would let him. He should smell the stench, so he could see what he had done.

Chapo was remarking, "Thanks for the tires and the good time."

The two men disappeared into the house, then there came a long, drawn-out bellow. Juana knew it was Chucho, who probably had forgotten about the body. The two men ran out of the house, Chucho looking like a wild man. He was shaking his head in disbelief, then he let out another bellow like a wounded animal. He fell to his knees and began to pound the wooden planks of the porch. Chapo stood by helplessly, looking as if he wanted to throw up.

Chucho moaned, "She's dead. Oh, God, she's still here, rotting . . ."

"We have to do something, Chucho," Chapo clumsily suggested, walking nervously around Chucho's kneeling body. Chucho was hitting the planks again. "It's not fair, it's not fair that life should rot!"

Juana could not bear it any longer. She ran across to him, kneeling by his side, taking him in her arms and kissing his forehead to stop his suffering. She had to tell him right away. "Chucho, the authorities are coming to take her body if we don't bury her right away."

"I looked at her face, Juana. She looked so peaceful, so young —but the stink!" There was a cosmic bewilderment on his face. Then it sank in. "To the crematory?"

"Yes . . ."

"I will never let them do that."

"Do you have any money left?" There was a ray of hope in Juana's voice. Chucho shook his head in despair, not only because the money was all gone, but because he could not bear the thought of Refugio being burned. He raised himself to his feet and picked up his clinging wife. He turned to Chapo. "She must not be burned."

"What can we do? There's no money left. We can return the tires."

"If we take the tires back, it wouldn't be enough even to buy a lot to bury her in, much less a coffin. You know what we can do? Let's go back to all the places we visited last night. Someone's bound to give us some of the money we spent on them."

"They were mostly strangers." Chapo was not optimistic.

Juana pleaded, "You can't leave me. The authorities will come. We can't leave her body in the house. Something has to be done now, right now."

"All right. We won't leave her here. We'll take her with us." Chucho knew it was an idea born of desperation. But what could he do?

"In Chapo's car? With both of you? Where are you going to take her?" Juana thought Chucho had gone out of his mind.

"We'll put her in the trunk." Chucho was serious.

"The stink, Chucho, the stink," Chapo reminded him.

Chucho remembered how, long ago, Refugio had talked about las yerbas de los yaquis which she kept in her herb bag. She had bragged that her medicine could cure anything, even the stench of death. He told Juana what they had to do. "Her herb bag, Juana, the one with the Yaqui herbs, do you know where it is?"

"Hanging in her closet."

"All right then, you and me are going back into the house, take some sheets, sprinkle all the herbs on her, wrap her up. Chapo and me, we'll put her in the trunk and tie her down real good. Come on!"

Juana could not move. The neighbor, taking her by the arm,

said, "Come, it's something. Better than the authorities. I'll help you wrap up the body."

The three of them went into the house and an hour later a mummylike bundle was tied securely in the trunk of the car. The trunk remained half open; it was the only way. So Chapo and Chucho used an extra rope to tie the open trunk to the rear fender. That way she wouldn't be left behind somewhere on the road. Chucho didn't waste any time; he got into the car and turned on the ignition. Chapo jumped in beside him and crossed himself. "¡Que Dios nos bendiga!"

Chucho stuck his head out of the car window. "If the authorities come, you know nothing. Do you understand? You know nothing."

The neighbor nodded her head in disbelief. Juana bit her lip and whispered, "Yes. I promise. I won't tell them anything."

When the car disappeared around the bend, the neighbor offered, "You can stay with me if you want."

"I have to clean the house before Chucho comes back. Put things away."

The neighbor walked away shaking her head in sympathy, and Juana sat down on the porch steps to watch the glorious colors of the dying sun. Her mother was gone. The traces of rain were gone. The sun had drunk all moisture in the desert. She looked at her mother's fruit trees. They needed water. The plants too. It was Chucho who watered the trees. He never failed to tend to them, bringing the water up the hill from the canal in huge white plastic milk bottles. It was a tedious and exhausting job. But he had done it for Refugio, for her Garden of Eden. Juana reflected how the trees would be there even after she herself was gone, as they were now that Refugio was gone. There was no mother now, no weekly ritual of waiting at the bus stop for her to come home from her job, no more stories from her mother about the outside world, no Chucho fighting with Refugio and laughing and talking to the rag man while they shared a bottle of wine. The trees grew in beauty with her mounting loneliness. Tears came to her eyes. She opened the palm of her hand to catch the tears. Little wet drops glistened in the glory of the sun's last rays, colors found in soft whispers. She looked for a jewel in her teardrops. She was lost in a world all her own.

*   *   *

Chapo's face was fiercely red with anger. He threw a finger in the direction of the store. "Ladrones, not even half of what we paid for the tires. Let's twist the tires around their necks. You want to take the money?"

"What for? It's not enough. The tires get us around." Chucho had expected just that.

"Where to?" asked Chapo, truly discouraged.

"To El Chapulín Colorado. I have to pick up the deed for the land."

"What deed?" Chapo's eyes widened.

"Last night when I told Don Tiburcio about Refugio, he took it hard. I didn't know he liked the old battle-ax that much. He cried," Chucho explained.

"I don't remember any of that. Where was I?"

"Dead drunk."

"I remember you dancing flamenco on top of the bar."

"That was before your first hundred drinks."

"I lost count. You kept buying free drinks. Everybody was your friend last night."

Chucho felt the warmth of good memories. "Nice, nice."

Chapo was curious. "Deed for what?"

"The land under my house."

"You bought it from him?"

"Didn't have to offer him a penny. Seems Refugio had asked to buy it many times and he had refused. He liked to have her beg cause she looked so soft—that's what he said. So, last night, he just confessed to me that he was giving it to her."

"But she's dead."

"Don't be stupid, Chapo. When people touch each other in life, they touch each other in death. He was going to sign over the deed to Refugio. He said that Refugio would know up in heaven where she is."

"There's the answer. You can sell the deed or borrow money on it for her funeral."

"Never! The deed belongs to Refugio. It is her land now . . . No."

"Are you going to ask Don Tiburcio for money, for the funeral?"

"Not him. He is doing something generous already. We don't ask him. We'll just look around for some of the people we bought drinks for last night."

They went into the Chapulín Colorado and found Don Tiburcio at the bar. "Two drinks on the house for my friends." Don Tiburcio was remembering the night before when Chucho had spent so much money at his place.

"Gracias, Don Tiburcio."

"I'm glad you came around. Here's the deed for Refugio. I know she knows. You say goodbye to her for me at the funeral. I can't go. I want to remember her alive. But you tell her, I will visit her on Sundays, take her some flowers, and we can talk about the days." Don Tiburcio's face revealed how very fond he had been of Refugio. Chucho did not have the heart to look around for familiar faces. He did not want Don Tiburcio to know that it was Refugio's funeral money that he had spent the night before. Chapo came up to Chucho and nudged him as Don Tiburcio went to take care of another customer. "Look, the Red Beard. He borrowed fifty pesos from you last night, remember? You want me to explain the situation?"

"No," Chucho protested nervously.

"No?" Chapo did not understand.

"I don't want Don Tiburcio to know I took her money. I'm just a thief, that's all I am. I took money from a dead woman. May the heavens strike me dead if I don't give her a decent funeral. I'll find a way."

The gypsy who had played the guitar for Chucho's dancing the night before came over. "Now it's my turn to buy you a drink. Two tequilas, Don Tiburcio."

Don Tiburcio came back with two tequilas while the guitar player strummed the song about the Mountain of Sorrow in Andalucía. The song was a plaintive melody about a lost love who followed fireflies into heaven. Don Tiburcio took out his handkerchief. He blew his nose and told the musician, "We lost a loved one only yesterday. Chucho's mother-in-law. She used to come on weekends and sit right where you're sitting. A fine, fine woman. I'm going to miss her."

There was a faraway look in the musician's eyes. "In Andalucía we not only sing about the loved ones who have left us, but we dance about them with the passion of our feet." He begun to strum a flamenco tune, the very one Chucho had danced to the night before when he had been quite drunk. But he was sober now. Too sober.

Red Beard came up to the bar and ordered a drink for his two friends. The guitarist asked Chucho, "Did you love your mother-in-law?"

Chucho had no idea why he said what he did, but he did. "Yes, I

loved her very much. She was a warrior. She scorned dreamers like
me because we don't take reality between our teeth. We don't face
up to the struggle. She was a coyote balasiada, a bullet-scarred
coyote who was not afraid."

"Dance it!" commanded the guitarist. Chucho jumped up on the
bar and proclaimed, "I dance for Refugio. I dare life and pain and
fear with my feet, as she did with her guts and her heart. I dance her
passions! Her laughter! Her spirit!" Faster and faster, Chucho dared
with his feet for the love of Refugio. The dance became unrelentless
until both Chucho and the guitarist were spent. Then silence, until
Don Tiburcio blew his nose again and commented, "That was a good
thing you did for her, Chucho."

"I should have done things for her when she was alive."

"No one cares about the living." These words of wisdom came
from Chapo.

"You know that her favorite season was autumn? Because it was
a time of realness, of harvest. Fruits were gathered and flowers gave
the last of their bloom." Chucho's memory of Refugio was full blown.

"I never heard her say that, Chucho."

"That's because she never confided in you. Only in the rag man,
Chapo."

"What rag man is that, Chucho?" asked Don Tiburcio.

"A clown I bought for her made out of rags."

Don Tiburcio started to cry again. Chucho put his arm around
Don Tiburcio and comforted the bartender. "She told me many
times how much she liked you, but that you were a dreamer, like
me."

Don Tiburcio nodded. "I am."

"You know why she didn't like dreams?"

They all listened intently to Chucho's words. "She used to say
that dreams were cruel because the waiting sometimes had no end."

"You talk as if you loved your mother-in-law."

Chapo could not believe Chucho's reply. "You are very right
. . ."

A stranger came into the bar asking, "Who owns a green car
parked outside?"

Chapo and Chucho looked at each other while the stranger continued, "There's a bunch of dogs sniffing and howling around it. I
think someone went to call the police."

Chucho and Chapo jumped off their stools and ran outside without a word. Outside, the neon lights were playing fiercely with the white bundle tied to the trunk of the car, as dogs tried to take a grab, then sniffed around it. Off and on, on and off, off and on, blue and red, green and yellow, neon lights claiming the body of Refugio. The two jumped in the car and rode off after kicking a dog or two.

"Where to?" Chapo asked.

"To Adela's."

"Chucho, she's stinking terrible."

"Not her life, Chapo, not her life."

"You know, they were right back there. You talk as if you loved her."

"I loved her—that's why I hated her so much."

"She used to call you a coward."

"She called me every name in the book. She had a big mouth. She was jealous of my freedom. She had a right to resent me, I suppose."

"I remember the time she cracked your skull."

"Why do you remember only the bad things?" Chucho shouted in Chapo's ear.

"I just don't think we're going to get the money," Chapo answered despondently.

"Adela has a heart." Chucho was not about to give up.

"She's a businesswoman."

At one time Adela had catered to the best clientele. The powerful police commissioner had been her protector and best client. Or at least that's what she claimed. Now in less prosperous times, she housed six girls in a dilapidated two-story building at the south end of the red-light district. One of the girls opened the door, then went to call Adela. The room where Chucho and Chapo waited was dimly lighted. It was not a busy night by the looks of the place. The madam came in, smiling in recognition. "You must have fallen in love with my girls, you came back so soon."

"I'm not here as a customer tonight," Chucho explained.

"Oh? Your friend, perhaps?" She turned to Chapo.

Chapo stood doggedly behind Chucho, who reminded her, "He was here with me last night for the show. We only saw the show, Adela."

"That's not like you, Chucho—just the show?"

"I've got a favor to ask, Adela."

"Favor?" Adela was now on guard.

"I tipped your dancers last night, a lot of money. I was very generous. Don't you remember?"

"I remember. My girls remember," Adela said pleasantly.

"Well I'm in a little trouble. I was generous with money that wasn't mine. So I thought, since you've known me all these years, you could make me a loan—mind you, not give the money back, just make me a loan, and I'll pay it back as soon as I can."

"For you, Chucho, I would do anything. But money? It is an ironclad rule in this house that we do not give money or lend money to any clients. It would be our ruin. We can't afford the luxury. Sorry."

"Just this one time." Chucho felt awkward begging. But it was for Refugio.

"Nope. Can't do that. If I break the rule once, I'll do it a second time. That's the way it goes. You understand. It's a hard life." It was a businesslike refusal.

"I see your point." It was Chucho's attempt at a gracious out.

"Here, a few pesos, since you were so generous last night." She handed him some money.

Chucho was too embarrassed not to take it. Out in the street, Chucho and Chapo put up the collars of their coats, for the wind was raw and cold. They got into the car without a word and drove around for a while.

"Well, our last bet is Chen's. We dropped a bundle there last night. There's another poker game going on." Chucho was still hopeful.

When the two drove up to Chen's Laundry, the place was in total darkness. Chucho jumped out and went to ask at the bakery next door. He came back with bad news. "Place was raided. Our last hope." The two men sat numbly, staring out into the darkness.

Chapo's voice had a finality. "We can't pay the criers, Chucho. No funeral for Refugio, no wake, no dancing, no eating . . ."

"To hell with all that, Chapo, what's so great about paying criers to moan and scream at your funeral?"

"We better do something about the body. They'll throw us in jail if they find it in our trunk."

"To hell with the criers. They're not good enough," Chucho concluded.

"They go with the grand funeral and that's what she wanted," Chapo sighed, waiting for Chucho, for an answer. Far off in the distance the howl of a coyote mixed with the laughter that spilled from a doorway.

"We are going to bury her ourselves, Chapo," Chucho decided.

"Now don't get crazy. Where? Not the cemetery . . ." Chapo was not up to that.

"Up there. The hill behind the church." Chucho was imagining the climb.

"Go up that hill? Who's going to dig a grave in this freezing weather?" Chapo was skeptical.

"You and me . . ." Chucho squinted in thought.

"We don't even have a shovel," Chapo protested weakly.

"I'll borrow two from the shed behind the church. Father Vallejo won't mind." Chucho had the whole plan in his mind.

"He's asleep, Chucho. We can't wake him up at this hour."

"We'll borrow them anyway." Taking the shovels without asking was the least of Chucho's problems.

"Now, Chucho?"

"Yes, now. But first we buy a couple of bottles with the money Adela gave me." He winked at Chapo.

*   *   *

It was close to midnight when they started the climb up the hill with two shovels and Refugio. The biting wind was torturous but most welcome, for it lessened the overpowering stench of the body. Their fingers and noses were numb with the cold. Up, up, they climbed, huffing and straining. The body was cradled in two huge horse blankets that Chucho had taken from Father Vallejo's shed. They supported the weight high on their shoulders, holding tight with both hands. The two shovels, alongside the body inside the blankets, would clank against a rock every so often. Chucho was very careful not to let the body drag. At intervals they would stop to rest and to drink tequila for warmth. The rest was brief, for it was better to keep moving, creating some body heat against the bitter wind. It took what seemed like an eternity to reach the top of the hill. Chucho's throat felt bruised with cold.

They scrambled to the top. The lights of the city shone bright against a dark horizon. Somehow distance diluted their glaring vulgarity. Chucho felt as if his nose and fingers were going to break off. The climb was over, and now they could build a fire to thaw themselves out. They laid the body down gently and began to gather sagebrush and branches broken by the wind. There was no protection from the swift and biting wind. Building a fire was next to impossible on open ground. Chucho led the way to a huge boulder that broke the wind; in time, they had a fire blazing.

"I'm one great big icicle, Chucho." Chapo put his hands out to pick up the scattered warmth of the fire. He kept his gaze on the fire, once in a while blowing on his hands. Chucho was already looking for a good burial ground. He soon found a high spot, next to a clump of trees. It was on the edge of the hill with a full view of the town, Refugio's town. Chucho walked the area round and round and dug his foot into the earth.

"We'll dig the grave here," he finally decided.

They took turns digging and, at times, they dug from opposite ends. Every so often, they stopped and rested from their labor to drink from the bottle. The warm glow of the liquor sent new vigor into Chucho's tired body. He looked down into the town that spoke of many lifetimes. Then he resumed his digging, his body aching from fatigue. He insisted that Chapo rest for longer intervals. After all, this was Chucho's way of asking forgiveness from a woman who had given so much to his life. He finished the digging himself, letting Chapo scoop earth out of the shallow grave. When the grave was deep enough, they went to the body where it lay, close to the boulder where the fire blazed. They moved it with great care and laid it next to the open grave. Chucho rested a hand on Chapo's shoulder. "Now we wait."

"Wait?"

"For the sunrise. I want her to see it one more time." Chucho felt the excitement of life's conspiracy with death.

Chapo did not answer, but took out the bottle and drank, then he handed it to Chucho who drank also. Chucho took a knife from his pocket. He squatted to pick up the upper part of the bundled Refugio and laid her head on his lap. He carefully cut the cloth that covered up her face. "There, now she can see."

The two men sat and watched the lights of the city disappear gradually as they waited for the sunrise. Chapo rubbed his arms vigorously. "Let's wait by the fire. Too cold here."

"You go. I want to stay with her. We must see the sunrise together."

Chucho's mind flashed with memories—Refugio's face full of a

softness when she talked of good things, of Juana as a child, of the
seeds she had planted breaking through the earth, of the men she
had loved. The softness had been for the realness of things that
smacked of life.

Chapo stayed, taking another drink. "You think where she is,
she knows there are city lights?"

"She's still here with us. She hasn't gone anywhere yet." Why
should she? thought Chucho. She had never been in any hurry to
go.

"I suppose soon she'll be in heaven."

"I hope heaven is half as wonderful as earth." Chucho really
doubted it.

"What do you think?" Chapo waited for Chucho to answer,
knowing his friend had answers for everything, but Chucho's mind
was still cushioned in the memories of Refugio.

"She suffered a lot, Chapo. When we drank together, she talked
about her husband. She cleaned houses for gringos on the other side
since she was thirteen. When she got together with a man, she kept
on working. She never stopped working. Before we built the house,
she had never had a house. She rented in a presidio all her life. She
would buy furniture, and her old man kept selling it for money, to get
drunk. But in spite of the bad things, deep down, she understood
how precious life was. We men are a bad lot, Chapo. Women are
much better creatures."

"Where are your balls? We are men!" Chapo looked like a little
rooster, posing manhood.

"We whore around, drink too much. That husband of Refugio's
kept selling every stitch of furniture, so she took after him with a two-
by-four, beat him up bad. He left town awfully scared. Went back to
his mother in Coahuila. Refugio saw him years later when she went
to visit her family. He recognized her. He was selling fake watches to
American tourists, but when he saw her he ran the opposite way.
Ha!"

"She was a fighter all right."

"Didn't have a man for a long time, that's why I gave her the rag
man. Something to hug at night, after a few drinks."

"Why didn't you do her the favor?"

"Sometimes when we talked about life and joked all night, and
she would grow soft in wisdom, I had desires—but I couldn't. There
was this respect I had for her . . ."

"You were scared of her." Chapo got up and danced about. The warmth of the fire had dissipated. "I'll get more wood. Fire's dead. I'm freezing just sitting."

The first light rose in the east. The city did not have long to sleep. Chucho sat Refugio up against his shoulder to face the east. "Look, Refugio, morning. Your face is the sunrise, mother-woman-friend . . ." He called Chapo. "Come back, Chapo. Her face is beautiful."

Chapo was looking down at Refugio's face. "She was a fine-looking woman."

Chucho held the stiff, dead weight of the woman in his arms. The stench had been forgotten. Tears filled his eyes. "Refugio, I couldn't give you your fancy criers, or the kind of wake you had in mind with five kinds of meats and candies and all the wine flowing free. I couldn't give you musicians and fireworks, and all your friends singing and dancing for you. I'm so sorry. There's only me, the poor fool who stole your money. This is all I can do for you. I wish I could do more. You deserved so much."

"She can't hear you, Chucho."

Chucho bent his face and kissed her fully on the lips. "Listen, I promise to keep the rag man company when I'm feeling blue. I'll get me a couple of bottles, and the rag man and I will wait for you. Don't forget. I love you, Refugio, for having lived."

With great care he laid the body gently down on the ground, then he jumped into the grave, took off his coat and made a pillow for Refugio's head.

"That's your only coat, Chucho," Chapo reminded.

"Here, help me." With effort and care, they got Refugio in the grave until her head rested on Chucho's coat. Then the two scuttled out of the grave, dirty, tired, half-frozen. Chucho looked down at the still form and became very conscious of death. The crying of the morning wind was the expectancy of something more. There was the morning and sunrise unexplained, like the life of each day. These things are better not explained, surmised Chucho.

The grave had to be covered. Then there were the coyotes. "Let's shovel the dirt, then we'll look for rocks to cover her grave," Chucho exclaimed with a note of finality.

They took different paths to find enough large rocks, each making a trip to the grave with their arms full. The rocks were finally gathered. The sun was high when they finally filled the grave and then sat down to fix the rocks in a mound. Again Chucho was pensive, thoughts spilling over to try to understand the coming of the sun, the waking life, the atmosphere diffusing light, all a song like the currents of a river, all beyond his understanding. If a skill is a form of freedom, thought Chucho as he formed a small mountain of rocks, then it belonged to death as well as life. Chucho became euphoric. He slapped Chapo on the back, and both men laughed. Then they wrestled like bears around the grave. Chucho took out his bottle and peered into it. "Hey, there's some." He took one gulp and handed the bottle to Chapo. A thought came to Chucho. "A plain cross with two good pieces of wood and her name on it. That will please her."

They found the wood, then sat down near the grave again to make a cross, sharing the rest of the drink.

The Paris Gown

"Cognac with your coffee, Teresa?"

"No, thank you, Gran—Clo." Somehow the word "grandmother" did not suit Clotilde Romero de Traske, sophisticated, chic, and existentially fluent. Teresa had awaited with excitement this after-dinner tête à tête. She knew so little about this woman who had left her home in Mexico so long ago. The young girl curiously searched her grandmother's face for signs of age. There were few. They were indistinguishable in the grace and youthful confidence exuded by this woman. Her gestures, eyes, flexible body, and above all her quick, discerning mind spoke of the joy of living.

Clotilde was an art dealer at the Rue Auber. Back home she was more than that. She was a legend. Tongues wagged incessantly recounting her numerous marriages, her travels, her artistic ventures, her lovers, and the rich and famous that frequented her salon. Then there was the hushed up scandal concerning her departure from Mexico so long ago. No one was willing to tell an innocent girl like Teresa how her grandmother had come to live in Paris. Back home, the wealthy women cushioned in static, affluent, stagnant lives had clacked tongues in furious gossip about the infamous Clotilde. Infamous or not, Clotilde Romero de Traske was to be admired.

"How do you like Paris, child?" There was a daring in her grandmother's eyes.

"Oh, I love it. It's so old-world—so rich in history and culture."

The older woman laughed. "Above all, Paris is a flesh and blood city, the City of Lights. Here the soul blossoms like a flower opening to the sun."

"Yes, I felt it. But I'm not clever enough to put it the way you did."

"You are most clever and lucky. Everybody should see Paris before they are twenty-five. I heard that somewhere. Can't remember where. But, there is no place like it in the world."

You should know, Grandmother, Teresa reminded herself. You've been everywhere, but you never returned. It was time to ask.

"You never returned home, Clo. Why?"

"Does anyone ever really go back home? We change so with time, but home remains the same, and so it's no longer home. Home to me is the pieces of my life that have fitted the puzzle called 'me.' Good or bad—ugly or beautiful. I guess I'm home."

"Were you always so wise?"

The grandmother laughed. "My dear, if you knew the idiotic things I've done. Wisdom is what you learn from the mountain of mistakes you make in life."

It was amazing, the beautiful clear depth of the "legend." Teresa felt a rush of admiration for the emberlike quality of her grandmother's spirit. It filled the room. She knows who she is, thought Teresa. How wonderful to have reached that comprehension of one's place in the universe. Teresa looked about the room and decided that it too was a piece of Clotilde, of what she had become in the life process. The art, the furniture, the flowers were all impressions of a great ferocity for living. Teresa caught herself. Why am I doing this? Analyzing rooms? My grandmother? Yet the feeling of the room could not be ignored. The colors were wonderful. They seemed to awaken feelings she could not really define. Maybe it's all a mystery beyond me.

"So—you are traveling with a university group?" Clotilde's expressive eyes searched her granddaughter's face.

She thinks I'm uncomfortable, thought Teresa. "I escaped."

"Escaped?"

"You know what I mean."

Clotilde laughed. "Assuredly, not in the same way."

"I can't believe the attitudes back home. They all live in the seventeenth century where I must not be exposed to the evils of the world." Teresa realized the petulance of her words.

"You really believe that?" Clo seemed amused.

"They're all stifling, sometimes my mother, my father, my aunts, you name it! Everybody back home is so—so proper."

Clo reflected, "Some moles, some eagles. I don't mean to judge, but you know what they say, 'different strokes'—"

Teresa laughed. "—'for different folks'. Of course. But you don't think 'old'!" Teresa saw the fairness in Clo's words.

"What is 'old'? Don't you think it's a knack for seeing what's real?" Clotilde put down her cup and walked to the mantelpiece over the fireplace as if she wanted to observe her granddaughter from a new perspective. Teresa also saw something new. A convex reflection of mood. Clo was the focal point in front of the wild, unkempt order of her art, a form liberated from civilized order. Teresa felt more than knew it, for she knew little about art.

"I love your paintings, your sculpture. The old mixed in with the new . . . I know very little about art, but this excites me."

"How discerning! Your feel for art is more important than knowing about it, art without doctrinaire implications."

"What does that mean?"

"You felt something. It left an impression perhaps relating to your experiences. You do not need rules or labels to understand."

Teresa felt inadequate. But it spurred her, so she asked, "Are you an artist yourself, Clo?"

"A very bad one, I'm afraid. When I was your age, I thought I had great talent. I was foolish."

"So you became a dealer in art?"

"It amounted to that after so many years." The collector went up to a massive piece of sculpture and touched its outline reverently. "Have you ever heard of Gaudier-Brzeska?"

"Heavens no." Teresa confessed her ignorance, knowing that she was about to be enlightened.

"Gaudier was a man of great passion, a primitive; he plunged into the world of feeling, and instinct, and energy. Free of barbarism."

This puzzled Teresa. "Primitive—barbarism—don't these go together?"

"Primitives? People of instinct and intuition—free—like children in their thinking, like animals when in fear—brutal. Savages, you might say, but savages do less harm than barbarians. Barbarians are a product of civilization. Artists attempt to preserve our humanity. Civilization destroys it, little by little."

Teresa was intrigued. "Artists are not barbarians?

Clo checked herself. "Some artists cannot be barbarians if they are artists. Remember, barbarians are associated with crudeness of taste, excessive greed, excessive cruelty, and a fondness to be on top. What does that sound like to you?" She did not wait for an answer but continued. "Politicians, big business, warmongers for great gain. All these are creatures of civilization."

"That's not what I learned in history books." Teresa was bewildered.

Clotilde looked apologetic. "I talk too much. I think too much for my own good. Gaudier made out of stone and metal what I have tried to make out of my life—to leave the field of invention open, to step out of apathetic and pathetic comforts."

"You're free . . ." Why had she said that? She didn't even know why the people back home considered Clotilde so infamous. If the result of infamy led to the kind of woman standing next to her, then it must have redeeming virtues. She touched the figure by Gaudier as if to add a part to herself, to understand what made her grandmother who she was. "I know now why you never went back to Mexico, Clo . . ."

"I may go back one of these days, if the fancy strikes me."

"Why? If I had a choice I would stay in Paris."

"Ah! But you do have a choice."

"No, no, my father would forbid it. You know how fathers are. They're so archaic." But no matter how archaic, I'll always obey him, do what he says, think what he thinks, Teresa realized. She asked Clo, "How old were you when you ran away from home?"

"I didn't exactly run away." Clotilde's eyes were full of memories.

Teresa did not want to press. She got up and walked around the room, looking at paintings, vases, bronze figures. She pondered aloud, "I can't imagine my father being comfortable in this room. It is too primitive and wild and free, without rules . . ."

Clotilde concluded, ". . . and fathers love rules."

"More than they love us?" Teresa looked at her grandmother intently.

"You want to know how I felt about my father's love?"

"Yes . . ." Teresa's voice anticipated.

"He was proud of me because I was pretty, because I was modest. But he was foremost a businessman and a very rich man. I'm not condemning him. He tried to be fair, but all the rules were his rules. I was a commodity to him, an investment. He could marry me off to a man of property. That was good business."

"That was not love. My father didn't want me to go to the university in Mexico City—but he gave in."

"It's a different time from my time, Teresa. Each generation has its dead ends for women." The grandmother's words were the words of experience.

"Did he try to marry you off to a rich man?" Teresa remembered that part of the story from back home.

"Oh, yes, he had decided to marry me to Don Ignacio, our neighbor, a widower about my father's age."

"I'm glad I live in this generation." Teresa felt a tinge of relief.

Clo's eyes were back in time. "It was something that rich fathers did. Quite commonplace. Then there were the alternatives: If you refused to marry your father's choice, there was the nunnery. Or—remaining single, an old maid, totally dependent on the charity of others, unwanted and ignored. There were times I considered running away with the stable boy. He was beautiful, so young and strong. But that choice led to poverty, sacrifice, discomforts. That's all there was until the day Tío Gaspar came to visit.

"He had squandered his inheritance living the life of a bohemian. I liked him; he treated my brother and me like people. He didn't talk down to us. Spent hours talking about his gypsy life and the freedom of artists. He painted—badly, but with heart. He bought some easels for my brother and me so we could try our hand at watercolors. When my brother showed his first picture to my father, my father was so proud he fooled himself into thinking that Manolo had great talent. But that was to be expected. He always raved about anything my brother did. The sun rose and set around my brother; after all, he was a boy, a varón, a macho, his future heir. I was only a girl."

"It's still like that with many families."

"Oh yes, traditions do not die easy. For thousands of years men have believed themselves superior to women. They do not mean to be cruel. They are just overwhelmed with this self-given image." Clotilde paused, then asked, "Do you have a young man?"

"I've fallen in love several times. Most men want to possess you. So I run away."

"Are you running away now?"

"In a way. The word 'love' confuses me," Teresa confessed.

"Your instinct is pure. You sense that love can destroy you when it is not love but the illusion of love. I myself have been so careful. I hear the wisdom of the prophet and use it to measure the quality of love. It's a good test."

"What prophet?" Teresa was intrigued.

"Kahlil Gibran. His words—'But let there be spaces in your to-getherness . . .' Real love respects separateness. I have chosen well."

Clotilde made her way to the French windows leading to her garden and opened them. She did not go outside but looked out from the doorway as Teresa came up behind her. Teresa was amazed. The garden was like the room—lacking neat symmetry, with a cob-blestone path leading to nowhere in particular and trailing vines snaking up cypress trees. Here and there flowers grew like surprises. A storybook garden—the secret garden—a garden found in dreams. What was that fragrance? Teresa inhaled it slowly, deliberately. "What is it?"

"Italian jasmine, a gift from a man who knows the pricelessness of our aloneness. That is a must: to find the heights of oneself, a solitary journey."

"Where is he now?"

"I don't know. He had a calling to walk the silence among pyramids. But he'll be back. He always surprises me."

"All those alternatives you talked about back home you didn't take any of them, Grandmother." She dared to use the word now. Clotilde's ember eyes accepted.

"My father bought my brother expensive artist's palettes and gave him lessons. But then, Manolo took advantage. He had no talent. His work was awkward and miserable. But he told my father he wanted to study art seriously; would my father finance a stay in Paris? He didn't want to study art, just have a good time. Tío Gaspar knew I was a much better artist. He bought me books on art and told me I must give it my full dedication if I were ever to go to Paris. An open door! My father could send me to an artists' colony, I could travel. When my father heard these plans, he was enraged. How dare I presume I could have such freedoms! I was only a girl! I should dedicate myself to learning the social graces, to embroidering, practicing meekness, to readying myself for a worthy husband. But I did just the opposite. I spent my days reading all the art books I could get my hands on. Mostly I took Manolo's, for he merely threw them aside and never bothered to read one. I worked and worked on land-scapes and painting with charcoal. I was truly convinced I had a talent. I had always competed with Manolo—to dare my father. I needed his approval so badly. My brother and I rode horses, and we loved to ride. I would ride my horse into the hills, without a saddle, my hair wild and unkempt. Again, all this angered my father. Nevertheless, one summer he bought a pair of stallions, beautiful horses, for Manolo and me. Every morning I would race Manolo and beat him every time. My father would watch, and after the race I would run to him, throw back my head, and look him in the eye, hoping for some word of praise. He was oblivious to me, his eyes on my brother, though he chided, 'A man must never allow a woman to outdo him. A varón can ride better than a mere girl. A man must master all things!' Funny, Manolo never mastered anything. I did all things well, but I never heard a word of praise from my father."

They walked into the garden in silence, watching a bird hop along a branch. The cypress looked silver in the slant of shadows and sun. From outside the garden walls came the sounds of moving traffic, whistles, muffled conversations, the splashing of rain puddles left from the night before, a wonderful cacophony touching only the edge of a life. Clotilde led her visitor along the cobblestone path that rambled to nowhere in particular. They came to a low stone bench facing an arched terrace lined with colored earthen pots full of flowers. How Mexican! thought Teresa. They sat absorbing sounds until her grandmother picked up the threads of her thoughts and feelings of long ago.

"Well, my brother did not want to go into the banking business, so he talked my father into sending him to Europe with Tío Gaspar to study art! He, of course, had no intentions of doing so; he wanted the good times of the idle rich. He would write letters to me from here, from Montmartre, about the great life, making new friends. He claimed people were alive in Paris. The phrase echoed again and again in my thoughts—where people were alive, where people were alive . . . I went to my father and asked him if I could go live with Manolo and Tío Gaspar to study art. I reminded him how much more talent I had than my brother. Papá thought I was insane. 'What! You're only a girl! It's time you thought about marriage.' That's when he told me about his plans for marrying me off to Don Ignacio; a great dream of his life—to merge two great estates. I had to pay the price for being *bien gentille*! I argued with him, told him I deserved better than the fates imposed on women in the town. I demanded equality with Manolo; I wanted the same trust and freedom. My mother accused me of wanting to drive my father to his grave. He was close to a nervous breakdown because of my selfish and willful behavior. Why couldn't I behave like a good daughter? Like a good woman?"

Teresa understood. "All choices were dead ends."

Clotilde rose and walked among the earthen pots, feeling the twinges of pain in the memory of a sad experience. Then she stood tall, looked at the blue-hazed sky and smiled down at her granddaughter, continuing her story:

"Dead ends, yes. I had to think of something, something to free myself from a prison that made me a lesser being. I took my horse and ran away into the hills. No, it was not running away, really. When I raced my horse I felt the only freedom I knew. I rode and rode, my mind, my body, my spirit melting in the wind, the wild nature of the hills. I stopped racing my horse when I could go no more! My poor little horse was so tired. It was dark and I realized I was lost. I heard the scurrying of some animal in the dark; it terrified me, so I huddled against a clump of bushes and cried myself into a numbness. Then I decided to die with the night's cold.

"I didn't die with the night's cold, but I almost died after three days of thirst, hunger, and exposure to the heat of the days and the cold of the nights. I had given up when my father's search party found me. He had been looking for two days. I remember how he picked me up in his arms. There were tears in his eyes. Poor dear father. In his blind way he loved me . . . Well, I came down with pneumonia and was delirious for a long time. There were no miracle drugs then. I awoke one afternoon to see my father hovering over me. He was so gentle and concerned. My first thought was to take advantage of that concern. In a weakened voice I begged him not to force me to marry old Don Ignacio, to let me go to Paris. I remember his eyes widening in angry surprise, a look of disbelief on his face. He gave me a long lecture on the consequences of my rebellion, my unloving manner toward my family, my ingratitude, and on and on . . . He stormed out of my room and refused to come visit me during my recovery. In a way, it was a blessing in disguise. I had time to think."

It was time to gather thoughts and feelings and to put them in perspective. Clotilde surveyed her garden as if it were some part of a triumphal memory. "Look around. This garden is so different from the garden in my father's house. It was an impressive garden, manicured to perfection. It had a pond with swans and flowers, all in symmetry, according to color and species. I remember hedge after hedge after hedge. I looked out my window during my recovery and saw some of my little cousins playing hide-and-seek just as I had when I was a child, running from one hedge to another. Two children around four years old were happily playing when a toddler ran toward them. They walked him over to the pond to play. When the child saw the water, he took off his clothes and went in. The water came up to his knees. I saw the nurse running to him, picking him up, shaking him in reprimand. She turned him around and spanked his little bottom. A curious episode of innocence. But the whole day the scene kept coming back into my mind. I was trying to find a solution to my life, and this scene kept intruding. Suddenly I had an answer, a real solution to escape my father's tyranny."

Teresa's eyes awaited the wonderful solution, but Clotilde merely motioned for them to return to the house. Teresa followed Clotilde back into the room where light and shadows played in whispered silences. Clotilde walked to the Gaudier sculpture and touched flowing curves that mated. She kept her hand on the figure as if transferring some unknown energy from the figure to herself. Then she went on with her story.

"After that I became the daughter that my parents wanted. I didn't argue or beg. I simply accepted their plans for my marriage. It was all a feigned acceptance, of course. I pretended great interest in an engagement party they were planning to announce my marriage to Don Ignacio. I was to have the best and most exclusive ball any young girl had ever had. Money was no object. My father, overwhelmed by my docility, told me I could have whatever my heart desired. My heart's desire! He had already forgotten what it was. He meant something he could buy for me.

"So I played his game. 'Papa,' I said, 'I would like a beautiful gown from Paris, by the best designer, elegant, expensive . . .' I remember how his eyes lighted up. To parade me around in finery that would show off his money, he liked that. 'Of course,' he said, the most expensive gown he could buy. Right away my mother and he set about getting hold of the best Paris couturier and ordering a gown to my specifications. In the following weeks I corresponded with a French designer and told him exactly what I had in mind. At the dinner table I would talk of nothing else, like some frivolous fool! My father was so pleased that I had finally fallen into the routine pattern of genteel women.

"Finally the gown arrived. It was a beautiful gown, with masses of tulle and lace and pearl insets, all done by hand. The French designer assured my father there was no other gown like it in the world. Then my life became a whirl of parties with the fawning Don Ignacio by my side. How I hated the man! What makes old, rich, doddering fools think they deserve a young wife? But I went through all the social rituals and pretended gaity. At night I would lock the door of my room and put on my Paris gown. I would stare at the image in the mirror, at the beautiful gown, at the face wanting courage, wanting enough valor to carry out the plan. I knew that what I intended to do would assure my freedom."

The afternoon sun had lost its full ardor. The pale coolness of early dusk came through the opened doors. On a line of light, pieces of shadows touched the coming night with a gentle sobriety. It was a time suitable for sadness, part of the long ago and part of the present. Clotilde picked up the threads of her design from so long ago. "I spent a lot of time after that planning a grand entrance at the ball. My father decided that at a precise moment he would make a champagne toast and direct the guests' attention to my entrance, down the long staircase. I would come down wearing my Paris gown. Both my father and Don Ignacio were looking forward to the occasion with great pride. How appropriate! My father would show off the precious possession he was turning over to his very rich friend!

"The night of the banquet I stayed in my room, making myself beautiful, but my thoughts were with my racing horse, the wind, and the taste of freedom. I could hear the music from downstairs, people talking and laughing. The gown was laid out on my bed in full glory. It was really a beautiful thing. But then, my plan was a beautiful plan. Close to the appointed time for my descent, I put the finishing touches to my face, my hair; then, I was ready. I had to be brave. When I opened the door, the orchestra had just begun playing the music for my entrance. My father's voice rose above the music for the toast, making some remark about the long friendship of the two families that were to be united, then the voice of Don Ignacio toasting our future happiness. In my mind's eye I could see all the glasses raised.

"I swallowed hard and slipped silently down the hall to the staircase. I could feel my whole body trembling, but I knew I could not falter. I was at the top of the staircase. I remember how cold the banisters were. My throat was tight and my head high. I did not look down. I guided my footing on each step as I counted. That was what was important, counting the steps to my freedom. There would be no marriage, no convent, no old maid existence for me. I remember

the next words that came out of my father's mouth: 'May I present
. . .' Then I heard the cries of disbelief and horror, yes, among all
present. Still, I held my head high and looked directly into their
faces, all frozen by shock. I saw my mother fall into a faint. And poor
Don Ignacio, his face was purple, his mouth gaping. He flung his
glass to the floor and left the room without ceremony. But no one
noticed because all eyes were on me. After all, how often had they
seen a girl of my upbringing, betrothed to the richest man in town,
come down a staircase—stark naked . . ."

Clotilde's hands played with the buttons of her blouse, lost in the
memory of her truimph. There was a sudden flurry of curtains
touched by wind. Teresa went up to her and kissed her cheek. "You
were so brave, so brave . . ."

Clotilde smiled as she talked about the consequences of her act.
"My poor darling father! I will really never know the full extent of his
distress, his shame. He couldn't abandon an insane daughter rejected by his best friend. But she couldn't remain in his house as a
constant reminder of the scandal she had caused. He had the solution. He would send her away forever with enough funds to stay
away. Poor darling father!"

"Were you lonely leaving everything behind?"

"Of course I was lonely, but I've never had any regrets."

"It was all worth it, then . . . the solitary journey."

"Oh, yes, it's all that matters, my child."

Both women looked out of the window and caught the last full
colors of the day.

If It Weren't for the Honeysuckle . . .

El Nido was one of many little villages lost deep in barranca country along the Sierra Madres in northern Mexico. Along a cluster of desert mountains, every so often a green hill rose and sank among mountains thick with dry brush, strewn with red stone, nearby muddy streams, and grass-covered crags. The village of El Nido lay on the eastern slope of a hidden mountain. Houses, huts, stores, a placita, and one large, abandoned mansion dotted this desert side, going down, down, until they reached low ground. A long time ago flash floods from a river on the western slope had driven people to high ground. But now the river was gone, dried up. Signs of a river existing in the past were visible where water still narrowed to dry patches surrounded by mud and arbustos polvorosos. Close to the top of the eastern slope a huge white church towered high and was visible from the western slope. From an ancient grove of wild elms, a footpath led for three miles from one side of the mountain to the other. The old riverbed on the west was banked by huge cottonwood trees, deep-rooted weeds of a primitive life. They were staunch and demanded little else than feeding from a deep subterranean river, for the source of life.

The only house around on this side of the mountain had been built on the dry surface of the riverbed; it was cradled in a world of greenness. One wall of the house was invaded by profuse honeysuckle vines. The house belonged to Beatriz. It had been built by Beatriz, who was now digging in the garden. She was a slender, small woman with wisps of brown hair and watery blue eyes. Her mother had had seven children. Two of them had died at a very young age, so Beatriz did not have a memory of them. But she had

47

grown up with four older brothers. There had been many "fathers," so her mother claimed, but she remembered only one who had been a gachupín. She was the only fair-skinned child, so her mother had concluded that the wandering gachupín must have been Beatriz's father, but she wasn't sure. Beatriz as a child had been full of shame when her mother repeated the story as a joke, so she had run to her abuelita, who loved her and made her feel that she mattered in the world. But that had been many years before, in a distant village. Now she was a woman of thirty-nine. Past her youth, she had become part of the riverbed, the honeysuckle, and the giant trees. Together they were the music of a symbiotic breathing. Her desires and her dreams were like the intricate patterns of underground roots, a silent wildness.

It was a cool early morning and she had worked with total concentration around the tomato plants in her thriving vegetable garden. She was content like the fragrance of the moist earth. She worked a while longer, then leaned her body back to rest. Squinting, she looked out to the steeple of the church. Sometimes she imagined the steeple was looking over the mountain to see how she was doing. She made a mental note of things she had to do. She would take her vegetables into the village to sell. With the money she could buy a pane for the broken window. She had to wrap the brown sugar melcochas she had made for the kermes tomorrow at the church . . .

The voice of Sofía broke her reverie. "Mofi! Mofi! Come back —Mofi . . ."

Beatriz watched Sofía limp toward the cottonwoods, then stop, calling piteously, "Mofi! Mofi! Where are you?"

Beatriz wanted to tell her that her cat was never coming back, but she didn't have the heart. Sofía looked over to Beatriz with big, dark, liquid eyes that pleaded. "Do you think he'll come back?"

"I'll get you another cat," Beatriz consoled.

Sofía shook her head. "No. I want Mofi. I miss him so."

The younger woman looked hopelessly at Beatriz who many times felt an impatience with Sofía's fearful dependency. If only she had a little courage. Beatriz had grown to feel protective of Robles's other "wife." Robles's victim was more like it; Sofía, in her early twenties, looked thin and gaunt, her pretty face lined with worry. Her shoulders hunched, she clasped and unclasped her hands and began to whimper.

"Mofi's chasing butterflies somewhere." It was a wish more than a

lie, and Beatriz said it only to stop Sofía's distress. It did make Sofía
feel better. She imagined, "You think so?"

"Cats do that sometimes."

"I—I hope he's happy."

Beatriz wondered what Sofía knew about happiness, poor thing!
The girl stiffened again and her face became distorted with fear.
Beatriz asked, "What's the matter now?"

"You know he's coming today. Aren't you afraid?"

Beatriz's voice was steady and sure. "Not anymore." What she
felt was loathing.

Sofía clutched Beatriz's arm, her eyes pleading for denial. "Today—he's coming today. I marked each day off on the calendar. The
afternoon—he always comes in the afternoon."

"Or the middle of the night. Try to put it out of your mind. You
make yourself miserable. Just keep out of his way."

"I'm so afraid . . ."

"I know . . . I know . . ." She reached out and held the younger
woman to comfort her. Beatriz could feel the frail body tremble. "He
wants you to be afraid. It gives him pleasure, don't you see?"

Sofía shook her head. "He broke my hip. A year ago . . ." She
began to sob hysterically.

"The doctor said it can be fixed. You just wait and see. You'll be
as good as new."

Sofía was wringing her hands; now she clasped them until her
knuckles went white. Beatriz firmly unclasped them. "Listen to me
. . ."

Sofía was not listening, still encapsulated in memories that terrified. Beatriz took her by the shoulders. "Look at me—I said look at
me! I will not let him harm you—do you hear? Not anymore. What's
going to kill you is pure fright. Do you know people have died of
fright? Now, do as I say. Look out there, look at the trees, the sky,
the climbing honeysuckle. Look! Everything is still wet from the rain,
the tears that wipe us clean. Now, breathe in and smell the world
. . ."

Sofía was responding to the world about. She was holding tight
to Beatriz's hand. "Now, let go of my hand and let's go over there
where I was digging. Yes, over there. Sit down. Here, beside me.
Look . . ." Beatriz took a handful of moist, sweet earth and put it in
Sofía's hand. "Smell it. Isn't it wonderful? When I do that it fills me
with a gladness."

Sofía did exactly what Beatriz prescribed. The lines of worry were now gone from her face—the beginning of peace. Beatriz laughed softly. "This place will be ours forever, and our lives will be good. Our days are already good, aren't they?"

"Except when he comes . . ." Sofía's voice was edged with fear.

Beatriz quickly reassured, "He's not going to be around forever. He's tired, sick, old, and drink will be the end of him. Forget him; listen to the river sing . . ."

"You always hear it singing. I can't."

Beatriz began a song that came from earth, wind, and sky; it flowed like light in currents, deep currents of a glad heart. Sofía's fears were temporarily stilled.

After a while Sofía spoke in an almost hopeful voice. "I'll make breakfast." She limped her way back to the cool kitchen. Beatriz tidied her hair, then she went to look at the wide, profuse tendrils of honeysuckle forming a geography of their own, vines extending in all directions. The tendrils crept in and out of the trellises Beatriz had made for their support. It had rained for three days and nights, making the greenness shockingly bright and heavy with sweetness. She looked up to the heavens, watching the clouds move with the secrets of raindrops. The tapestry of earth and sky spelled out such a beautiful order to her, and she loved order above all things.

She had clipped and trimmed the honeysuckle so that it wouldn't choke itself. Its breadth was free to reach for the sun. But now she noticed that she had neglected the bottom growth close to the ground. Here the honeysuckle tangled chaotically. There were no ins and outs, but an overlapping and an entanglement that made her decide to clip and trim it that very afternoon. Six years before, she had planted the honeysuckle, two years after the house was finished. The joy of her house!

What had life been before the house? She remembered the little village of San José. She remembered four brothers and a mother. Most of all she remembered the grandmother who had bought old, tattered books for her to read. She recalled how she had met Robles through her brothers. At fourteen she had ridden her little donkey to town during la feria. The fair was held every year, and every year she and her brothers dyed turkey feathers to make headdresses to sell. Her grandmother had been dead a year, and she was not happy at home where she washed, ironed, and cooked for the family. She was a good workhorse to the family and nothing else. When she reached her brothers' booth she noticed an older man drinking with them. She listened to him talk about all the places he had been and was impressed because she had never been anywhere. How stupid she had been at fourteen! The forty-year-old Robles talked about all the things he would buy for her and all the places he would take her if she ran away with him. Her brothers, half-drunk and unconcerned, had kidded Robles. "Hey, leave her alone. You like them young, eh? Apestoso, you have a wife in every pueblo."

All of this had meant nothing to Beatriz. The prospect of a new dress and travel, the flattery of attention, and the thought that she would no longer be a slave to her coarse brothers and a mother—who cared little for her because she was only a girl—it was enough for her to take up Robles on his offer. At fourteen, there had been no thoughts about consequences.

The lunacy of being a woman! She had run away with Robles in his vegetable truck; for three years she had lived in the back of it. Yes, he had bought her a dress, the only thing he ever bought her. Three years of utter misery, for Robles was worse than her brothers. He went into violent rages when he was drunk. He beat her and raped her at intervals, and there was nothing Beatriz could do. From village to village, three years of sleeping on dirty vegetables or piles of manure, with no cover against rain or freezing weather. She planned to run away, so she memorized how to start the truck and drive it— all in her head. One time he had left her on the outskirts of a pueblo while he visited one of his "wives." She stole the key without his knowing and took off in the truck. But as fortune would have it, she had driven the truck straight into a tree. Dazed and bleeding, she tried to flee on foot, but Robles caught up with her and beat her unconscious.

She lay bruised and swollen in the back of the truck without food or water, wishing she could die, while he drove for two days along a road she had never seen. When she felt better, hunger became an awful gnawing in her stomach. She raised herself up to a sitting position and reached for some turnips to eat. Her mouth was parched and she longed for a drink of water. Robles was driving down a road following a dry riverbed. As they reached the bottom of the hill, she noticed that the world had turned green. Suddenly the truck stopped.

Robles got out of the truck and walked to a broken-down, skeletal shack in the middle of the riverbed. Beatriz, spying a little stream snaking through cottonwoods, found her way to the water. She was washing her face after a long drink when Robles came up behind her and announced, "This is my land."

"Your land? You mean you own it?" She could not believe it; an excitement began to grow. "You mean we're home?"

He laughed disdainfully, as if he had heard a bad joke. "Home? What home?"

Beatriz was beside herself. She ran to the shack, touching its walls, walking into the windowless, doorless, single room that lacked even a roof. "Home . . ." She savored the word as if it were holy.

He laughed his cruel laugh again and ordered, "Get back in the truck. We're leaving."

"Why did you bring me here?" she demanded.

"To show you I am a man of property. It's good land. The river's underneath. But I don't stay in one place. You know that. Let's go."

"I'm staying. I'm going to build a house right here."

"You're crazy." He spat out the words. "Stay—I don't care. When I come back, I'll find only your bones. You'll be a good meal for the coyotes up in the hills." Then he had left.

She ran back to the truck to salvage her grandmother's Bible. That night she had prayed to the Virgin Mary. In the dark she visualized the kind face of her grandmother who had truly loved her. She remembered the thin, veined hands that had held the Bible, the wisps of white hair that had escaped a tight bun at the nape of her neck. She remembered the smell of the old woman's apron as she had laid her head against her abuelita's breast while being taught to read. Oh, the warmth of that love! Oh, the magic of words! Her only possession was her grandmother's Bible, but she had also left her a legacy—a passion for reading. Alone, in the cold, dark shack, when the wind moaned and coyotes howled in the hills, she held the Bible close to her heart and envisioned la anciana who had loved her so. It warmed her; courage glowed.

On the second day, hunger made her go into the village to find work. She had found work in a taquería, washing dishes, then later becoming the cook in the small restaurant. There was enough money now to take care of her small needs and a few extra pesetas to save in a glass jar. When she had saved enough, she began to buy wood, nails, adobe, a hammer. It had gone so slow, so slow, the building of her house—never enough pesetas, never enough time for building. But she never stopped, never gave up. It was the only thing with meaning in her life.

She shook herself free of the memories. There was too much to do. She went back to the house and found Sofía busy in the kitchen. Lucretia was asleep on the cot. Over the wall hung a calendar with a picture of the Virgin wearing a painted smile, passive and calm. Beatriz stared at the bright aura around the saintly face and wondered if she heard their prayers every night, prayers for the safety of the girl-child sleeping so soundly, so innocently. She must never be another victim.

Sofía was pouring water into a pan for cereal. She stood waiting for the water to boil, staring at it with a numb, forlorn look on her face. When it began to boil, she poured in some dry cereal and stirred it round and round. So many things baffled Sofía, so many terrors invaded her life, that Beatriz understood these moments of blocking out existence, this floating into a nothingness. All dreams had been beaten out of Sofía.

She had come into their lives furtive and lost. Robles had found her on a mountain road. She had crossed Snake Mountain and its terrors. Suffering from exposure and starvation, Sofía had taken the liquids given to her by Beatriz with the frozen look of death on her young face. But she had recovered, and recovered quickly, but not soon enough so that Robles would stay to abuse her and use her for his pleasure. Sofía had been the first victim Robles had brought to her. Beatriz had ministered to her needs with patience and compassion for she had been a lost creature in the world herself.

Sofía had become very attached to her. In time she had told Beatriz her story. She had lived in a poor farm in San Angelo with her parents, two teenage brothers and a three-month-old baby sister. They all had died violently. Her father and two brothers had been killed in a feud over the piece of land where their house had stood. The killers had burnt down the house, but Sofía, her mother, and the baby had escaped. They had found themselves crossing La Montaña de las Víboras. The mother had made the choice out of hysteria and desperation. It was a deadly mountain, a mountain of stone and poisonous snakes. But it was the dead heat of the days and the cold of the nights that had given the mother a fever, driving her to her death. The baby had died of hunger when there was no more milk from the mother. Sofía dug their graves with her hands and buried them; she had wanted to dig a grave for herself, to lie in it and wait for death. Instead she had fallen asleep in total exhaustion. She slept a long, long time; then, half out of her mind, she made the perilous climb to the top.

Beatriz listened to the story of the sixteen-year-old with tears in her eyes and a wanting to protect the girl from Robles. He had ordered Beatriz to clean her up so he could take her for a "wife." The older woman shuddered at the horror awaiting the girl. She had to be warned. "Sofía, the man who brought you here is a beast. He wants you for his 'wife.' You know what that means?"

The girl nodded. "Are you his wife?"

A bitter laugh from Beatriz. "He has women all over. Victims, like you and me. Go, go, while you can."

"Why do you stay?"

"This is my house. My house. I built it. But you can still escape. I'll take you to the village. Sometimes he stays away for a long time. When I was building this house, he stayed away for five years. He never goes to the village. A long time ago he cut up a man badly in a bar fight, so he stays away. I'll help you find a job there."

But Sofía had found a protector in the world. She felt safe in the house with Beatriz. She could not be convinced. So it had happened, as it had happened to Beatriz so long ago, the violation, the cruelties. Somehow Sofía had survived it all, but she had been crippled in body and spirit by Robles and had become totally dependent on Beatriz.

Sofía shuffled over to the sleeping Lucretia, and Beatriz knew she was thinking the same thing: "How are we going to save her from him?"

She looked at Beatriz beseechingly. "He's coming this afternoon. What are you going to do?"

Always, she had to have the answers; always she was to be the buttress. She loved Sofía and pitied her helplessness. She had no solution. Yet there must be a solution. Ways came to her mind. "We can tell him she died."

"Of cholera?" Sofía was not satisfied.

"That's the way he brought her to us. He expected her to die."

"Yes, he did . . . yes, he did." There was a tinge of hope in Sofía's voice.

"We'll get her out of the house." A plan was growing in Beatriz's mind. "We'll send her to the church to help with the booths for the kermes. Señora Acosta can feed her supper at the rectory. I'll send a note to Father Ruiz asking him to put her to work until we get there."

"Get there?"

"For rosary services this evening."

Doubt hovered in Sofía's voice. "He won't believe us. What if he goes to the village?"

"He never goes to the village."

Sofía sat down, her body quivering. "He'll kill us. Everytime he comes, I tell myself today is the day, the day we die."

Beatriz s face tightened with impatience as she pulled Sofía out into the garden. "Now stop it. You want to awaken her? Frighten her?"

Sofía remembered. "She doesn't even know about Robles . . ."

"Do you see how important it is to get her out of the house? It's the beginning of a plan. I'll work out the rest. Right now let's do something sensible. Work puts things together, makes things clear." Beatriz really believed it. It had been a point of salvation in her life. "We're out of herbs. Let's cut some herbs."

Beyond the vegetable garden was her bed of herbs growing profusely. Beatriz knelt down and started to loosen the earth around her plants. There was altamisa and estafiate for stomachache, carcomeca for cleaning out the body, masta for the nerves. Beatriz began to cut the té de tila from the mountain of the Yaqui seers. Sofía recognized it. "Isn't that the tea you brew for Robles?"

"Yes. It numbs pain and relaxes the body. Here, taste it. It's sweet."

Sofía took a leaf and put it in her mouth, chewing it slowly. Again, a thought. "I wish it were poison."

"We'll make him some tila to make him sleep."

If only he would sleep forever, thought Beatriz. There must be a way . . .

Lucretia appeared at the kitchen door. "Why did you let me sleep so late?" Then she reminded the two women, "You left the cereal on the stove. It boiled over."

Beatriz stood up, her apron full of herbs, and walked up to Lucretia. She kissed the girl's cheek. "I don't feel like eating cereal anyway. We can have fruit, bread and butter, and a good cup of coffee. How does that sound?"

Lucretia laughed. "Oh, yes!"

Beatriz and Sofía looked at the girl-child with soft blowing hair and bare feet, a child of god, full of love, full of trust. Beatriz and Sofía looked at each other. Their eyes said, Our child is happy and content. Garden, sun, morning, birds—all were a symphony of peace.

Beatriz led the way into the kitchen. "Let's make some breakfast then."

* * *

Lucretia had been informed about her day helping out for the kermes.

"All day?"

"Yes, they'll need you all day. Give Mrs. Acosta my note, and she'll fix supper for you and Father Ruiz."

"Why can't you come?"

Beatriz fumbled for an answer. "Sofía needs help with the dolls she's making for the kermes."

Lucretia searched Beatriz's face with a question. "Where did you get all the books you have?"

Beatriz was somewhat startled by the question. "Books?"

"Yes, you have so many."

"Why do you ask that?"

"Because Father Ruiz told me you have read more books than all the people in the village, including the doctor. You told me you never went to school. Where did you get them?"

"I got them." Beatriz's words were strained and tight. She changed the subject. "Time to get started, before the sun gets too hot."

"I'll wait for the both of you before rosary," Lucretia remembered as she made her way up the path toward the road. She waved at the approaching Sofía who had been out looking for her cat. Both women watched her until she disappeared behind the bend of cottonwoods. Sofía brought Beatriz back to the reality of Robles. "He'll come soon."

Robles, a man who crushed souls between his teeth. Robles who came in kicking furniture, breaking things, cursing, full of drink. The rage had to be vented. He would find his favorite victim, Sofía. In the beginning, Beatriz would interfere when he beat Sofía, so he had turned on her, until she could no longer endure it. Again and again she warned Sofía, "I can't come between you and Robles when he's in a rage. Go—hide—don't let him see you. If you're not around, I can calm him down much better."

"I can't leave you alone with him." Sofía didn't understand.

"He's afraid of me," Beatriz explained. "But he smells your fear like an animal. It excites him. He's rotten."

Sometimes Sofía disappeared into the woods when they heard his truck on the road. But there were other times when he caught them unaware. Poor Sofía! Nothing could stop him when the rage was high. Soon Sofía lay crumpled and whimpering on the floor. Beatriz would step in when the rage was nearly spent. She would place a firm hand on his arm and say ominously, "No more."

He would stare with incredulous, bleary eyes but, with a slobbering, hanging mouth, he would obey. And she knew why. There had come the day when she could no longer take his blows. After beating her, he had fallen asleep in a drunken stupor. Beatriz had taken the small, sharp ax she used to cut vines and jumped on the bed, straddling his bloated belly. She grabbed him by the hair and beat his head against the headboard until he came to his senses, bleary and stinking of panic. Full of hate, holding the ax high over his head, she had threatened, "If you ever lay a hand on me again, I'll split your head." Gulping his astonishment and fright, Robles looked into the eyes of a woman who would not hesitate to kill. She had hissed menacingly, "I can do it while you're asleep—any time."

But now, at the mention of his name, Beatriz shared Sofía's dread. It crawled through her skin. How could they save Lucretia? She would never allow the filthy animal to take the child's innocence. It was up to her. It was always up to her.

Sofía's face flushed darkly. "Let's go away. The three of us. The city—he'll never look there."

Beatriz felt a rush of anger. "To beg in the streets? To sleep in alleys? To starve? This is my house!"

Sofía was relentless. "Your house is on his property. Everytime he comes, he claims the house—says it's legally his. Let's just leave. He's going to throw us out anyway."

"Didn't you hear? This is my house! My house!" The fury in Beatriz's voice made Sofía cringe.

"My house is my life," reasoned an anguished Beatriz. "It's my self. It's my reward for suffering, for the pain of degradation. It's my haven, my ordered world." How could she make Sofía understand that she would never leave it? Leave the house? Struggle out in the

world without anything? Never again. "Out there, Sofía, it's no different from the mountain where your mother died, no different from
the violence of the men who killed your family. It destroys the spirit
inside. This house, it's our haven, our peace, our order, a place to
raise our girl, to see her go to school, even make a good marriage."

"A good marriage . . ." Sofía savored the words without really
understanding.

Beatriz continued, "The earth beneath my feet wants me here.
The house wants me here. I gave up my soul for this house."

"Your soul?" Sofía held her breath in disbelief, expelling it with
the same self-question, "Your soul?"

"Hurricanes die down, floods recede, and volcanoes stop vomiting their fire. Somehow, I don't know why, an order comes about
afterward, and flowers grow, like honeysuckle, sweet as the breath of
heaven."

"Are you all right?"

"I'm fine. So many terrible things have happened to me, to you.
Don't you see? We deserve this place, this peace."

The sudden clatter of birds' wings reminded Beatriz of things to
be done, of finding a way out of a hell called Robles. She must keep
busy to dispel a growing fear, a fear that could overwhelm. Work,
put something in order, then things would be clear, and hope would
find some kind of solution. She had to trim the honeysuckle. Oh, the
greenness of the world! There she could find a wondrous tranquility,
a good clean impartiality, for a little while. She approached Sofía,
put her arm around the frightened woman, promising, "I'll find a
way. I'll make things right."

She felt some of the tenseness leave Sofía's body. Beatriz told
her, "I'm going to keep busy. That's when I can sort things out. I
have to trim the bottom of the honeysuckle."

Sofía walked to the kitchen door, stopped, turned, and asked in
soft compliance, "Shall I make something?"

"He'll expect food. What do you have? Oh, I know, the
chicken."

"I already cut it up for soup. He likes chicken soup."

"Let's both keep busy then." She repeated the words to herself.
Beatriz had no doubt there was salvation in work. She picked up her
ax and a rusty spade and made her way to the honeysuckle vines.
She examined the bottom and found incrustations growing in a wil-
derness. Traces of three days' rain everywhere. Her strokes with the

small hatchet were swift and trained. The vines could hardly breathe. She set about to give the bottom of the vines some kind of space, a path for the vines to find the sun. She worked in full absorption for a while. The church bell had announced the noon hour as she came to the side of the wall where there was little sun. Moisture was visible on leaves and petals. She lifted the vines to find the main artery, the one to lie salvaged when the rest were cut away. In the cool darkness of the undergrowth she saw a whiteness gleam.

Three white, fruiting, amanitas, full blown, forming the usual fairy ring. The ring was completed by smaller stumps of spores that had failed fruition. But the three, the three, these beautiful three were a blown reproduction of a whiteness found in dreams. Beatriz stared in fascination. An excitement grew in her and her blood found a song, "I shall find a way, a way . . ." She looked up at the climbing honeysuckle and felt its triumphal presence. A breathing, smiling god looked down at her, the vestal maiden. The honeysuckle had given her a gift, an answer to her problems. She did not doubt; she touched the white glories with a growing assurance. But she had to be careful, for the pollen of the amanitas burned the skin. She swiftly cut them with the ax and put them in her apron pocket. Then she went back to her work, cutting the small, overlapping vines away from the main stem. The flowers on the honeysuckle vines had a brilliant timbre—trumpets of freedom, trumpets of freedom. She had to tell Sofía. She went back to the coolness of the kitchen and found Sofía cutting up cilantro and garlic. The chicken was already simmering in a pot. Sofía looked furtively toward the door when Beatriz entered.

"We're going to have an abundance of squash and onions this season," Beatriz informed Sofía as she made her way to wash her hands.

"He'll come anytime now. Are we going to do it? Tell him Lucretia's dead?" Sofía's questions were thick with doubt.

"Yes, died of cholera. We couldn't save her. She died like the rest of her family."

"The plan will do for today, but what about the next time he comes?"

"There won't be a next time." Beatriz's words rang clear, mixing with the soft shadows in the room. When she heard the impossible, Sofía turned and looked at Beatriz intently, narrowing her eyes in disbelief. "No next time?"

"I've found the answer. How we can rid ourselves of the beast."
"Rid ourselves?"
Beatriz reached into the pocket of her apron and took out the three amanitas. "They are the gift of the honeysuckle."
"Poison mushrooms?"
"Yes."
"For Robles?"
"Yes . . . the fruit of freedom."
"No, not that way . . ." Sofía recoiled at the thought.
"Then what way, Sofía? You asked me to make things right. Well, this plan was fated by the gods."
"What gods? Don't talk like that. You frighten me."
"I need your help."
"I can't." Sofía was crumbling again.
"You rather he rape Lucretia? Throw us out of my house? Beat you to death? He can, and he will one day. This way is so easy, Sofía."
"To take a life?" Sofía asked righteously.
"To kill the dragon with seven heads."
"It's murder, Beatriz."
"Listen to me! I'm tired of picking up the broken pieces. You snivel and cry and grovel in fear all day long, clinging to my skirts like the coward that you are. You left it up to me, remember?"
"Not this way, please, not this way!"
"For once in your life, be brave. The gods are on our side."
"There are no gods on our side. You're thinking crazy."
"He's forcing our hand. It's his doing, Sofía. He comes into our lives like a bellowing wounded pig, destroying everything in his path, maiming. He's so miserable. You really think he wants to live?" Beatriz had to defeat Sofía's convictions.
"Everybody wants to live," Sofía answered lamely.
"Like Mofi?" Beatriz knew this was her trump card.
"What do you mean?"
"I saw him kill Mofi. He grabbed Mofi by the tail and smashed her head against the wall after you ran out, after he beat you."
"He killed Mofi?" Sofía's stricken face refused to believe.
"He'll do the same to us." Beatriz knew she had won.
"Killed Mofi? Killed my furry ball of love? For no reason . . ." The weaker woman folded in pain.
"Robles? Reason?" Beatriz's voice was strident with scorn. Sofía's

eyes were wild, all the terror in her life welled. She was full of the energy called hate. She walked up and down, all moral convictions were pushed away, giving place to rage.

"You're right! Dragon with seven heads! No, no—he's a scorpion. I used to kill scorpions in the fields. They would leave me with the babies, the women who gave birth out in the fields. I was just a girl then. I would wrap the baby and cover it with sand up to the shoulders, always under a shade tree. The cool sand would keep the baby alive. The mother would go back to work in the fields. It was my job to kill any scorpions that came near the baby. I killed them with a rock. I can kill a scorpion."

Then Sofía floated into a pain all her own. She sang her pain for Mofi. "No, no, no, no . . ." Beatriz waited quietly for the pain to spend itself. Then she broke the silence. "How else can we save our child?"

*   *   *

Beatriz had cut flowers for the table. The chicken soup was simmering on the stove. She removed the pot from the fire and set about to washing and slicing the amanitas. When they formed a little heap on the cutting board, she stared at the brownish-white pile. Mixed feelings were mounting. A kind of wary anticipation, a tinge of fear, but there was no sense of guilt. Why don't I feel any guilt? she asked herself. She pushed the thought aside as she looked for a smaller pot to pour the portion of chicken soup that was to be Robles's. She poured it into a blue enamel pan, then she threw in the mushrooms. She glanced over at Sofía who sat immobile, numb. She knew her companion was paralyzed by fear and guilt. She was waiting for the sound of Robles's truck. After watching the pieces of mushroom float and dance in the liquid, mixing well with the cilantro and small potatoes, Beatriz sat down at the kitchen table and faced Sofía. She knew why she felt no guilt. She knew too well and she had to tell someone. "I know it's wrong, Sofía, I know it'll work, and I know why I feel no guilt."

"I wish I could be calm like you." Sofía's tearful voice wavered. "Look at you! You even put flowers on the table. Why did you put flowers on the table?"

Beatriz knew it was an accusation. It didn't matter. She smiled at Sofía as she explained. "I feel as if we have been caged for a lifetime, and now we have the key to open the door to freedom. Don't you feel that?"

Sofía shook her head. "Free? What about the weight of the guilt I'm feeling?"

Beatriz confessed. "I only feel this—this pleasure in my guts. The thought of seeing Robles dead . . ."

"Stop!" Sofía clenched her hands and lowered her head.

"Sofía, is there something wrong with me?" Beatriz reached out and put her hands over Sofía's. "I feel as if there were something unholy and heartless in me. Maybe, maybe because it isn't the first time—the first time I've taken a life.

"You've . . . you've . . ." Sofía dared not even think it, much less say it.

"Don Carlos. You know that big mansion, the one that's all boarded up in the village? That was his house. I used to work for him."

"I heard he died of a heart attack. Didn't he?" Sofía's soft eyes were pleading for an answer.

Beatriz was caught in painful memories. "Day after day after day, the exhaustion, the defeat. I would fall asleep with a saw in my hand, nails in my mouth. I could not stop, I could not rest—the house, the house had to be built. Many times I went hungry; I bought adobes instead. I would forget I had not eaten for days and went on working and working on the house. It was like a fever that kept me going, never stopping, until my body just collapsed. I would pass out, then come to, deluding. In my head—or maybe I really saw it—I imagined it, so real, so real. I'd see the house completed—windows, walls, doors, all finished. Delirium? Perhaps. Deep, deep down I knew I didn't have the strength, the money, or the time to build it by myself . . ."

"But you did it."

"No, no—not by myself. I went to work for Don Carlos as a housekeeper. The job paid a little more than what I made at the taquería. I had heard that Don Carlos was a wise and learned man. When I saw his study, with books covering wall after wall, I knew it was true. In the winter the long walk from here to his house left me frozen. I would make the walk before sunrise so I could go into the house early on these cold mornings, make myself a cup of tea, and then go to his study and read and read and read. He slept late into the morning, so the old man never knew. It was so wonderful, all the worlds that opened up to me . . ."

"The books in your room. That's where they came from?"

"They were his."

"He gave them to you."

"No." Beatriz's face was taut with bitter memories. "He knew about the house. He would make jokes about it, not in a vicious way. But he knew I would never be able to do it by myself. One day he handed me this paper to sign, an agreement, he said. If I promised to stay for one year and do everything he said, he would give me enough money for materials and workers to help me finish the house. Of course I signed it. I never imagined . . . I thought he was a man to be respected for his years and his position in the town. One day I was changing the bedding in his room when I saw him at the door, watching me. I knew what he wanted. He told me to take off my clothes and lie on the bed. Oh, the obscenity of that bed! It was his playpen and I became his plaything. I felt so unclean, so worthless."

Beatriz covered her mouth as if to stifle a scream, her body shuddering with remembered disgust. He hurt my body, maimed my soul. Two months later, he caught me reading. For some reason he awakened early and found me in his study. He grabbed the book from me and hit me across the face. He was enraged. How dare I read his books! My mere touch defiled them; to him I was no more than an animal. Then he laughed. A joke, he said, a joke! How did I learn to read, a nothing like me? He threw me out of the room and had a locksmith put a lock on the door. The only key hung on his key chain. Oh, he was old and feeble and had a bad heart. When I went to work for him he had given me careful instructions about his medicine. Oh, the gods are just! The very next afternoon, after the lock had been put in, he was playing like an idiot with my naked body when he started to choke and his face turned purple. I knew it was a heart attack. He pointed a bony finger toward his medicine, his eyes pleading. I did nothing. Then, while he watched helpless and dying, I found his key chain, took the key that unlocked the study, dangled it before his face, and walked away. I had mercifully refused him his pitiful life."

Sofía was moaning, "I'm so sorry, so sorry . . ." Beatriz was by her side, comforting. "It happened a long time ago. It's all gone now. I remember going down to the study, opening the door, and taking book after book. There were so many. While he lay dead on his bed, I found some boxes, packed the books. I paid a boy to take them to the rectory. Days later, they found him dead and closed up the house. Little by little I brought all the books here. They never questioned me about his death or about the books. So you see, I helped him to die. I felt the same pleasure then as I feel now. I feel no guilt. Absolutely no guilt . . ."

The sound of Robles truck broke the silence of the outside world. Sofía's eyes widened in terror. "It's h—him."

Beatriz went to the door, then gave rapid, short orders to Sofía. "Wipe that look from your face. Don't say anything. Keep out of his way. Whatever you do, for our sake, don't break down, understand? Let me handle him."

Sofía was looking around the room in desperation, as if trying to find a place to escape to. A wild question came to her lips. "Where's Mofi? Did you bury Mofi?" She moaned, her hands clenched in prayer, eyes tightly closed to erase the world. "It's him—it's him . . ."

Beatriz took Sofía's face in her hands and observed harshly, "He's clever, he can read what's on your face and you're going to get us killed. Is that the way you want it?"

Sofía's horror mounted with the truck door's slam and the sound of heavy trudging steps coming to the door. The uneven steps were muffled by loud cursing. Fungus of the world, thought Beatriz. He was drunk, but that was in their favor: he would be dull witted, thick tongued, and wanting sleep. Yes—yes, it was better that way. The swollen poison stood in the doorway. Beatriz felt no fear.

Robles was breathing hard and his face was pale. His eyes were unseeing. He made his way unsteadily to a chair and slumped down heavily. His head fell forward into his hands as he made deep retching sounds. He was going to vomit, Beatriz was sure. Yes, he stood and headed for the bathroom. He pushed Beatriz roughly aside, then disappeared into the other room. Soon the sounds of heaving and vomiting filled the room. Beatriz motioned to Sofía to stay in the shadows while she sat at the table calmly until he emerged from the bathroom. He looked like a sick animal as he tried to focus through his bleariness.

"I feel sick."

Beatriz smiled. "Want to lie down?"

"Eh?"

"You should lie down. I'll get you a cold compress."

Robles nodded, stumbled to the cot, and fell heavily on it. In the dark corner Sofía grimaced and closed her eyes tightly. Beatriz quickly and efficiently rose to get a basin which she filled with cold water, then she found a wash cloth and made her way to the cot. She sat down by his side, wrung out the cloth, and placed it on Robles's forehead. She did it several times until he mumbled his satisfaction. "Ahhh."

Beatriz motioned to Sofía with her head. "Put the tea kettle on. A cup of tila tea will settle his stomach. It'll help him relax. That's what you need—your cup of tea."

He groaned his answer. "Awww."

Beatriz turned to Sofía who was already lighting the stove. "Take out the whiskey." She wiped Robles's face again. "You'll feel much better. I'll even put a little whiskey in it."

He opened his mouth, exposing rotten teeth. "Ahhh."

Beatriz informed him, "We have a whole bottle of whiskey, don't we, Sofía?"

Sofía stuttered, "Y-y-yes."

"Whiskey?" Robles showed signs of interest.

It's better than the tequila you've been drinking all day." She had to find out how much he had drunk.

"Beer," was the sullen response.

"Beer? You must have finished a barrel." Beatriz calculated the alcohol in the man.

"Uh-huh," was his thick response.

He'll fall asleep—he'll fall asleep right after we feed him the chicken soup. He'll give us no trouble, thank God. Beatriz relaxed, coaxing, "I'll take off your shoes, bring you a basin with warm water and baking soda to soak your feet."

"Vieja." A tinge of suspicion in his voice.

"¿Sí?"

"You're still getting out of my house, you and that cripple!"

Her mind clicked—the injustices of the world—men had decreed that living things were not equal. Men had decreed that women should be possessions, slaves, pawns, in the hands of men with ways of beasts. It had been decreed that women should admire a manhood that simply wasn't there.

Beatriz gave no answer to his threat. She just sat by his side, her face carved in hate. She had to help Sofía with the tea. She made her way to Sofía who was already pouring the tea into a cup, the cup precariously sliding on the plate held by her trembling hand. Beatriz took the whiskey bottle and poured some into the cup, then took it to Robles, saying, "It'll make you feel so much better."

Robles, slumped against the wall on the cot, turned to face her, groaning and moaning. He sat up shakily, with great effort, then stood, reeling, his body swaying in a circle. "I can drink it myself, cabrona. Give it to me!"

He snatched it out of her hand, spilling the tea all over his shirt. The drunk let out a howl like a maddened bull and struck Beatriz across the face. The blow froze her. Robles glared at her, his eyes wondering why she had taken the blow without a word. Sofía fell into a chair, head in hands, swaying back and forth, whimpers writhing out of her throat. Robles taunted, "Beatriz, where's your ax, eh?"

Beatriz smiled resignedly. "I'll get you another cup."

She went to the stove and filled the cup again, pouring whiskey with a steady hand. With a subservient gesture, she offered it to him again. He gulped it down, then threw the cup against the wall, screaming his demand, "Give me the whiskey!" Without a word, Beatriz handed him the bottle. As he took it, he glared at her warily, then drank, slurping, as it ran from the sides of his mouth. He looked around the room. "Where's the girl?"

Sofía was sobbing now. Beatriz had to be careful. He might not believe her. "Lucretia died, Robles."

"Died?" He would not believe it. Sofía's wild sobs angered him. "Shut up! Shut up! You cripple!" He glowered with disbelief, repeating, "Died, eh?" He grabbed Beatriz's arm. "You're lying, you piece of shit!"

Disdainfully, she removed his fingers from her arm. She felt her senses floating in a great calm. There is no storm, no storm. Again a power suffused her, the same feeling as when she had denied Don Carlos his medicine . . . a savoring of revenge. Now, to function on volition, deliberate machinations, to appease him, to dull his senses, a mortal gesture against the kind of death Robles brought with him every time. Any fear in her had dwindled away. Robles was screaming in her ear, "Where is she? Don't you try to fool me, you slut!"

"Don't you remember? She was so sick when you brought her to us. You told us her whole family had died of cholera. How could she survive?"

"When did she die?"

"About a week after you left her here."

"I know a lying whore when I hear one," he hissed vehemently. Suddenly he turned on Sofía. "I'll get the truth out of that sniveling coward!" He made a grab for the cowering woman, dragged her by the hair, then, twisting her arm, he brought her to her feet. Sofía screamed in pain. "The truth, you garbage!"

A long scream of pain came from her throat. "She's d-e-a-d!"

He twisted her arm as if to break it. Sofía was choking in her own pain. She could stand no more. "She's in the village . . . the . . . village . . ."

He threw Sofía to the floor to confront Beatriz. But Beatriz did not give way: she looked him in the eye. "We did it for you."

"For me?"

Beatriz saw bewilderment on his face. She continued, "Look at you! You want Lucretia to see you like this? Is that the way a bridegroom should look? You need a shave and a bath and, above all, rest—so you can be at your best for your new bride. I have a clean shirt for you. Don't you want her to be proud of her husband? She's waiting for us to fetch her."

There was a mixture of confusion and anticipation on his face. He couldn't believe, but he wanted to believe, his feelings and thoughts in disarray. She smiled at him with unafraid eyes. He asked, "Waiting?"

"Yes, Sofía and I are going for her when you're ready. Now you tell me, you don't want her to see you like that. You want to be in your full manly vigor when you take her. To have that kind of strength, you need food and rest, then you'll be like new."

She could tell he liked what she was saying. She continued the coaxing, easy and calm, for she knew she had the upper hand now. The beast would eat out of her hand. "I made a pot of chicken soup for you. I know you haven't eaten for days. I made it just the way you like it, with small potatoes, celery, garlic, cilantro. You eat and rest. It's three miles to the village. By the time we come back with her, you will have rested."

Sofía picked herself up while listening to Beatriz as if it all were happening in a dream. She was caught, mesmerized by the confidence Beatriz exuded. Beatriz pulled out a chair for Robles. "Now you sit down, and I'll get you a bowl of delicious soup. Then I'll go look for your shaving things."

Robles sat down at the table. There was what might have passed for a smile on his face. When Beatriz brought him his soup, he inquired, "Pretty, eh, after you cleaned her up?"

"Beautiful! Eat your soup. Doesn't it smell delicious?" She turned to Sofía, asking with a lightness in her voice, "Bring glasses. We have to drink to Robles and his future bride."

Still dazed by Beatriz's euphoric state, by her daring, Sofía did as she was told. Beatriz poured some whiskey in each glass, then handed one to Robles and another one to Sofía. She raised her own. "To you, dear Robles. May the future bring all you deserve."

The three drank the whiskey, then Beatriz sat opposite Robles and watched as he took the first mouthful of soup. "It's not too hot, is it?"

Robles savored the first spoonful, then commented, "It has mushrooms. You forgot to tell me it had mushrooms."

Sofía could not stand it anymore. She silently slipped out of the house. Beatriz knew the poor woman was repelled by the smiling cat playing with the mouse. Robles had eaten his bowl of soup too fast. "Here I'll fill your bowl again, then I'll leave you to enjoy your food. Remember, it's a long way to the village. So you have time for a nap. You can clean up afterward, long before we return."

He merely nodded and continued eating. At the kitchen door, Beatriz turned to look at him one last time. Lucretia had been saved from the pestilence. Her skein of order would be maintained, with no more furies to defile it. She stepped into the yard, breathing in the brightness of the sun.

*   *   *

The waiting had created new tears. Sofía asked desperately, "How long does it take?"

"I looked in and he had gone to bed. He's sleeping peacefully."

"Maybe he's dead already. I don't believe it. It was too easy."

Beatriz assured her, "It'll be soon. He probably passed out with all that drink in him."

"Isn't there any pain, any symptoms?"

"Usually there are cramps, dizziness, vomiting. He's snoring like a pig."

"Aren't you afraid?"

"Of what?"

"Of going to hell . . . after what we've done."

"A merciful thing, Sofía. He's old and tired and so miserable."

Beatriz knew Sofía did not believe her. Their two different worlds were forever bound by a single action. Hell? wondered Beatriz. I don't believe in a hell. Words from the Bible began to run in her head. They fell from her lips with joy. " 'And the earth was without form and void, and darkness was upon the face of the deep. Then God divided the light from the darkness and He said, "Let the earth bring forth grass, the herb yielding seed, and the fruit tree yielding fruit after its kind." ' Oh, Sofía, look at all the gladness God made. This house, this yard, is a piece of his heaven."

"I don't think you believe in God," Sofía accused. Still, she asked, "Do you?"

"I don't know, Sofía. I believe in the greenness of the earth. Listen! The river's singing again. Can't you hear it?"

"No. It's only a dry riverbed."

"I will teach you how to listen. I have such plans for us. First, our trip to the city to fix your hip. Then Lucretia must go to school . . ."

"I don't want to hear them now. How can you be so sure he's going to die?"

"I'm sure."

"You sound so evil."

"No, Sofía, not evil. I love order around me more than anything. Yes, there's a wildness in me from all the things that have happened in our lives, the sadness, the loneliness, the violences. They grow inside us—mix—and become something I cannot explain. Remember when we were walking home from church one Sunday evening and we saw a couple in the park? They were kissing—remember?"

"Yes. You said the moon hurt so much."

Beatriz replied in sweet cadence, "It wasn't the moon. It was not knowing the love of a good man. Maybe that's what happens: we cannot love or believe—for a while. We'll have to learn, Sofía."

"You really think there are good men in the world?"

"Oh, Sofía, there must be—somewhere."

The sun was deep in the west now, the sky a darker blue. They sat on the sweet grass, listening. No sounds came from the house. But the sounds of the world combined into a distant and shadowy beginning. The steeple of the church shone with the setting sun. Beatriz intuitively knew it was time now. She stood up, then cleaned off her skirt and tidied her hair, a ritual. She put out her hand and helped Sofía to her feet. Together they walked toward the house with fresh momentum, a sturdy confidence. Beatriz went straight to the cot where the figure of Robles lay. Sofía followed her. Sofía whispered, "Is he dead?"

"Not yet. He's in a coma."

Robles eyes were wide open, and his mouth had a slight twitch that looked almost like a smile. Suddenly, the death rattle cut the silence like a filament of hollowness, something without roots, something lost in the course of evolution. For the two women, peace wore a bright design. Beatriz came to the next order of things. "We have to bury him."

"Bury him?"

"Yes, and I know exactly where. Where I found the amanitas, in that soft dark corner, underneath the honeysuckle vines. I'll get the shovel."

They dug for a long time, using the shovel and a bucket. They finished when the dark had fully cloaked the light. They wrapped him in sheets, dragged him out, and laid him gently in the moist earth where a fairy ring had once grown. Then they covered up the grave, an offering to a god dressed in honeysuckle vines.

Later, as they walked along the road leading to the church, they heard the vespers bell. They hurried to meet Lucretia for rosary services.

The Burning

The women of the barrio, the ones pockmarked by life, sat in council. Their minds were a dark, narrow tunnel that had long ago withered their souls. They had gathered in this heath all as one to condemn an enemy, to accuse her, to punish her. One old woman added fuel to the fire of hate. "This Lela changes light into darkness. I've seen her with my very own eyes!"

"You know the caves outside the town?" A woman dressed in black added to the fuel. "At night, when she stays in the caves, she goes through their open mouths into the long darkness and stays there days on end. When she's there I have seen lights appear like fireflies. It's her black magic! She's working some evil against us."

One with wild eyes nodded her head in affirmation. "She makes this potion. She says it's medicine for the sick. I say that it's the bitterness of good; I think she makes it for herself. What could it be but the red honey milk of evil?"

A cadaverous old woman pointed to the darkened sky. "I hear thunder. Lightning is not far."

A murmur rose in unison. "We could use some rain, but rain will not cleanse her evil."

The oldest one among them, one with dirty claws, stood up with arms outstretched to the sky, sniffing the sky of night as lightning flashed. Her voice was harsh and came from ages past. "She must burn! She's a witch! A witch!"

As the women circled the heath, a cloud, black and tortured, dug into the sky. Each pair of eyes looked into another pair—were they all in agreement? There were only grating sounds of frenzy, tight and straining. Thunder was riding the lightning now, directly over their heads. But still no signs of blistering words to justify the deed to come. Some women found their voices; anger, heavy like the cloud, crouched and waited for further accusations. Another soul took up the dirge. "The Devil's pawn! On nights like this, when the air is heavy like thick blood, she sings among the dead, preferring them to the living. I have seen her chase the dead back to their graves."

A feverish assent from another member of the group: "She stays and stays with those who die, like one possessed. You know what I think? I think she catches the fleeing souls of the dead and turns them into flies. She doesn't want them to find heaven."

They chorused, "A plague!"

Another clap of thunder reaffirmed. An old one, with nervous, clutching, spidery hands, made the most grievous charge, the cause for the meeting. With bony gestures the old woman shaped the anger in her heart. "She's the enemy of God! She put her obscenities on each doorstep. She wants us Christians as accomplices. She has committed sacrilege against the holy church!"

The fervor rose like a tide. "Burn her! Burn her! Burn her!"

The council howled that she must burn that very night. The sentence given could only have been born of night. Fear takes the disguise of outrage at night. The craved human sacrifice. The accused, a woman called Lela, was the eye of the the storm. She must be erased from the world to make them whole when the earth turned to light. It was a tempest grown in narrow margins where slavish minds punish the free. "Lela! Lela! Lela must burn!"

* * *

Lela had crossed the blue mountain to their pueblo many years before. It was one ranging south in La Barranca de Cobre. She had walked into San Angelo a bloody, ragged girl. In her apron she had carried some shining sand. She had hesitated on the outskirts of the pueblo, like a frightened fawn, to be asked into the village. The people gathered around her, wondering where she had come from. She had fallen to the ground in exhaustion. The people of the town did not take to strangers, especially to barranca Indians, los descalzos, for they were thought to be savage and uncivilized. She was a frightened child, hungry and lost, but she was a human being needing help. They took her in reluctantly. She remained a stranger to them, all that time. She refused baptism and never attended the Catholic church. She said her pagan prayers and shaped little pagan gods from clay. She sang songs to her nature gods in her dialect and kept her native tongue, learning just enough Spanish to make herself understood. The pueblo knew she was a Tarahumara from Batopilas, but it was her refusal to convert to Christianity that made people suspicious and hostile toward her.

She was kind and gentle and hard working, and she was able to cure the sick with her miracle sand. She was able to cure people with skin diseases, sores, or open wounds. Some wondered if the sand was the evil magic of her gods, but the results of the cure were sure and clean, so she became their curandera, outside their Christian lives.

She became the potter's helper since that had been her mother's trade. The potter was old, and some years after her arrival, he died. She now made beautiful things with clay for the village and surrounding villages. She became the favorite healer for many villages; her life was a busy one. But there were no suitors and few friends. Besides curing with medicinal herbs, she learned to set bones with great success; still, she was never invited to a baptism or wedding. Certainly never to a dance or a village festival. The role of outcast could have been hard and unacceptable to her, but she was in tune to the cycles of the universe, and her imagination and her beliefs sang the song of stars and seasons. She knew down deep that life simply passes unto life. Each of her days had a pattern of firmed senses and feelings. A current flowed through her from the earth, thus she intuitively knew the close mystery of her source. And the loneliness in her life, the emptiness, was filled with a steadiness and grace for necessary things. In time the loneliness became a silent love for the people of the village. Were they not miracles? She would listen to the silence, the nothingness and the allness of which life was made, learning to live happily in the oneness of herself. Many times she made plans to go back to Batopilas, but there was always someone who needed her. The welfare of the people came first.

Each day she lived the memories of her faith and that was what gave her the greatest joy. Her mother and father, and all her family before her, circling the centuries, had been the magic potters for the holy temples. They were endowed with a spirit that ran through their fingers, a spirit transferred to the clay figures of the little gods. Now they could hear the prayers and supplications of the people. Her mother and father had taught her how to shape the little gods, the household gods that shared family blessings and family problems. The stone images of the greater god, like the awesome Tecuat, who

commanded silence and obedience, were sculpted by the holy artists, the elder wise. The greater gods were ritual gods that never got
close to the people. They were the Lords Above and existed mostly
to punish the weak and sinful.

She remembered as a child going to the rituals in honor of
Tecuat. She would make her offering in front of the forbidding figure, then run off with a sigh of relief. But the little gods! Ah! They did
everything human beings did: laugh, sing, dance, make love, enjoy,
and she learned to mold them in the manner of the act. Each home
had its little god. He lived with members of the family as a friend, a
confidant, and a comforter. They did not rule or demand obedience
but were a source of hope, companions to the people. Little gods,
born of river, sky, fire, seed, birds, and butterflies, were hidden in
small niches in the woods, in the hills, along the river, in the caves,
and in the natural grottoes behind the waterfall.

When she was growing up, Lela would often go god-hunting in
the woods and hills and river paths. She would find a god in a cave
or in a hidden niche overgrown with vines. A special, holy time, a
time of prayer and meditation, and of talk. The little god, smiling at
her, would accept her prayers and her simple offering. She would sit
cross-legged, her eye level to his, and confide her dreams and fears.
Both dreams and fears were intertwined in the mind of the young
girl. She dreamed of venturing out beyond her village to discover
new worlds, to learn new things, but she feared leaving her parents
and her friends. Her longing to leave frightened her because she
dreamed about it every day; she was ashamed of telling anyone she
was restless and desiring new things to learn and do.

One day she walked too far toward the pines, too far toward a
roar that spoke of rushing life. She followed a butterfly that must also
have heard the command of dreams. It flitted toward the lake; she
followed, looking for little gods in the glint of the sun and in the open
branches that pierced the absoluteness of the sky. The soft breath of
the wind was the breath of little gods, and the crystal shine of rocks,
polished by wind and water, was their winking language.

When she reached the lake, Lela stepped into the water, feeling
the cool mud against her open toes. She gently touched the ripples
of the broken surface with her fingertips, ever so lightly. After a while
her feet felt no more bottom, so she cut through the water with
smooth, clean strokes, swimming out to the pearly green rocks that
hid the roar. She floated for a while, looking up at the light filtering

through eternal trees. The silence spoke of other than itself; it spoke in colors born of water, plant, and sun. She swam all the way to the turn that led to the cradle of the roar, the waterfall.

This became her favorite place until the day god-hunting became a child's game. She was no longer a child, and the dream of going beyond her world possessed her every thought. She could think of nothing else. So one day she went beyond the waterfall without telling any one, beyond the purple trees that led to the mountain that hid the other worlds outside of Batopilas.

If she could cross the desert, she would find another village, other people, other ways. In her innocence she never realized that people could be different from her. The spirits of the little gods protected her. Feeling safe in their protection, she journeyed one whole day, the piercing sun beating down mercilessly. She lost all sense of direction; the terrain was all new to her, so she made her way toward the horizon. At dusk her dry, parched skin welcomed the coldness of the night wind. But not for long, for the wind grew cold and was just as merciless as the sun had been. She found a clump of mesquite behind some giant saguaros. This became her shelter for the night. Cold and hungry, she curled up and gazed into the garden of stars which comforted her until she fell asleep.

At first light she awakened and quickly resumed her journey. She was halfway up the mountain by noon. She rested for a while, then set out again. Her mouth felt like sand and her stomach gnawed as she followed a path made narrow by a blanket of desert brush. Thorns tore the flesh of her legs and feet as she made her way up, up to the top. But before she reached it, climbing became a torture—no sure footing until the path lost itself in a cleavage of rocks. Night again, but she was not afraid, for the sky was full of blinking little gods.

Making her way along a zigzagging path, she lost her footing, falling down, down into a crevice between two huge boulders. As she fell, her lungs filled with air, then her body hit soft sand. On the edge of her foot she felt the cutting sharpness of a stone. She lay stunned for a while, feeling a sharp pain on the side of her foot. Somewhat dizzy, she managed to sit up to look at it. It was bleeding profusely, blood soaking the soft sand. The huge boulders loomed upward, rebuking her helplessness. She began to cry. She quickly dried her tears and set about stanching the blood. She tore off a piece of her skirt to use as a bandage. While wrapping her foot, she noticed the sand. It was crystaline and loose, shining in the light of a rising moon. Lela took a handful of the sand and let it spill from her fingers, fascinated by the flow of silver grains.

"The sand of little gods," she whispered to herself. She. took some sand and rubbed it on the wound before she wrapped it. Burning with fever she tried to sleep. The fever filtered into dreams of delirium. But as the night went on, she dreamed of the sand becoming the faces of happy little gods. She slept until dawn passed over her head.

The Indian girl rested, then awakened feeling well. She had no fever. She examined the wound, and to her amazement, there was no swelling or infection, only a healthy scab. If it had healed normally, it would have taken weeks to reach that stage of healing. She stood and felt no pain when she put weight on her foot. She kneeled and kissed the shining sands. The sand was too precious to leave behind. It could cure many wounds. She would take as much of the miracle as she could. She took off her apron and filled it with sand, securing it before climbing up the crevice. When she reached the top, she circled the crevice for miles, finally ending up on the other side of the mountain. Below her was another world. She made her way down, fatigued and half-starved, into the arms of strangers.

This place was to be her home for a lifetime. The indifference of the people, their coldness, grew into a long loneliness. One day while exploring the caves on the side of a mountain, she found an entrance where feldspar and black tourmaline formed adventures of light which filtered through the narrow opening to the sky, a ladder of light where little gods danced a skein of colors. Here she found the warmth of a lost sun. Here she wove the delicate dreams of loneliness. But weaving dreams was not enough. She brought clay and dyes to the cave to shape and mold her little gods.

Years flew by, she was old now and her body must give way. One day her little gods, the many kept on shelves in her little house, sang a song of truth, of a long life lived well—a song of returning back to Batopilas, to her origin. For the cold of the snake had never touched her heart; she knew it was the price she had to pay for not giving up her faith, the way of her people. Soon the journey began, a journey to discover the Oneness of herself and the Allness of living things. They told her to race back to the waterfall. Yes! Yes! Of course she would go back with her little gods, but first she had to leave something behind to show the people of the village how much they meant to her as human beings, even if they had shunned her for a lifetime. I must let them know I love them, she decided. An answer came: she would give them a part of herself, something holy, something happy. She would shape a little god for each of them and leave it on their doorstep.

In the cave, she happily shaped a little god for each family, and when she was done, by the light of the moon, she reverently placed one on each doorstep. When the act of love was finished she went back to her house to await the journey back to where water laughed and the earth smiled. It would be a life-giving road back to her origin.

*   *   *

And the women who sat in council? They were caught in a fearful sweep of hate. Spiderlike, apelike, toadlike, in their smallness, they were tortured minions. They could not be stopped now. The scurrying creatures gathered firewood in the gloom. With antlike intentions, they hurried back and forth carrying wood to build the fire that would burn Lela, the witch. They piled the wood in a circle around her house, singing their brittle song, "Burn her! Burn her! Tonight! Tonight!"

"The circle of fire will drain her powers!" shouted the old one with claws. She and the others were piling wood when the parish priest came running from the church. He commanded with raised arms as he ran among them.

"Stop! Stop this madness!" The thunder and lightning seemed to ask, What is evil? No evil—only the vacuum of good. What is good? The empty ones turned a deaf ear to their priest. They were dead wood themselves. "Burn! Burn! Burn!"

The priest pleaded with one woman, then another, begging until his voice was raw, taking the wood from their hands. He tried to reason. "All is forgiven, my children. She only made some figures of clay."

There was a hush. The old woman with claws came up to the priest and spit the condemnation in his face. "Only figures of clay! She took our holy saints, so pure, that pray and look up to heaven, she took our Joseph, our Mary, and so many more and made them obscene. How can you defend the right hand of the Devil? She left them undressed, fornicating, drinking, winking, singing, dancing. Can you forgive that? Can anyone forgive it?"

"All of you," the priest said simply, without hope. What the women saw in those figures was the filth of humankind, the celebrating of sin itself! They could not believe their ears. The priest that blessed them with holy water wanted to forgive the rape of their holy saints who knew not sin or lust, whose eyes saw only heaven. Why did he contradict his own teachings? The old one with claws said triumphantly, "She turned our holy Christian saints into pagan devils!"

The priest shook his head, realizing the futility of the struggle. "They are not sinful in her beliefs. She did not sin."

They all turned their backs on the priest and continued piling the wood. Soon the pile would be high enough to set a match to it. Soon it would burn the sin and the sinner.

*   *   *

There was no thought, there was no dream in Lela's dying body. She was waiting for another wave of pain. She was savoring the calm before the pain's return. She fell asleep. A brief sleep, because the pain took over, and she writhed upon the bed, the sheet clinging to her body, her face dripping with perspiration. A moan funneled from her throat; when would the body give way? Give way, give way, she begged in torment. After a long struggle, the pain broke into a blackness. She tried to use her mind against the pain. Memories came, bright and real—the waterfall! She was back in the grotto behind the waterfall, the song of the cascading water filling her with happiness . . . her hermitage of dreams about new worlds. She did not regret; alone, always alone, she had found the Oneness of herself. Life had knitted all the little gods inside, within her being. She had found a wholeness with the earth itself.

New pain tore her body in two. She gripped the edge of the bed to withstand the pain. In her half-consciousness, white blurs whirled into black, black into white, again and again, until another interval of peace returned. She looked at the shelf above her bed holding rows of smiling little gods, humble and human like herself. Their eyes wore a fierceness for life, a wonder for having life. They were guardians over their maker. She whispered, "Is it time? Is it time to go back to the waterfall?" Their smiles said yes.

As the women outside the house lit the fire, another roll of pain took Lela's body; it rolled, rolled, rolled itself into a fiery redness. Between pain and breath, she saw the kind face of the goddess Ta Te, born of the union of clean rock and blue flowers. She was beckoning, "Come, child, come home . . ."

Lela saw the little gods becoming whirls of light, like falling silver sand. The body was giving way now; still, there was one wish, her dying breath. "Oh, find me a clean burning, a dying by fire, give my ashes to the wind, the destiny of all my fathers . . ."

The little gods were racing to the waterfall.

Leaves

A lemon-colored leaf free-floated down from the cottonwood, landing on Isabel's toes, onto a hard, calloused toe whose nail was beginning to curve into the flesh. The sudden flare of color disturbed the hollow, merciless realization that consumed her thin, trembling, little body. For a moment she forgot the terror she was experiencing. The weight of her pain left her for that moment. She breathed deep and looked up at the cottonwood. The resplendent face of the tree wore no despair. It was there as it had always been, whole in itself. She gazed upward, past yellow leaves to the blue of sky. Gray patterns were already clinging to rooftops and a side of the presidio wall. She turned her head to look at the mountain with the crimson lacquer of late afternoon. Nothing's happened, she told herself. Everything is the same. But she knew it wasn't true. The horror that lay in the small, dark room was still there. She felt a sorrow rising to her throat.

Life is out here, she told herself, swallowing hard. I'm still here. Mrs. Gómez is watering her geraniums across the street. Don Tomás is waiting for the bus. I can hear the Esparzas' radio. She suddenly realized her feet had gone to sleep. Limbs throbbing, she stood up from the street curb where she sat and began to stamp her feet on the concrete. When the blood warmed, she sat down on the curb again and rubbed the numbness. It did not leave her, the grief that suffocated, that cut off her ability to breathe. It ran through her veins as the thought of her mother, lying dead in their cold, cramped room, overwhelmed. Isabel wanted to die too. Yes, yes, dead is better. What was there to living anyway? Her life tangled in vomit-soaked sheets and the pervasive toilet stink that awakened her in the mornings to the calamity of her life. Thoughts tore mutely through her mind—memories, something in her reminding her that not all had been bad. Mamá was a good, warm memory. Mamá lying dead with a heroin needle still in her arm—the comforter, the protector, the dreamer, the loved one—would be the first to tell her that life was indeed worth living. Why? Sobbing hard, she brought her head down to her knees.

After a while she felt she could cry no more. She felt a knotted stiffness along her spine. From a deep wellspring inside her came a temporary peace. She looked up at the cottonwood just in time to see a rush of lemon leaves rain down on her. She closed her eyes and whispered, "Mamá . . ."

Presentiments of the good that was yet to be. There would be miracles. Isabel was thirteen and every pore in her body was awakened, breathing in the early evening, the colors of the horizon, the sounds of people. Imprints. Like Pepe making love to Mamá. How many times had she listened in the darkness when they thought she was asleep? It had been a music, the smell of their bodies, the greediness of soft whispers, pleasure flowing, passions not yet understood. Pepe and Mamá in the beginning had been good. Pepe had been the only father she had ever known. She would keep the memory of the beginning. She fell to her knees in the autumn dusk and began to pick up leaves as if it were the only task in the universe.

A stir of wind began to blow the leaves away. Why was she doing this? There were more important things to do. Someone must be told. The world must know her mother was dead of an overdose. She began to shiver, wanting the dark to erase her from existence.

"What's the matter?"

Rico Mariposa was standing by her side. Linda, his older sister, was by her too. The Mariposas were good friends of her mother. Linda's voice was full of concern. "You've been crying."

Rico sat down beside Isabel on the curb. "Wanna tell us?"

The words came out small, scattering in the darkness. "Mamá's dead."

*   *   *

Ferment—the smell of wind washed in rain—Isabel's sense of terror in the hollow of her loneliness—faces full of the ritual of death . . . The priest was at the head of the grave praying for a woman he had never met. It doesn't matter, Isabel wanted to cry out. Prayers won't bring her back. What would happen to her mother's hair? Her eyes?

What would happen to her under the earth? No! Her mother wasn't dead. What if she opened her eyes inside the coffin? But the coffin was closed. She wanted to scream, to stop them from putting her into the ground.

"Take a handful of earth." Someone was speaking to her.

"What?" Isabel recoiled. She was supposed to throw the first handful of earth into the grave. She fell to her knees on a mound of sweet-smelling earth and dug her fingers deep. "Don't put her in the ground—not in the ground . . ."

The words rasped in her throat, whispers, moans. She felt Linda's arm around her, helping her up, leading her away. A gentle rain began to fall.

*   *   *

Isabel was wrapped in a worn blanket, her small, wan face lost in the hugeness of the covering. She had been living with Linda at the Vaquero Apartments for a couple of weeks. The apartments were on Alameda, a few blocks east of Evergreen Cemetery where her mother was buried. Linda and Rico were playing gin on the kitchen table. Linda, with her long, lovely hair that reached all the way to the seat of her jeans, was looking at her cards with a frown as Rico placed his on the table. They're strangers, thought Isabel. They're really strangers.

But she also knew that they cared for her. Really cared. She could tell. Isabel turned to stare out of the window where bloodred flowers tapped on the pane. There were only a few, for most of them had given in to autumn. She turned back to watch Rico with a rising warmth. He was one of the miracles. Isabel knew that he saw only the child in her. Many a time she wanted to reach out and touch him, tell him that she knew about love, tell him about Mamá and Pepe.

"Hey, Isabel, want some hot chocolate?" Linda was putting on a sweater to go to work. Isabel shook her head.

"Rico will help you with the dishes." Linda was already at the door.

Isabel's heart quickened. She would be alone with Rico. It was the first time. She got up, still wearing the blanket, and followed Linda to the door. "Thank you . . ."

"For what?"

"For letting me stay here. For being my friend."

"Sure, kid." Linda was gone and Rico sat at the table deep in thought. Isabel made her way to the sink and began to stack the dishes.

"Leave them alone. I want to talk to you. Come over here and sit down."

Isabel obeyed. She sat down across from him and waited.

"You have a grandmother in Tornillo," Rico informed her.

"I didn't know . . ."

"It took Susan a long time, looking her up."

"Who's Susan?" Isabel looked perplexed.

"The social worker who asked you all those questions."

"Oh, Miss Espinosa."

"Yeah, her. She's fixing it for you to go live with her, your grandmother, I mean."

"Why can't I stay here?"

"You have to go to school. Your grandmother wants you. She's family."

"I want to live with you—like Mamá and Pepe used to live together." The words came easily to her, without hesitation or embarrassment.

But Rico looked uncomfortable, confused by her words. "You don't know what you're talking about."

"About love . . ."

"You're just a kid, and Pepe didn't love your mother."

The words from his lips hurt. It was cruel of him to say that. She protested hotly. "They loved each other! You don't know."

"It was Pepe who got your mother hooked on the stuff. No good punk. Don't tell me you've forgotten."

She wanted to forget, but dark flurries came into her mind. Pepe hitting Mamá. Mamá clutching at him, begging him to stay. Mamá writhing in bed, alone, holding her cramping stomach, sweat pouring from her thin body, her large burning eyes staring in a mirror, planning the next fix. If there was none to get, her mamá disappearing into the night in a desperate search, staying away for days. She shook her head to erase the terrible memories. She stared at Rico across the table, feeling the insurmountable barrier between them. She heard the tap, tap, tap of the flowers outside the window, desolate in their aloneness in a season of ripe death. But she knew miracles would happen. Her mamá always spoke of wonderful things that were to be. Miracles were not a farce. She had seen one with Pepe and

Mamá in the beginning. Now she wanted to get away from Rico who had no eyes for dreams. "Go away . . ."

Rico, surprised by the whispered vehemence, did not argue. He picked up his jacket and left the apartment. She was left alone without solutions. She washed the dishes, listening to the tapping of the flowers. The tapping became a dance of delirium. She belonged with Mamá, the mamá who had talked of dreams, of owning a little house someday, even a garden—a mamá who had laughed once, who had peeled oranges for her as she wove wonderful tales about their future —the mamá who had pointed out the beauty of moonlight caught on an edge of a curtain—a mamá free in her passions and her giving. She belonged with Mamá. Mamá was waiting.

*   *   *

It was late afternoon when Rico and Linda walked through the cemetery to look for Isabel. The mother's grave was along the fence that looked out onto the railroad tracks. November gold filled all directions. The light of day was contracting itself into a softness as sounds from the living world outside the cemetery brazenly filled the afternoon, sounds soaked into falling leaves. Leaves fluttered to the ground live substances of fancy following the path through tombstones.

Isabel was sitting by her mother's grave, her knees drawn up against her tear-stained face. She was thinking about leaves. Did the fallen leaf hanker for the mother tree? Did it miss the sweetness of its mother's veins? She watched some leaves huddled in the wind; then, with a sudden gust, they rose to dance themselves into the wire fence, then up again, dispersing, in constant movement, spiraling, falling free. She looked up to see Rico and Linda coming toward her. Linda was by her side. "Let's go home."

"This is home as much as any place." Isabel's words rang true. There was a silence. Rico, squinting in the sun, leaned against a tombstone to look at her. He shook his head. "You sure stubborn— just like a kid."

Isabel said nothing. She was looking at an ancient, gnarled tree stretching its bare limbs far beyond the touch of tombstone. A few leaves clung to the mother tree, but they would fall soon enough. That was the way it was meant to be from the first day of their conception—leaves prepared to fall from the tree, the separation point itself so fragile that the slightest gust of wind would set them free to fall, to tell the tale of a mother tree, rushing forth among tombstones, then blown asunder. Isabel informed them, "Mamá was right."

"About what?" Linda asked, reaching out to stroke the younger girl's hair.

"Miracles. They're all around."

"We can't stay long. It's getting cold." Rico's voice was matter-of-fact. He walked over to Isabel, his eyes capturing hers, steady, almost expressionless. He reached for her hand. Isabel did not give him her hand, but he took it anyway. "Come on."

Isabel did not stir. Rico repeated himself a little roughly this time. "Let's go."

"It's hard to break free." Soft sobs broke from her throat.

"You better come with us. Linda and me, we don't want to waste time with the dead." He pulled her gently to her feet, holding her hand firmly. She did not resist.

The three of them walked slowly away from the grave that held a woman, a mother, who had died with a heroin needle in her arm. They wove their way through tombstones, leaving behind them pulseless shadows, leaves everywhere, the colors of chaos reconciling themselves to immortality, for miracles never die.

Looking for God

Josefa, at ten, always felt God in the silent church where candles flickered before the Virgin. His presence seemed to float in the shadows like flower petals broken by a gentle wind. It was a favorite place, the church, for here, in the quiet of afternoons, God had become her unseen playmate. At times she imagined Him in the rushing fingers of light streaming from the stained glass windows. It broke the secret of the shadows, silent and still, in the corners of the church.

Many times she wondered if God's voice was like the voice of Father Tomás, who spoke in a solemn tone on Sundays. Sometimes he spoke in rapid, complicated words full of feeling, and faith, like a murmur, grew from a single whisper to a multitude of voices breaking into song. The bigness of God awed her on Sunday morning when all eyes shone with belief in Father Tomás's words.

God was different when she was alone in the church. Then he became the laughing sun pouring himself into the silent emptiness. She could touch Him then, breathless as she reached out of the darkness to the streaming light. She was enclosed in a stillness all her own, wanting to assure Him that she felt Him, that she was His friend.

Josefa had few friends, for her grandmother, who was Father Tomás's housekeeper, kept her away from the barrio children. La abuelita considered the little barefooted barrio Indians too rough and loud, claiming that they were too common as they clammered in the hot sun, running, shouting, and spitting on the desert ground. Through the securely locked kitchen screen door, Josefa would watch them play, wishing she could be one of them as they kicked up dust, colorless and dead. She would press her little face against the door screen, tasting and smelling the dust, watching the crowd of children run toward the main square of the barrio. Beyond that was a red desert leading to a series of hills. After that, the lake.

Now, in the shadows of the church, Josefa came upon the glass case where they kept the crucified Jesus. It lay there, so still, the whole year until the coming of Lent. During Passion Week it had a place beside the altar. She looked about, then lifted the glass top and leaned her shoulder against it, leaving her hands free to touch the painted wounds on the plaster face of the son of God. She looked intently at the closed eyes, the mouth curved in forgiveness. She wondered if the face of the real Jesus had looked so in the throes of death. The thought made her put the top down quickly. She suddenly ran out through the open aisles.

She almost ran into the figure of her grandmother carrying a white tower of clean, ironed altar linens. The old woman frowned, shaking her head as Josefa looked at her with eyes full of her adventure in the empty church.

"Where have you been?" scolded the grandmother. "If Father Tomás catches you . . ." The old woman handed her the stack of clean linens. "Here, put these away."

The grandmother did not wait for an answer, but left Josefa with the pile of linens in her arms. Josefa walked thoughtfully into the room beyond the sacristy. On top of the chest where the linens were kept was a ram's horn full of sacred oil. Father Tomás had brought the ram's horn all the way from Barcelona, for when he was very young he had been sent all the way from across the sea to be the parish priest in San Lorenzo, all the way from Spain to the small Mexican village in Baja California. Josefa picked up the horn to touch the mystery of its ribbed hardness. Outside the window, the fluttering of birds could be heard. Her heart skipped. A swallow had lighted on the window sill. A swallow!

In her excitement she dropped the horn, oil spilling from the narrow opening, forming a dark, round stain on the worn rug. Josefa stared at the stain for a second, then knelt to touch the oil with her finger. Sacred oil! She looked at the glistening, oily substance on her fingers, then quickly formed a cross on her forehead. The oil had not been wasted. But now, she was looking out the window again. She could see birds lighting on the branches of the tree outside the window. It was the coming of the swallows to San Lorenzo. Almost miraculously, they always came to rest along the lake and on top of roofs and trees in the town. If only she could go to the lake to watch

the swelling life of birds—but the lake was forbidden. Her grandmother had forbidden that she walk alone as far as the lake.

Father Tomás had explained how in the spring when the winter
nights were gone, the sun called back the birds. The swallows would
cross Baja California, the sky black with wings. It took them many
days to cross the desert, stopping in low, wet lands to rest. Behind
them were the cold winds of March. Josefa imagined the birds clinging to frozen weeds at night. But now they were flying north in huge,
dark, moving clouds, over pueblos and mountains. They would be
coming to the lake with beating wings, circling as they did every year,
looking for seeds, rest, and warmth.

Josefa went to the door and looked out on the main square. She
saw birds drinking in the stone fountain. Many, many, so many!
Josefa ran out into the heat of the sun. She had forgotten that her
grandmother had forbidden her to go to the lake. She was thinking
of the birds coming to the lake as she made her way to the outskirts
of the barrio. She had passed the adobe presidios without seeing
anyone, for the red heat stopped people from venturing out in the
middle of the afternoon.

As she crossed the red strip of desert her cheeks burned dry with
the heat. The air was hazed with the heaviness of sun as she reached
the hill that led to the lake. Beyond that hill, the trees would make
things cool. As Josefa ascended the long, gradual hill, the red sand
of desert disappeared and tall pine thickened. The world was now
green. After a long while she reached the top of the hill, then started
down toward the lake that lay broad and clear and still. She was halfway down when she came to a tree, its thick trunk twisted like a
cradle, sprouting profuse branches. With one rapid movement, she
thrust herself up on the trunk. Space wavered before her as she listened to the sound of voices somewhere in the distance. The voices
were soon overwhelmed by the clattering of wings. The birds were
coming!

She saw them cutting the sky, squadrons finding the hill. She
heard continuous warbles mixing with the humming of bees. So
many birds! How beautiful! Birds hastening toward the open ground,
voyaging creatures, sweet voiced, their song a growing sea of sound.
One lone bird had lighted on a dark green bough close to where she
sat. Josefa watched it, drawing in breath softly, her face bright with
wonder. The bird's gray feathers spread in balance, its voice rising

tremulously as if commenting on the clearness of the lake. Again, Josefa felt God as she had in the silver shadows of the church.

A coarse, blurring shout broke the chorus of the birds. Josefa turned to see some boys from the barrio slithering down the hill. They came to a stop at the bottom of the hill, then El Lobo, their leader, shouldered his way to the front of the group. Josefa saw the slingshot carelessly slung around his neck and felt a fear like heat caught in overhanging weeds. She looked up to see the birds creating lines in the air. The boys found their marks. Birds fell. Josefa screamed.

She ran down the hill dragging earth behind her, her eyes focused on El Lobo, who was killing birds with great enjoyment. She had to stop them! Stop them! Stop them! She was now among them as they aimed their slingshots at the screaming sky.

"Stop it! Do you hear? Leave the birds alone!"

Josefa struck out clumsily at the burly boy who stood before her. The other boys pushed and stumbled around their leader. Josefa's knees ached. She choked back tears. A whispered plea broke from her lips as she saw the bird in El Lobo's hands. "Please, let . . ."

She knew already they would not mind, for they were mimicking her plea, "Let the bird go, let the bird go." The snickering became heavy, dark laughter, and El Lobo looked blankly at her. His face broke into a fearful grin as he motioned with his head and another boy came forward with a knife. Some boys were around her now, holding back her arms, eagerly waiting for her terror. She could see the bird in El Lobo's hand, the underside of the wings spread out as the other boy handed him the knife. Josefa saw the heartbeat; then El Lobo, with one stroke, cut through the breastbone. There was only a muffled squeak from the little bird. She saw the open beak, the spilled intestines. The world shrank to pain, and the boys jeered and laughed louder than before.

"Squish it, squish it in her face!" They threw Josefa to the ground, one boy holding her face to the sky, now blotted out. All she could see was the dead bird in his hand.

What was it she tasted? Tears? Blood? She shivered in the heat and the prickling of her skin was moist. She did no more than turn her body around, her mouth and nostrils tasting earth.

She did not want to turn around, not for a long, long while. She cried and cried until there were no more tears. She listened for sounds, the wild sounds of birds dying, of boys screaming, but there were none. All she heard was the buzzing of bees. Once she heard the croaking of a frog. She no longer felt the heavy, honey hotness of the sun upon her back. But still, she did not turn around. She could not. She did not want to see the dead birds, shriveled, no longer soaring joyfully, immortal in the sun.

In time the terror vanished; so did the day. She felt the shadows cooling her cheek. She felt the stillness of darkening sky and silent lake deep inside her. She sat up finally, eyes closed, a breeze blowing across her temples. She opened her eyes to see the moon rising, seemingly caught among tall trees. She looked up beyond the moon to the evening star. She felt so alone in the vastness of trees and lake.

She made her way tn the edge of the lake filled with the gentle light of the moon. It seemed to tremble, full of tiny light crystals. But an emptiness was still stretching through her body, now numb in the cold darkness that smelled like pine. She looked up at the face of the moon, beseeching, "Where are you, God?"

Village

Rico stood on top of a bluff overlooking Mai Cao. The whole of the wide horizon was immersed in a rosy haze. His platoon was returning from an all-night patrol. They had scoured the area in a radius of thirty-two miles, following the length of the canal system along the Delta, furtively on the lookout for an enemy attack. On their way back, they had stopped to rest, smoke, and drink warm beer after parking the carryalls along the edge of the climb leading to the top of the bluff. The hill was good cover, seemingly safe.

Harry was behind him on the rocky slope. Then, there was the sound of thunder overhead. It wasn't thunder, but a squadron of their own helicopters on the usual run. Rico and Harry sat down to watch the 'copters go by. After that, a stillness, a special kind of silence. Rico knew it well; it was the same kind of stillness that was a part of him back home, the kind of stillness that makes a man part of his world—river, clearing, sun, wind. The stillness of a village early in the morning—barrio stillness, the first stirrings of life that come with dawn.

Harry was looking down at the village of Mai Cao. "Makes me homesick." He lit a cigarette.

Rico was surprised. He thought Harry was a city dude. From Chicago, no less. "I don't see no freeway or neon lights," he joked.

"I'm just sick of doing nothing in this goddamned war."

No action yet. But who wanted action? Rico had been transformed into a soldier, but he knew he was no soldier. He had been trained to kill the enemy in Vietnam. He watched the first curl of smoke coming out of one of the chimneys. They were the enemy down there. Rico didn't believe it. He would never believe it. Perhaps because there had been no confrontation with Vietcong soldiers or village people. Harry flicked away his cigarette and started down the slope. He turned, waiting for Rico to follow him. "Coming?"

"I'll be down after a while."

"Suit yourself." Harry walked swiftly down the bluff, his feet carrying with them the yielding dirt in a flurry of small pebbles and loose earth. Rico was relieved. He needed some time by himself, to think things out. But Harry was right. To come across an ocean just to do routine checks, to patrol ground where there was no real danger . . . it could get pretty shitty. The enemy was hundreds of miles away.

The enemy! He remembered the combat creed—kill or be killed. Down a man—the lethal kick: a strangling is neater and quieter than the slitting of a throat; grind your heel against a face to mash the brains. Stomp the rib cage to carve the heart with bone splinters. Kill . . .

Hey, who was kidding who? They almost made him believe it back at boot camp in the States. In fact only a short while ago, only that morning, he had crouched down in the growth following a mangrove swamp, fearing an unseen enemy, ready to kill. Only that morning. But now, as he looked down at the peaceful village with its small rice field, its scattered huts, something had struck deep, something beyond the logic of war and enemy, something deep in his guts.

He had been cautioned: The rows of thatched huts were not really peoples' homes, but "hootches," makeshift stays built by the makeshift enemy. But then they were real enemies. There were enough dead Americans to prove it. The hootches didn't matter. The people didn't matter. These people knew how to pick up their sticks and go. Go where? How many of these villages had been bulldozed? Flattened by gunfire? Good pyres for napalm, these Vietnamese villages. A new kind of battleground.

Rico looked down and saw huts that were homes clustered in an intimacy that he knew well. The village of Mai Cao was no different than Valverde, the barrio where he had grown up. A woman came out of a hut, walking tall and with a certain grace, a child on her shoulder. She was walking toward a stream east of the slope. She stopped along the path and looked up to say something to the child. It struck him again, the feeling—a bond—that people were all the same everywhere.

The same scent from the earth, the same warmth from the sun, a woman walking with a child—his mother, Trini. His little mother who had left Tarahumara country and crossed the Barranca del Cobre, taking with her seeds from the hills of Batopilas, withstanding suffering, danger—for what? For a dream, a piece of ground in the land of plenty, the United States of America. She had waded across the Río Grande from Juárez, Mexico, to El Paso, Texas, when she felt the birth pangs of his coming. He had been born a U.S. citizen because his mother had had a dream. She had made the dream come true— an acre of river land in Valverde, the edge of the border. His mother, like the earth and sun, mattered. The woman with the child on her shoulder mattered. Every human life in the village mattered. He knew this not only with the mind but with the heart.

Rico remembered a warning from combat training, from the weary, wounded soldiers who had fought and killed and survived, soldiers sent to Saigon, waiting to go home. His company had been flown to Saigon before being sent to the front. And this was the front, villages like Mai Cao. He felt relieved knowing that the fighting was hundreds of miles away from the people of Mai Cao—but the warning was still there: Watch out for pregnant women with machine guns. Toothless old women are experts with the knife between the shoulders. Begging children with hidden grenades, the unseen V.C. hiding in the hootches. Village people were not people, they were the enemy. The woman who knew the child on her shoulder, who knew the path to her door, who knew the coming of the sun—she was the enemy.

It was a discord not to be believed by instinct or intuition. And Rico was an Indian, the son of a Tarahumara chieftain. Theirs was a world of instinct and intuitive decisions. Suddenly he heard the sounds of motors. He looked to the other side of the slope, down to the road where the carryalls had started queuing their way back to the post. Rico ran down the hill to join his company.

* * *

In Rico's dream, Sergeant Keever was shouting in code, "Heller, heller!" Rico woke with a start. It wasn't a dream. The men around him were scrambling out of the pup tent. Outside, most of the men were lining up in uneven formation. Rico saw a communiqué in the sergeant's hand. Next to Keever was a lieutenant from communications headquarters. Keever was reading the communiqué:

"Special mission 72 for Company C, Platoon 2, assigned at 2200

hours. Move into the village of Mai Cao, field manual description—
hill 72. Destroy the village."

No! It was crazy. Why? Just words on a piece of paper. Keever
had to tell him why. There had to be a reason. Had the enemy come
this far? It was impossible. Only that morning he had stood on the
slope. He caught up with Keever, blurting out, "Why? I mean—why
must we destroy it?"

Sergeant Keever stopped in his tracks and turned steel blue eyes
at Rico. "What you say?"

"Why, I said."

"You just follow orders, savvy?"

"Are the Vietcong . . ."

"Did you hear me? You want trouble, Private?"

"There's people . . ."

"I don't believe you, soldier! But okay. Tell you as much as I
know. We gotta erase the village in case the Vietcong come this way.
So they won't use it as a stronghold. Now move your ass!"

Keever walked away from him, his lips tight in some kind of disgust. Rico did not follow this time. He went to get his gear and join
the men in one of the carryalls. Three carryalls for the assault; three
carryalls moving up the same road. Rico felt the weight and hardness
of his carbine. Now it had a strange, hideous meaning. The machine
guns were some kind of nightmare. The mission was to kill and burn
and erase all memories. Rico swallowed a guilt that rose from the
marrow and with it, all kinds of fear. He had to do something, something to stop it, but he didn't know what. And despite all those feelings there was a certain reluctance to do anything but follow orders.
In the darkness, his lips formed words from the anthem: "My country
'tis of thee . . ."

They came to the point where the tree line straggled between two
hills that rose darkly against the moon. Rico wondered if all the men
were of one mind—one mind to kill. Was he a coward? No! It was
not killing the enemy that his whole being was rejecting, but firing
machine guns into a village of sleeping people . . . people. Rico remembered when only the week before, returning from their usual
patrol, the men from the company had stopped at the stream, mingl-
ing with the children, old men, and women of the village. There had
been an innocence about the whole thing. His voice broke the silence
in the carryall, a voice harsh and feverish. "We can get the people
out of there. Help them evacuate . . ."

"Shut up." Harry's voice was tight, impatient.

The carryalls traveled through tall, undulant grass following the dirt road that led to the edge of the bluff. It was not all tall grass. Once in a while trees appeared again, clumped around scrub bushes. Ten miles out the carryalls stopped. It was still a mile's walk to the bluff in the darkness, but they had to avoid detection. Sergeant Keever was leading the party. Rico, almost at the rear, knew he had to catch up to him. He had to stop him. Harry was ahead of him, a silent black bundle walking stealthily through rutted ground to discharge his duty. For a second, Rico hesitated. That was the easy thing to do: carry out his duty, die a hero, do his duty blindly and survive—hell, why not? He knew what happened to men who backed down in battle. But he wasn't backing down. Hell, what else was it? How often had he heard it among the gringos in his company?

"You Mexican? Hey, you Mexicans are real fighters. I mean, everybody knows Mexicans have guts."

A myth perhaps. But no. He thought of the old guys who had fought in World War II. Many of them were on welfare back in the barrio. But, man, did they have metals! He had never seen so many purple hearts. He remembered old Toque, the wino, who had tried to pawn his metals to buy a bottle. No way, man. They weren't worth a nickel.

He quickly edged past Harry, pushing by the men ahead of him to reach the sergeant. He was running, tall grass brushing his shoulder, tall grass that had swayed peacefully like wheat. The figure of Sergeant Keever was in front of him now. He had a sudden impulse to reach out and hold Keever back. But the sergeant had stopped. Rico did not touch him, but whispered hoarsely, desperately, in the dark. "Let's get the people out—evacuate . . ."

"What the hell . . ." Keever's voice was ice. He recognized Rico and hissed, "Get back to your position, soldier, or I'll shoot you myself."

Rico did as he was told, almost unaware of the men around him. But in the distance he heard something splashing in the water of the canal, in his nostrils the sweet smell of burnt wood. He looked toward the clearing and saw the cluster of huts bathed in moonlight. In the same moonlight he saw Keever giving signals. In the gloom he saw the figures of the men carrying machine guns. They looked like dancing grasshoppers as they ran ahead to position themselves on the bluff. He felt like yelling, "For Christ's sake! Where is the enemy?"

The taste of blood was in his mouth, and he suddenly realized he had bitten his quivering lower lip. As soon as Sergeant Keever gave the signal, all sixteen men would open fire on the huts—machine guns, carbines would erase everything. No more Mai Cao—the execution of duty without question, without alternative. They were positioned on the south slope, Sergeant Keever up ahead, squatting on his heels, looking at his watch. He stood, after a quick glance at the men. As Sergeant Keever raised his hand to give the signal for attack, Rico felt the cold, metallic deadness of his rifle. His hands began to tremble as he released the safety catch. Sergeant Keever was on the rise just above him. Rico stared at the sergeant's arm, raised, ready to fall—the signal to fire. The cross fire was inside Rico, a heavy-dosed tumult—destroy the village, erase all memory. There was ash in his mouth. Once the arm came down, there was no turning back.

In a split second Rico turned his rifle at a forty-degree angle and fired at the sergeant's arm. Keever half-turned with the impact of the bullet, then fell to his knees. In a whooping whisper the old-time soldier blew out the words, "That fucking bastard—get him." He got up and signaled the platoon back to the carryalls as two men grabbed Rico, one hitting him on the side of the head with the butt of his rifle. Rico felt the sting of the blow as they pinned his arms back and forced him to walk the path back to the carryall. He did not resist. There was a lump in his throat, and he blinked back tears, tears of relief. The memory of the village would not be erased. Someone shouted in the dark, "They're on to us! There's an old man with a lantern and others coming out of the hootches."

"People—just people . . ." Rico whispered, wanting to shout it, wanting to tell them that he had done the right thing. But the heaviness that filled his senses was the weight of another truth. He was a traitor, a maniac. He had shot his superior in a battle crisis. He was being carried almost bodily back to the truck. He glanced at the thick brush along the road, thinking that somewhere beyond it was a rice field, and beyond that a mangrove swamp. There was a madman inside his soul that made him think of rice fields and mangrove swamps instead of what he had done. Not once did he look up. Everyone around him was strangely quiet and remote. Only the sound of trudging feet.

In the carryall, the faces of the men sitting around Rico were indiscernible in the dark, but he imagined their eyes, wide and confused, peering through the dark at him with a wakefulness that questioned what he had done. Did they know his reason? Did they care? The truck suddenly lurched. Deep in his gut, Rico felt a growing fear. He choked back a hysteria rising from his diaphram. The incessant bumping of the carryalls as they moved unevenly on the dirt road accused him too. He looked up into the night sky and watched the moon eerily weave in and out of tree branches. The darkness was like his fear. It had no solutions. Back at the post, Sergeant Keever and a medic passed by Rico, already handcuffed, without any sign of recognition. Sergeant Keever had already erased him from existence. The wheels of justice would take their course. Rico had been placed under arrest and temporarily shackled to a cot in one of the tents. Three days later he was moved to a makeshift bamboo hut, with a guard in front of the hut at all times. His buddies brought in food like strangers, awkward in their silence, anxious to leave him alone. He felt like some kind of poisonous bug. Only Harry came by to see him, after a week.

"You dumb ass, were you on loco weed?" Harry asked in disgust.

"I didn't want people killed, that's all."

"Hell, that's no reason, those Chinks aren't even—even . . ."

"Even what?" Rico demanded. He almost screamed it a second time. "Even what?"

"Take it easy, will you? You better go for a Section Eight." Harry was putting him aside like everyone else. "They're sending you back to the States next week. You'll have to face Keever sometime this afternoon. I thought I'd better let you know."

"Thanks." Rico knew the hopelessness of it all. But there was still that nagging question he had to ask. "Listen, nobody tells me anything. Did you all go back to Mai Cao? I mean, is it still there?"

"Still there. Orders from headquarters to forget it. The enemy were spotted taking an opposite direction. But nobody's going to call you a hero, you understand? What you did was crud. You're no soldier. You'll never be a soldier." Rico said nothing to defend himself. He began to scratch the area around the steel rings on his ankles. Harry was scowling at him. He said it again, almost shouting, "I said, you'll never be a soldier."

"So?" There was soft disdain in Rico's voice.

"You blew it, man. You'll be locked up for a long, long time."

"Maybe." Rico's voice was without concern.

"Don't you care?"

"I'm free inside, Harry." Rico laughed in relief. "Free . . ."

Harry shrugged, peering at Rico unbelievingly, then turned and walked out of the hut.

La Yonfantayn

Alicia was forty-two and worked hard at keeping her weight down. Not hard enough, really, and this was very frustrating for her —to never quite succeed. She wanted to be pencil thin like a movie star. She would leaf through movie magazines, imagining herself in the place of the immaculately made-up beauties that stared back at her. But in essence she was a realist and was very much aware of the inevitable bodily changes as years passed. She often studied her face and figure in the mirror, not without fears. The fantasy of glamor and beauty was getting harder and harder to maintain. It was no easy task, getting old. Why didn't someone invent some magic pill . . .

Sitting naked, defenseless, in a bathtub brimming with pink bubbles, she slid down into the water to make the usual check. She felt for flabbiness along the thighs, for the suspicious cottage cheese called tired, loose fat on her underarms. Suddenly she felt the sting of soap in her eye. Carefully she cupped water in her hand to rinse it out. Damn it! Part of her eyelashes were floating in the water. It would take close to an hour to paste new ones on again. Probably Delia's fault. Her girl was getting sloppy. Mamie was a new face at the beauty parlor, anxious to please the regular customers. Maybe she would ask for Mamie next time. No dollar tip for Delia after this. The soapy warmth of her body was almost mesmerizing. In her bubbly, pink realm Alicia was immortal, a nymph, sweet smelling, seductive, capable of anything.

Heck! She had to get out of the bath if she had to paste the damned eyelashes on. She stood up, bubbles dripping merrily off her nice, plump body. She had to hurry to be in time for her blind date. She giggled. A blind date! She could hardly believe that she had agreed to a blind date. Agreed? She smiled with great satisfaction and murmured to herself, "You insisted on nothing else, my girl.

You wanted him served on a platter and that's the way you're getting him."

Rico was her yard boy, and at Katita's wedding she had seen Rico's uncle, Buti, from afar. Such a ridiculous name for such a gorgeous hunk of man. From that moment on she had been obsessed with the thought of owning him. It was her way, to possess her men. That way she could stay on top—teach them the art of making her happy. "Oh, I have such a capacity for love!" she told herself. Humming a love song, she stepped out of the bathtub and wrapped a towel gracefully around her body, assuming the pose of a queen. A middle-aged queen, the mirror on the bathroom door told her. There are mirrors and there are mirrors, she gloomily observed. She sucked in her stomach, watching her posture. But the extra pounds were still here and there. Time had taken away the solid firmness of youth and replaced it with extra flesh. She turned away from the mirror, summarizing life under her breath. "Shit!"

The next instant she was all smiles again, thinking of the long-waisted bra that would smooth out her midriff and give her an extra curve. Then there was the green chiffon on her bed, the type of dress that Loretta Young would wear. She visualized herself in the green chiffon, floating toward Buti with outstretched hand. There would be the inevitable twinkle of admiration in his eye. In her bedroom she glanced at the clock on her dresser. It was late. With rapid, expert movements, she took out creams, lipstick, eyeshadow, rouge, and brushes from her cosmetic drawer. She wrapped a towel around her head and had just opened the moisture cream when she remembered the eyelashes. Did she really need them? She remembered Lana Turner with her head on Clark Gable's shoulder, her eyelashes sweeping against her cheeks. Max Factor's finest, Alicia was sure of that.

Hell! She rummaged hurriedly around the bottom drawer until she found a plaster container with the words "Max Factor" emblazoned on the cover. Anything Lana did, she could do better. She took out a bottle of glue, then carefully blotted the excess cream from her eyes and began the operation.

*   *   *

"Hey, slow down!" yelled Rico as Buti made a turn on two wheels.

Rico turned around to check the load on the back of the pickup. They were returning from Ratón where at the ranger's station they had gotten permits to pick piñones in the Capitán Mountains. Buti had presented the rangers with a letter from Don Rafael Avina giving him permission to pick piñón nuts from his private lands. Buti had also signed a contract with the Borderfield Company to deliver the piñones at the railroad yards in Ancho, New Mexico, where the nuts would be shipped along with cedar wood to Salt Lake City. His first profitable business venture since he had arrived in the United States. He had a check from Borderfield in his pocket. He was well on his way to becoming what he had always wanted to be—a businessman. From there, a capitalist—why not? Anything was possible in the United States of America. He even had enough piñones left to sell to tienditas around Valverde and a special box of the best piñones for his blind date, the richest woman in Valverde. Things were coming up money every which way. He had had qualms about letting Rico talk him into the blind date until Rico started listing all the property owned by Alicia Flores: two blocks of presidios, ten acres of good river land, an office building. That made him ecstatic. Imagine him dating a pretty widow who owned an office building! There was no question about it—he was about to meet the only woman in the world that he would consider marrying. By all means, she could have him. It was about time he settled down.

All that boozing and all those women were getting to be too much for him. What he needed was the love and affection of one good, wealthy woman. Yes, ever since he had met Don Rafael things had gone for the better, Only six months before he had even considered going on welfare. Poker winnings had not been enough, and his antique shop had not been doing very well. He had resorted to odd jobs around Valverde, a new low for Buti. Then he had met Don Rafael at El Dedo Gordo in Juárez.

At the Fat Finger everybody knew Buti. That's where he did the important things in his life—play poker, start fights, pick up girls, and most important of all, drink until all hours of the morning. It was his home away from home. His feet on native soil and mariachi music floating through his being—that was happiness. One early dawn when only Elote, the bartender, and Buti were left at the Fat Finger —they were killing off a bottle of tequila before starting for home— who stumbles in but this little fat man with a pink head, drunker than a skunk. He fell face down on the floor soon enough. Buti helped him up, dusted him off, and led him to the table where Elote had already passed out.

"You sit right there. I'll get us another bottle." Buti wove his way between tables and made it to the bar. The little man just sat, staring into space until Buti nudged him with a new bottle of tequila.

"Where am I?" the little man asked, clearing his throat.

"In the land of the brave . . ." Buti responded with some pride.

"Where's that?"

"The Fat Finger, of course."

The friendship was cemented over the bottle of tequila. The little man had been a good ear. Focusing on the pink head, with tears in his eyes, Buti had unloaded all his woes on the little fat man. Buti recounted how he had tried so hard to become a capitalist in the land of plenty to no avail. He tried to look the little fat man in the eye, asking, "Are you a capitalist?"

"Yes," assured the little man, with a thick tongue. "I am that."

"See what I mean? Everybody who goes to the United States becomes a capitalist. Now—look at me. Great mind, good body— what's wrong with me?"

"What you need is luck," advised the little man with some wisdom, as he reeled off his chair.

Buti helped him up again and shook his head. "That's easier said than done. I know the principles of good business—contacts, capital, and a shrewd mind. But where in the hell do I get the contacts and the capital?"

"Me," assured the little fat man without hesitation. "Me, Don Rafael Avina will help you. I'm a millionaire."

"That's what they all say." Buti eyed him with some suspicion.

"Don't I look like a millionaire?" demanded the little man, starting to hiccup. The spasmodic closure of the glottis caused his eyes to cross. Buti looked at him, still with some suspicion, but decided that he looked eccentric enough to be a millionaire. "Okay, how're you going to help me?"

"First you must help me," said Don Rafael between hiccups, "find my car."

"Where did you park it?"

"I don't know. You see, I have no sense of direction," confessed Don Rafael, leaning heavily on Buti. "It's a green Cadillac."

That did it. A man who owned a Cadillac did not talk from the wrong side of his mouth. "Can you give me a hint?"

Don Rafael had gone to sleep on his shoulder. Now is the time to be resourceful, Buti told himself. How many green Cadillacs can be parked in a radius of six blocks? Don Rafael could not have wandered off farther than that on his short, little legs. It would be a cinch, once he sobered up Don Rafael enough for him to walk on his own speed.

It took six cups of coffee, but Don Rafael was able to hold on to Buti all the way to Mariscal, where Buti spotted a lone green Cadillac parked in front of Sylvia's place, the best whorehouse in Juárez.

"Hey, Don Rafael." Buti had to shake the little man from his stupor. "Is that the car?"

Don Rafael squinted, leaning forward then back against Buti. "Is it a green Cadillac?"

"A green Cadillac."

"That's my car." Don Rafael began to feel around for the keys. "Can't find my keys." Buti helped him look through all his pockets, but no keys.

"You could have left them in the ignition."

"That would be dumb." Don Rafael kept searching until Buti pushed him toward the car to look. Sure enough, the keys were in the ignition.

"There are your keys and your car." Buti gestured with a flourish.

"Then let's go home."

"Your home?" queried Buti.

"Why not? You can be my guest for as long as you like—if you can stand my sister . . ."

"What's wrong with your sister?"

"Everything. Does everything right, prays all the time, and is still a virgin at fifty."

"See what you mean. You could drop me off at my place in Valverde."

They drove off, and it was not until they were crossing the immigration bridge that they heard the police sirens. A police car with a red flashing light cut right across the path of the green Cadillac. In no time, three police officers pulled Buti and Don Rafael roughly out of the car.

"What is the meaning of this?" demanded Don Rafael, sobering up in a hurry.

"You're under arrest," informed a menacing-looking officer.

"What are you talking about?" Buti asked angrily, shaking himself free from another officer's hold.

"You stole that car," accused the first officer.

Don Rafael was indignant. "You're crazy. That's my car!"

"That's the mayor's car. He reported it stolen."

"The mayor's car?" Buti was dumbfounded. He would never believe another little fat man with a pink head again.

"I have a green Cadillac," sputtered Don Rafael. "I demand to see my lawyers."

"Tomorrow you can call your lawyer. Tonight you go to jail," the third officer informed them with great stoicism. All of Don Rafael's screaming did no good. They wouldn't even look at his credentials. So the two had to spend a night in jail. Buti diplomatically offered Don Rafael his coat when he saw the little man shivering with cold, and even let him pillow his pink head on his shoulder to sleep. Buti had decided there was more than one green Cadillac in the world and that Don Rafael threw his weight around enough to be rich. Don Rafael snuggled close to Buti and snored all night.

They were allowed to leave the next morning after Don Rafael made a phone call and three lawyers showed up to threaten the government of Mexico with a lawsuit for false arrest. Outside the jail stood Don Rafael's green Cadillac from heaven knows where.

On the way home, Don Rafael gave Buti a written permit to pick piñones on his property for free, so Buti could count on a clear profit. Don Rafael wrung Buti's hand in goodbye, making him promise he would come up to Ratón to visit him and his sister, which Buti promised to do. Yes, Buti promised himself, he would soon go to Ratón for a social visit to thank Don Rafael for the piñones. He was well on his way to becoming a capitalist . . .

"Hey, Buti," called out Rico, "you just passed your house."

Buti backed the pickup next to a two-room shack he had built on the edge of his sister's one acre of land. The two-room house sported a red roof and a huge sign over the door that read "Antiques." After the roof and the sign, he had built himself an indoor toilet of which he was very proud. That had been six years before when he had come from Chihuahua to live with his sister and to make a fortune. He had fallen into the antique business by chance. One day he had found an old Victrola in an empty lot. That was the beginning of a huge collection of outlandish discards—old car horns, Kewpie dolls, wagon wheels, a stuffed moose head, an old church altar. At one time he had lugged home a huge, rusty commercial scale he claimed would be a priceless antique someday. The day he brought home the old, broken merry-go-round that boasted one headless horse painted blue, his sister, Trini, had been driven to distraction. She accused him of turning her place into an eyesore and ordered him to get rid of all the junk.

"Junk!" exclaimed Buti with great hurt in his voice. "Why, all these antiques will be worth thousands in a few years."

Rico had to agree with his mother—the place was an eyesore. After parking the pickup, Rico reminded Buti about his date with Alicia that night.

"Put on a clean shirt and shave, okay, Buti?"

"Baboso, who you think you talking to?"

"She's a nice lady, don't blow it," Rico reminded him.

"Sure she is. I'm going to marry her," Buti informed his nephew, who stared at him incredulously.

"She's not the marrying kind, Tío," Rico warned him.

"She's a widow, ain't she? She gave in once."

"That's cause she was sixteen," explained Rico.

"How old was he?" Buti inquired.

"Seventy and very rich."

"Smart girl. Never married again, eh? What for?"

"She's had lovers. Two of them."

"Smart girl. What were they like?"

Rico wrinkled his brow trying to remember. "The first one was her gardener. She took him because she claimed he looked like Humphrey Bogart."

"Humf—what?"

"Don't you ever watch the late late show? He was a movie star."

"What happened to him?"

"Humphrey Bogart? He died."

"No, stupid, the gardener."

"He died too. Fell off the roof fixing the television antenna."

Buti wanted all the facts. "What about the second lover?"

"He had a cleft in his chin like Kirk Douglas," Rico remembered.

"Another movie star? What's this thing with movie stars?"

"That's just the way she is." Rico added reassuringly, "But don't worry, Tío. She says you are the image of Clark Gable."

* * *

After the dog races, Buti took Alicia to Serafín's. It had become their favorite hangout. For one thing, the orchestra at Serafín's specialized in cumbias, and Buti was at his best dancing cumbias. No woman could resist him then. He could tell that Alicia was passionately in love with him by the way she clung to him and batted those ridiculous lashes. As he held the sweet-smelling, plump body against him and expertly did a turn on the floor, she hissed in his ear, "Well, are you going to move in?"

"Haven't changed my mind," he informed her in a cool, collected voice.

"Oh, you're infuriating!" She turned away from him, making her way back to the table. He noticed that the sway of her hips was defiant. Tonight could be the night. She plopped down on the table. "I've had it with you, Buti."

"What do you mean?" He tried to look perplexed.

"Stop playing cat and mouse."

"Am I suppose to be the mouse?" His voice was slightly sarcastic. "I've never been a mouse."

"Let's put our cards on the table." Her voice sounded ominous.

"Okay by me."

"Well then, don't give me that jazz about you loving me too much to live with me in sin. Sin, indeed! When I hear about all those girls you run around with . . ."

"Used to run around with," corrected Buti, looking into her eyes seductively. "I only want you. You are the world to me. Oh, how I want to make love to you. It tortures me to think about it. But I must be strong."

"There you go again. Come home with me tonight and you can make love to me all you want to." It was her stubborn voice.

"Don't say those things, my love, I would never sully our love by just jumping into bed with you." Buti was proud of the fake sincerity in his voice. "Our love is sacred. It must be sanctified by marriage."

"Marriage be damned!" Alicia hit her fists on the table. She was really angry now. He could tell. She accused him, "You just want my money."

"You're not the only girl with money. But you are the only woman I could ever love." Buti was beginning to believe it himself.

"You liar! All the girls you've had have been penniless, submissive, ignorant wetbacks from across the river." Her anger was becoming vicious now.

"Wait a minute." Buti was not playing a game anymore. He looked at the woman across the table, knowing that she was a romantic little fool, passionate, sensuous, selfish, stubborn, domineering, and full of fire. That's the kind of woman he would want to spend the rest of his life with. Nevertheless, he took affront. "What am I? I'm penniless—not quite, but almost. You could say I'm a wetback from across the river. And you, in your mindless way, want me to submit. Stop throwing stones. We seem to have the same likes!"

She looked at him with her mouth opened. She had sensed the sincerity in his voice. She could tell this was not a game anymore.

She knew she had been ambushed, but she would not give in.

"If you love me, and I believe you do, you'll come live with me, or—" there was a finality in her voice, "I simply will not see you again."

"I will not be another notch on your belt." There was finality in his voice too.

*   *   *

"Hell!" Alicia slammed the half-empty can of her beer against the porch railing. She hated the smell of honeysuckle, the full moon, and the heavy sense of spring. She hated everything tonight. And look at her—this was her sixth can of beer—thousands of calories going straight to her waistline. She hated herself most of all. Buti was through with her. He must be, if what Rico had told her was true. He had come over to help her plant some rosebushes, and she had casually asked him how Buti was doing these days. According to Rico, he spent a lot of time up in Ratón visiting his friend Don Rafael Avina and his unmarried sister.

"Is she rich?" Alicia asked nonchalantly.

"Very rich," Rico answered in innocence, setting the young rosebushes up against the fence.

She didn't ask much more, but knowing Buti, she could put two and two together. He had found himself a greener pasture and a new playmate. He loves me. I know he loves me, but I've lost him forever, she despaired. She couldn't stand it anymore—the moon, the smell of honeysuckle. She went back into the house and turned the late late show on television. She threw a shawl over her shoulders and huddled a corner of the sofa. She sighed deeply, her breasts heaving under her thin negligee.

She recognized the actress on the screen. It was Joan Fontaine
with her usual sweet, feminine smile and delicate gestures. She always looked so vulnerable, so helpless. Clark Gable came on the
screen. Oh, no—why him? Even his dimples were like Buti's. Damn
it all. She wanted to see the movie. They had had some kind of quar-
rel and Joan Fontaine had come to Clark to ask forgiveness, to say
she was wrong. Joan's soft, beautiful eyes seem to say, You can do
what you wish with me. You are my master . . . Alicia began to snif-
fle, then the tears flowed. Especially when she saw big, strong,
powerful Clark become a bowl of jelly. All that feminine submissive-
ness had won out. Joan Fontaine had won the battle without lifting a
finger. Hell, I'm no Joan Fontaine, though Alicia. But Clark was
smiling on the screen, and Alicia couldn't stand it any longer. She
turned off the set and went out into the night wearing only a
negligee, a shawl, and slippers. She didn't care who saw her. She
was walking—no, running—toward Buti's shack almost a mile away.
The princess was leaving her castle to go to the stable; it was her
movie now, her scenario. She was Joan Fontaine running toward
the man she loved, Clark Gable. It mustn't be too late. She would
throw herself at his feet—offer him all she had. She suddenly realized
the night was perfect for all this!

The lights were on. She knocked at the door, one hand against
her breast, her eyes wide, beseeching . . . in the manner of Joan
Fontaine.

"What the hell . . ." Buti stood in the doorway, half of a hero
sandwich in his hand.

"May I come in?" There was a soft dignity in her voice. Buti took
a bite of his sandwich and stared at her, speechless. She walked past
him into the room, and when she heard the door close, she turned
around dramatically with outstretched arms. "Darling . . ."

"You're drunk." Buti guessed.

"I only had five beers," she protested hotly, then caught herself.
"No, my love, I'm here for a very good reason . . ." Again, the Fontaine mystique.

Buti took another bite from the sandwich and chewed nervously.

"Don't you understand?" She lifted her chin and smiled sweetly
like she had seen Joan Fontaine do it hundreds of times. Buti shook
his head unbelievingly. She began to pace the floor gracefully, her
voice measured, almost pleading. "I've come to tell you that I was

wrong. I want to be forgiven. How could I have doubted you? I'm so ashamed—so ashamed." Words straight from the movie.

Buti finished off the sandwich, then scratched his head. Alicia approached him, her hand posed in the air, then gently falling against his cheek. "Do you understand what I'm saying?"

"Hell no, I think you've gone bananas."

She held back her disappointment with strained courage. "You're not helping much, you know." She bit her lip, thinking that Clark Gable would never have made an unkind judgment like that. She looked into his eyes with a faint, sweetly twisted smile, then leaned her head against his shoulder. She was getting to him.

There was worry in his voice. "Are you feeling okay?"

She began to cry in a very un-Joan Fontaine-like way. "Why can't you be more like him?"

"Like who?"

"Like Clark Gable, you lout!" She almost shouted it, regretfully.

Buti's eyes began to shine. She was beginning to sound like the Alicia he knew and loved. "Why should I be like some dumb old movie star?"

"Don't you see?" She held her breath out of desperation. "It's life . . ."

"The late late show?" He finally caught on—the dame on television.

"You were watching it too!" She accused him, not without surprise.

"Had nothing else to do. They're stupid, you know."

"What!" Her dark eyes blazed with anger.

"Those old gushy movies . . ." He gestured their uselessness.

"That proves to me what a brute you are, you insensitive animal!" She kicked his shin.

"Well, the woman, she was kind of nice."

"Joan Fontaine . . ."

"Yonfantayn?"

"That's her name. You're not going to marry her, are you?" There was real concern in her voice.

"Yonfantayn?" He could not keep up with her madness.

"No—that woman up in Ratón."

"Berta Avina?" The whole scene came into focus. Buti sighed in relief.

"Rico told me she is very rich."

"Very rich."

"Is she slender and frail and soft-spoken like . . ."

"Yonfantayn?" Buti silently congratulated himself on his subtle play.

"Yes . . ."

Buti thought of Berta Avina, her square, skinny body, her tight lipped smile. He lied, "Oh, yes. Berta is the spitting image of Yonfantayn."

"I knew it. I knew it!" Alicia threw herself into his arms. "Please please, marry me. You beast, I love you so."

"Can't marry you tonight, querida. We have better things to do." He pulled her roughly against him, with the Clark Gable smile, and then he kissed her again and again. Still relying on his dimples, he picked her up without too great an effort and headed for the bed. She tried to push him away, protesting coyly, "No, we can't. We mustn't. Not before we are married."

He stopped in his tracks, not believing his ears. This was the woman who had nagged him and begged him to jump into bed with her. Now he couldn't believe his ears. "Say that again."

"I said, not until we're married."

"Why? That's not my Alicia talking."

"Well, that's what she would say."

"Who would say?"

"Joan Fontaine, silly!"

"Well, I saw a movie myself last night, something about the wind . . ."

"*Gone with the Wind.*"

"Yes, that one with the guy you like, the one that looks like me."

"Clark Gable."

"He says to this beautiful, strong-willed, bossy woman—'Frankly, my dear, I don't give a damn!' "

He winked at her and threw her on the bed.

Rain of Scorpions

"Hey, Miguel, how about a semita?" Fito sat on a stool in the middle of Papá At's tiendita. He sat facing the door, his crutches on the rungs of a stool. Miguel, who was sweeping the floor, nodded and hurried to the bread counter. Wiping one hand on his shirt, he reached for a semita and took it to Fito, anxious to please his hero. Fito stuffed the sweet bread in his mouth as Ismael gulped down his coke and headed for the door. Fito called out, "Got you where it counts, eh, college boy?" Ismael did not even look back. The shadow of a bitter smile carved itself on Fito's face, then he turned to Miguel, the tinge of bad memories melting away. "Gimme another one, Miguel." The twelve-year-old handed Fito another semita, then went back behind the counter to fill brown bags with pinto beans, scooping them up from a sack. Watching the outlined shadows of the door framed by the sun on the floor, Fito relished his semita. Ismael's voice rang in his ears, "You're going nowhere, man!" Where could a cripple from Smeltertown go anyway? he asked himself. In the stillness of the afternoon, his eyes saw dead ends on the ceiling, the walls, the counters of the little store.

Miguel was behind him. "That Ismael is a prick. He's jealous. You're a hero in this town." Fito had lost a leg in Nam. Blacks and browns dying for their country in Nam. The poor sent out as cannon fodder by the rich. What the common man will do in the guise of patriotism! "Life's a setup, Miguel."

Miguel did not know what he was talking about. Fito could see it on the boy's face. Miguel's answer was a struggle to understand.

"You mean we can't do what we want?"

"Depends on the cards life deals you. If you're dealt a card that says you're Chicano and poor, you better believe it."

"Yeah," Miguel countered, not wanting to believe. "El Indio Tolo got away from the pony soldiers."

Fito smiled. Everytime El Indio Tolo had killed a pony soldier he had climbed his mountains. Knew those mountains like the back of his hand.

Miguel wanted the story again. "How many men did he kill?" Fito looked up at the ceiling and shrugged his shoulders. Who wanted to count the number of men killed? His friend Papá At had told the story over and over. All the barrio kids knew it by heart, and always the same question from the kids. How many men did El Indio Tolo kill? Some civilized world when people had to kill people to live free! Something screwy about that.

Miguel took a coke from a tin tub where the soda pop was snuggled in ice. He opened the bottle and handed it to Fito. "On me." Then Miguel went back to filling his bean bags. Fito drank the syrupy liquid. "I'm stuck. What good am I even in Smeltertown? What good is a man with only one leg?" In the cage of circumstances, the bars were all the things that imprisoned Chicanos—poverty, prejudice, exploitation. Yes, Ismael would be out of the cage. Book learning was setting him free; or was it? Maybe a new kind of cage, the trap of words and ready-made propaganda. Each gringo building his death house, a pyramid, bigger and bigger until they were trapped. Ismael would call it success. Why not?

Papá At walked into the store followed by la viuda Gómez. At sixty-three her days were spent complaining about her liver problem. Papá At was listening, nodding his head, patting her hand. The old woman signed laboriously. "Los viejos no servimos pa' nada. I need some camphor oil and four cans of Carnation milk. Put it on my bill." Buying from Papá At on credit was a way of life for the ancianos in town. Papá At would erase the debt by dismissing it with a wave of the hand. "What's mine is yours."

The old man had a couple of acres of farmland in Canutillo. Enough to grow fruit and vegetables to stock his tiendita. He also had a small pension. That was enough. The old people came to him with their problems because Papá At listened and found solutions, always from the heart. Mrs. Gómez was used to crying on his strong shoulder. "My arthritis is bad now."

Papá At's eyes were full of genuine concern. He promised her, "I'll come by after I close up. We'll talk about Tomás." Remembering her husband, now dead fourteen years, always made the pain disap-

pear for a little while. Fito knew for sure that Papá At would keep his
word. When Mrs. Gómez left, Fito glanced up to see the old man's
bright green eyes on him. Papá At had already picked up on his feelings.

"This is a wonderful land." Papá At was trying to make him feel
better. "There's nothing like the bigness of our desert. See that
mountain? It changes colors seven times each day."

"I have no time for mountains." There was impatience in Fito's
words.

"Make you feel better," Papá At promised. "That's the Indian
way."

Fito grinned. In his eyes swam good feelings toward the old man.
He stood and reached down for his crutches and made his way carefully to the door, then turned, wishing for a practical good-bye. "Got
to fix a radio."

Out in the hot sun, anger returned. Damned crutches. They sure
slowed down a guy. The advice of the cheerful army doctor floated
in memory. "You'll be fitted for an artificial leg in a couple of
months."

Fito's eyes had deliberately looked at the man's healthy leg, then
at the major's insignia and the look of detachment on the officer's
face. The corporal had asked, "You think that's a fair exchange for a
flesh and bone leg?" He had not waited for an answer.

Outside the store, he walked down the barrio street, pondering
his sad state in life. Shit! Shit! He had to do something about the bile
spilling in his guts. His crutches came down on loose gravel, crunch-
ing rhythmically "Wha . . . hope . . . wha . . . hope."

*   *   *

Miguel was among the school kids on the bus, lower grades on
the front seats, upper grades in the back. Some of his friends in the
sixth grade were sitting with the eighth-grade boys telling dirty jokes.
All the school children were returning from the clinic where their
blood had been tested for levels of sulphur dioxide. It was a known
fact that the air in Smeltertown was pure poison. A long time ago the
ASARCO plant had turned black from the poisons spumed out of
the second tallest chimney in the world, at one time the tallest, until
Japan built a taller one. For decades now the people of Smeltertown
had breathed the poisoned air.

In the seventies a growing ecological conscience had discovered the condition in Smeltertown, and the scientific findings of sulphur dioxide pollution were alarming. Disclaimers were put out by ASAR-CO: nothing was wrong with the pollution emanating from their chimneys. Still, they decided that the evacuation of the people from Smeltertown was the wise thing to do. The expense involved was a worthwhile one for it could offset law suits. Now was the time to do it when the voice of the environmental groups was dim. Expediency is a key word in big business. Take the people out of the town at minimal cost, find housing for them wherever. Evidence would no longer exist. The breaking up of a human nucleus of life, the warm web of human daily existence that identified a community, was not a consideration in decision making at ASARCO. People, after all, were expendable—never profit. This was the bottom line.

But to the barrio people of Smeltertown the decision of the dinosaurs was a deathblow. The breakup of the town was the breakup of their spirit, their identity, their very soul. They could not say it, but they sensed it; their hearts told them an abyss would grow in their lives. What would happen to longtime friends and loved ones? The people were confused, apprehensive, lost, angry, vulnerable. These chaotic feelings threatened their self-respect. They were awakened to the reality of their helplessness. The children on the bus, being children, perhaps, did not grasp the seriousness of the situation. But Miguel, a thoughtful and sensitive boy, had long thoughts about the breakup of the barrio.

Someone threw a Hershey bar over his head. It landed on the bus driver's head. "You damned kids! The brakes screeched to a stop at the corner of Main Street. "Out, out! Clear the bus!"

Then came a stampede. The bus driver, sitting, ignoring the mayhem, stared blankly out the window as the boys and girls scampered wildly off the bus.

It was past noon and they did not have to go back to school. Felipe caught up with Miguel. "Going to Papá At's?"

"Yeah, for a while." It was payday and he had to meet his father at Pepe's Bar.

Felipe went on ahead. "See you there."

It was a ritual between Miguel and his father, a worker at the smelter. Mamá had taught Miguel to wait at Pepe's Bar for Papá on paydays. Papá would give his week's earning to Miguel, keeping a few dollars for beer. After all, a family had to be clothed and fed.

Miguel liked to sit and watch the tired workers come into the bar. He liked to watch Papá's friends take off the weight of weariness. In Pepe's Bar eyes shone bright with expectancy and a warmth grew and bounced around the dark, cool bar. Laughter and the rapid compadre talk had the soft cadence of dreams.

Once Miguel had the pay envelope in his hands, he would rush home and put it into his mother's hands. The ritual had to wait until the four o'clock whistle blew. Until then he would go to El Amigo de Los Pobres.

When Miguel got to the grocery store it was full of children, the ones on the bus. Papá At was putting bubble gum and peppermint sticks into grubby little hands. On Fridays Papá At told stories about nature gods and Indians. Miguel knew all the stories by heart and so did his friends. Felipe and Sergio were already there drinking sodas. Sergio was throwing pieces of ice in the air then catching them in his mouth. Suddenly he took a piece and dropped it down Felipe's shirt. Sergio wiggled deliciously. The children were already seated around Papá At, waiting expectantly for their story. The three older boys savored their cold drinks and leaned against the counter to listen. No one ever tired of Papá At's stories, for there was a magic in his voice. He pointed to the mountain in the east, the only one still pregnant with greenery, not the black skeleton mountains dug into by ASAR-CO. "Over there is El Indio Tolo's cave."

A little boy asked, "Have you ever seen him?"

"His spirit is all around." This truth was strong in Papá At's voice. No one could doubt.

"That's where he keeps his gold," another boy informed the group. "That's why the cave shines at night."

Papá At shook his head. "El Indio Tolo was not interested in gold. That light at night is fox fire, fool's gold. Maybe sometimes it's not the light of metal fumes. . . ." He paused. "There are times when we can see the fire of the Red Wind."

Someone laughed, "Winds don't have fire."

"The Red Wind has an aura of light when he plays with Gotalla-ma," Papá At explained.

Miguel's imagination glowed. He loved the stories about the Red Wind. The song of the Red Wind was the song of all the voices of the world, at the beginning, now and forever. The song lived in the heart of all Indians.

Papá At sang the words, "We are all brothers and sisters of the Red Wind as El Indio Tolo is."

The thought became a soft drawn breath in Miguel's throat.

"When you hear the song of the Red Wind you hear the song of the earth breathing, of stars growing, and the whisper of seasons." Papa's words were a wild song.

An echo from the centuries grew and expanded in Miguel. Red Wind! Red Wind! The roar of an ancient, secret root found its home in Miguel. He glanced at his friends. They were caught in the same excitement. He looked at the mountain.

It seemed to mix and melt into Papá At's words. "The universe breathes and changes all the time. It does not have one voice, but as many voices as you can imagine. We cannot listen to the great sounds of the universe. It is too big for a single person, for we are very small."

Very small, thought Miguel, almost invisible. He remembered another time when Papá At had compared people to caterpillars making cocoons. People make cocoons, an individual order, so they can understand the small universe they themselves put together to feel safe and important. To hear a harmony, for the chaos, the chaos of the universe, would make everyone deaf.

A boy with limpid eyes asked, "What happened to the Indians who were here long ago?"

A tinge of sadness touched the old man's voice. "They were killed by the white man, the buffalo were slaughtered, and the lands of los indios were stolen. And when the white man conquered the Indians who survived, they were herded into desert reservations. The white man's way was like a twister in the desert destroying everything in its path. The moan of the twister was pain, a killing force, like hail, floods, earthquakes."

The children knew what floods were because the main street in Smeltertown had often been flooded during heavy rains that came seldom, but suddenly.

"Now I shall tell you about the Indian that never died."

The children chorused excitedly, "El Indio Tolo! El Indio Tolo!"

Papá At began the tale. "Well, when Geronimo gave up, his people were driven to a reservation up in the mountains of Ruidoso. El Indio Tolo was sixteen and hated the white man for leading his people to a living doom. He would rather be dead than trapped on a reservation. To be Indian was to be free, part of mountains, trees, and sky. So one night, in the Guadalupe mountains, he escaped. He followed an old Indian trail away from the pony soldiers.

"He was alone. One Indian in the universe. But when the Red Wind sang, El Indio Tolo felt the universe inside him, so loneliness became an aloneness that linked itself to nature gods, to sky, to running river. In the bitter cold of winter his feet would freeze and his stomach gnawed with hunger. He heard the song of the Red Wind become the snow howl of the canyons. But spring came, and springs were new beginnings. All around were the voices of hidden streams, of swaying trees and winking stars. The Red Wind would return to keep him company.

"One day the pony soldiers saw him and chased him through the canyon, but he was able to lose them, unmindful of his way. He did not recognize the land that he had come to, but he kept going on and on, until he found the cave."

Papá At paused in thought until a little girl asked, "Is he still there now?"

"Only the Red Wind knows. He may be living in the green valley far inside the cave."

Another little boy spoke out. "Tell us, what happened to him in the cave?"

Papá At continued. "He walked deep into a silence for a long time. Then he came to a place where water ran on purple rocks deep in the cave. So when he came to El Hoyo, he was not afraid. El Hoyo is a chasm that never ends. At its entrance is a guard made of stone sculpted by Gotallama. El Indio Tolo braved the crossing to the other side. There he found the colors of the world caught in water turned to crystal; here he felt a presence. He drank from a pool of clear water then fell asleep. He slept in a silence turned sweet by singing crystals. He slept a long, long time. When he awakened, before him stood Gotallama, god of waters and fire."

An excited young voice full of the tale added, "And they became friends."

"Yes," Papá At's eyes twinkled with a new mystery. "Gotallama led the way to the green valley."

There were hushed whispers of agreement. Papá At went on. "The secret valley is where nature gods live. El Indio Tolo became the only human being who knew the way to the green valley. Even now, the spirit of El Indio Tolo walks with Gotallama."

"Have you ever seen the green valley, Papá At?"

"No one has gone beyond El Hoyo."

The voice of a realist asked, "Is it really there?"

Papá At's words sounded like a clear bell. "It is so. No one doubts."

Miguel closed his eyes and saw the greenness. El Indio Tolo knew the way; perhaps he had left a map for other Indians to find. Surely there was something in the cave that could lead them to the green valley.

The story was over. The older boys led the children out of the store. Clamoring and laughing, they disappeared into the sun. Papá At had gone to the back of the store to cook his supper. Felipe and Sergio helped Miguel clear the counter and pick up gum and candy wrappers from the floor. The aroma of cooking tomatoes and onions smelled delicious as the boys left the store.

The beginning fall of the sun was glorious red and purple as they walked along the presidio street. Miguel's eyes caught Mrs. Gómez's curtains fluttering in a slight breeze. This had been her home for forty years. Where would she go if there was no more barrio? Felipe and Sergio went their ways as Miguel headed for Pepe's Bar. Along the way Miguel thought of water over purple rocks, El Hoyo, and the green valley. Smeltertown was like a giant mud hole. He realized this, but to him it was also as beautiful as the green valley where nature gods lived. He thought of the poison, of being poor. These things were not as important as the good things about the barrio. But grown-ups were different. They worked too hard and made plans that never came true. Maybe that was why they were so full of worries and anger, except in Pepe's Bar. The bar was like a waiting place. Sort of free of all worries and problems—a waiting place, where the hard edges of a confusing world were smoothed out. When grown-ups went into the bar, years seemed to peel off. They were no longer old. Their faces were no longer tight and they laughed as if they were free, as if they were important.

"Amorcito corazón"—the song floated from the jukebox in la cantina out into the growing shadows of the day. Once inside, Miguel heard the whirring of the ceiling fan in the cool darkness. He sat on a stool at the bar and watched Pepe wash glasses, setting them up to be rinsed. There were three people in the place. Champurrado, who was famous for making the best gorditas on the face of the earth and the best champurrado ever made. He would get up at three every morning and fix twenty dozen gorditas. The corn gorditas he would buy from the tamale store the day before. Then he would place them in a warm oven until his mixture was ready. He would cook brisket in beer with lots of cilantro, garlic, and cumin, then mix tomatoes, potatoes, and the beef and sauté everything in butter. Then he would fill each gordita with the mixture and top it with cheese and lots of lettuce. He would wrap each dozen in wax-paper and, by eight, he was out in his vending cart ringing his bell. The rush for his gorditas was a sight to see. Women gathered around his cart with ready money, shoving the other housewives so as not to be left without. The husbands who were lucky would find gorgitas in their lunch pail. On holy days, when kermeses were held at the church, Champurrado would prepare miztamal: goat's milk, choco-late, cinnamon, and sugar, a delicious drink. He sold all his cham-purrado in no time at all.

But Champurrado, the man, was not happy. His wife, fifteen years his junior, had run away with a mojado, a wetback she had met by the river. Champurrado had started a little business for his wife. He made jalea de membrillo and sent his wife out in the cart to sell it. One afternoon she was tired, so she stopped by the river's edge and took off her shoes and stockings to put her legs in the water. Lo and behold, a face came out of the water right in front of her. She saw a handsome young man with smoldering eyes, grinning at her. She could do no less than take him home, dry him out, and feed him. When Champurrado got home his wife convinced him he needed a helper because he was not getting any younger. After a time, Gregorio, the illegal alien, became her lover. She would wait until Champurrado left with his gorditas, then she would jump into bed with her energetic young man. One day Gregorio told her he was too good to be just a cook's helper. He was going to leave for Califas and find his fortune. She could come if she wanted. There was no ques-tion about it. Without a second thought for poor old tired Champu-rrado, the lovers left one midnight: while Champurrado was snoring.

It had happened ten years before, but Champurrado was still consumed by the betrayal. He was alone now, and his family were the guys who frequented the bar. He practically lived there after the gorditas were delivered each day.

He was sitting with Narizón. Narizón was a tailor and a garage mechanic. He owned a commercial Singer sewing machine which he used to make hilpas, a sacklike cotton dress. He used just one pat-tern and made dozens in bright colors. These hung in racks outside his small garage, where he fixed tires and carburetors. Narizón had a nagging wife and six children, so he divided his time between his garage and Pepe's Bar, going home only to provide for his family. Once, he took a new hilpa to his wife who threw it in his face. Narizón was not a happy man.

The third man sitting with them was a stranger. Miguel had never seen him before.

"Where Sergio?" Pepe asked. Sergio was his son.

"He went home." At least, Miguel thought he had gone home.

"The good-for-nothing is supposed to be here helping me."

Miguel went behind the counter to where Pepe was rinsing. "I'll do that."

Champurrado was calling for another beer. Pepe wiped his hands to get him one. Champurrado thanked Pepe, his voice mixing with the whir of the ceiling fan as he called out to Miguel, "Chaval, ¿qué traes? Still helping out Papá At?"

Miguel nodded as he placed the last of the glasses on the rack, then he walked over to their table. Champurrado looked up and winked. "How are Papá's gods?"

Miguel grinned. "Sure, sure. Ha, ha! Who am I to know?' He wondered how Champurrado felt about the evacuation to come. "What do you think about ASARCO breaking up the barrio?"

"Bastards! Let them try. Listen, kid, I have a shotgun, the one I should have used on that whoring wife of mine."

Miguel looked at Champurrado disbelievingly. "You're going to shoot the bosses?"

"If I have to. This is my town. Nobody makes me leave." Champurrado drank the rest of his beer in one gulp in defiance.

"You'll go like the rest of us," Narizón, the defeated one, assured him.

"Chingón. How much you bet?"

"Five dollars?" Narizón proposed, doubt in his voice.

"Five dollars for putting my life on the line?" There was mocking incredulity in Champurrado's voice. "Me against ASARCO?"

The stranger gave a hearty laugh. "David and Goliath. Where are you going to get five dollars, Narizón? I don't think you've ever had five dollars. Your wife wouldn't give you five dollars."

Miguel offered a solution. "There's a better place to go, better than Smeltertown."

Champurrado took hold of Miguel's arm. "What's the matter with you, Chico? This is paradise; it is home."

The stranger added, "If you like breathing poison."

Narizón was curious. "Where's this place you're talking about?"

"A green valley, deep in El Indio Tolo's cave. If we can find it— then everybody from here could go there."

Champurrado slapped his knee, laughing boisterously. "Papá At makes you believe anything! I suppose Gotallama's there."

Miguel's voice was sure. "Yes."

Champurrado rubbed his chin. "Papá At is a pagan. But that's good. That's good . . ."

"What's so good about it?" The stranger was curious.

Champurrado explained, "The old ways are better." He turned and put his arm around Miguel. "And your green valley, if Papá At says it's there, it's there. Did you know that gods play? They drink beer, sing, and tell jokes . . ."

"Shut up, you're confusing the kid." This from the stranger.

Pepe came in from the back with a huge plastic bag of chicharrones. He sold a bowl of crackling for twenty-five cents. Miguel returned to rinsing glasses until the smelter whistle blew.

* * *

As he came home on the bus from the veteran's hospital, Fito's thoughts ran as swiftly as the passage of towns and deserts. The man sitting next to him suddenlly spoke. "So much empty space."

Fito gave no answer, still looking at the blurred passing of cacti, brown arbustos and a desert breathing in its own vegetation.

The man tried again. "You from around here?"

"Yeah, next stop." Fito pointed at a broken-down wooden building high on a hill.

The man looked at Fito with kind, interested eyes. "Going home?"

Fito repeated the words, woven into the weight of memories. "Going home."

Fito felt the stranger's frank scrutiny. Strangely enough, he felt an unexplained kinship with the stranger. Funny, he never felt comfortable around gringos. The smokestack was now visible at a far distance.

The stranger commented, "That's a big one."

Fito laughed, his voice edged with bitterness. "Second highest in the world. Features poisoned air, Smeltertown."

The man nodded. "Carbon disulfide."

Fito nodded. "The whole town is covered with carbons. Our souls are covered with ash."

The man laughed lightly. "You don't like the way progress treats people, eh?"

"You kidding? Progress?"

"You're right, progress is a relative word. Progress for a few at the expense of the rest of the world. It's always been like that."

Now Fito knew why he had a good feeling about this man. He pointed to his missing leg. "Nam. My gift to the U.S A. who poisons me and my people."

"It's not only in this country; all nations have used the powerless to their advantage. Look at the millions who died building pyramids for pharoahs. Same thing. It's in nature too—anthills. Progress is a kind of death for the poor."

Fito's interest had been kindled by the general parallels. A question came to his mind. "It's for different reasons, isn't it? Ants do it for survival, slaves built pyramids for death."

"Exactly. . . . What is your name?" The man was genuinely interested in who he was.

"Fito."

"I'm John."

Fito smiled warmly. "Hello John." They both stared out the window, ideas growing. Then Fito realized in words, "You know, we Mexicans are both ants and Egyptian slaves. We work at ASARCO to survive, and we die on the installment plan creating comforts and pleasures for the rich and powerful. That's the real definition of progress."

The man spoke beyond the immediate. "Little by little the numbers will grow and come to their senses. The unenlightened, whom we used to call the unwashed, even the middle classes all over the world, are slowly realizing the unfairness of it all. But it's such a slow process, the opening of eyes and heart. Still, it'll happen, and you and I can help to make it happen."

Fito was skeptical. "Not in our lifetime."

The man laughed. "Probably not."

The bus had come to a stop. Fito was home. He held out his hand and John grabbed it. For a moment they were one in accord.

Fito could not help saying, "Listen, John, I have a little repair shop, televisions, appliances, has a sign—Fito's Repairs—can't miss it. If you ever come this way again you're more than welcome."

John fished into his pocket and gave him a card. "I teach history at a university. My phone numbers, home and office, if you ever get to California."

Fito took the card and could not help asking, "Why the bus?" Fito knew that few professionals traveled by bus.

John laughed. "Wanted to see the country at eye level. Good-bye, Fito. Good luck."

"Thanks." Fito picked up his crutches and got off the bus. He watched it disappear in the density of sun, catching the sharp, pungent smell of burned fuel. He slowly made his way to Papá At's. The sights and sounds of main street were stirrings of the heart. Home, yes, home, where he belonged. Nine guys from Smeltertown had joined the army, all ended up in Nam. Three had survived but only he had come back. He had wanted to come back. He stopped for a moment deep in thought as Manuel's old dog sniffed at his leg. Manuel had a shoe repair shop on the corner. As old Migaja continued sniffing his leg, Fito accused himself of coming back to Smeltertown because he had been crippled. But something deep inside told him it was more, something he could not touch with words. As he turned the corner the sight of the old sign over Papá At's store brought back the sense of childhood. "El Amigo de Los Pobres"; yes, Papá At had always been that. Fito went into the store, anticipating a cold drink.

The friend of the poor was sitting on the floor, bundling corn husks for tamales. His old eyes wrinkled as he smiled a welcome.

Fito grinned. "Sure nice seeing your old face." He made his way to the tub and took a Pepsi. He set his crutches against the counter, leaning against it to recount his experience at the veterans' hospital. "Getting a new leg. Doctor said it is better than the one I lost. Great kidder, eh?"

He drained the can and watched the old man make strips out of husks. With expert fingers Papá At wrapped the pieces around dried yellow bunches. Yes, he was home. Good, strong memories melting into the familiar again, a beautiful place, Papá At's store, a place heavy with meanings. In silence he glanced at the rotted timber that made up the roof, heard the song of dancing shadows, and breathed in the wonderful eating smells, but most of all, he absorbed the sight of Papá At. Fito's heart expanded like a growing universe. "Papá At?"

"Yes?"

"You've always been content. I've never heard you say you wanted more."

"I have everything." Papá At's voice was a clear bell.

"What about money, power, success . . .?" Fito knew these words were only words, far from dreams, to Papá At. But this was one old man who knew what human beings were all about.

Papá At stopped bundling and kindly searched Fito's face. "What's wrong?"

"Trying to sort things out . . ."

"All things in their place? Life isn't that way. All of us are lopsided puzzles. Like in the universe, order and chaos inside of us, same outside. We must accept without anger."

"I have a right to be angry. I lost a leg. I live under the shadow of what America is all about. It poisons the air I breathe. They're going to do away with the barrio. Aren't you angry about that?" demanded Fito.

A longing shimmered in the old man's eyes. "I wanted to die here in this town. I belong where I have lived. But hate does not solve anything. Long ago when my people had to move because of drought, no game, they followed the river . . ."

"Papá At, they stayed together, they tried together. There's not much of a river to follow here. ASARCO doesn't plan to find a single place for the whole town. They could care less."

Papá At shook his head, "I have no solution. If we are separated, we shall suffer like El Indio Tolo."

"Papá, that's a myth born from dreams, a way to hold back the ugliness of what's real. Abuelito, you think this tiendita is the whole world! What do you know about out there?"

Papá At's eyes grew somber. "The world? It is the universe that guides me. It is the universe that gifts its secrets to me. People— they're part of nature. The world does not matter that much."

Fito knew Papá At's vision was different from his, but he wanted the old man to assure him that what he was about to do was the right thing. He thought about the man on the bus. "I met this man on the bus, a professor, who teaches history. He said people are like ants, you know, patterns, systems. The poor are like ants, working and dying for the rich."

Papá At walked behind the counter, folding his hands. "Life is not money."

Fito turned to face him. "That's what it's all about. I remember a poem in school about an ant named Jerry who died in the middle of doing his work. The other ants just pushed him aside. People do that to people. Look at me, at all of us. The men in the town spent a whole life at the smelter, taking shit, eating poison. Guys around here who went to war joined up because there were no jobs or they quit school."

Papá At's face was perplexed. "No matter the unfairness, most of us stay human. That's important."

Fito laughed. "Not the ants on top! That's why the world's going to hell."

Papá At looked about the store and sighed. "You're right. I know little of the world; this place is enough for me. I never fought in a war, and I never think of the powerful and rich."

"I know. I wish I could be like you."

Papá At nodded, then went back again to his bundling. He sat on the floor and stretched out his legs. Fito picked up his crutches and made his way to the old man. In direct line to Papá At's eyes were the crutches and the one good leg. Papá At's eyes welled with love for the confused young man. "You must see clearly. You must feel open; anger has no doors." Papá At got up slowly to face him, "What is it that you want to do?"

"To have a meeting."

"What kind, hijito? Why?"

"I want the whole town to take a stand. We must tell the world something together. If they force us to leave Smeltertown, we must stand up and demand a place where all of us can go. Our families go back generations! We mustn't behave like slaves, like ants."

"That's a wonderful idea, Fito! We should come together and listen to you."

"Am I talking wild? You think it's possible, the whole barrio speaking as one?" Fito felt a wave of lostness.

Papá At put his arm around Fito's shoulder. "No, it's a good dream and the best in us is dreams."

*   *   *

Lupe looked out her bedroom window at a dark sky then walked away, avoiding the mirror of her dresser. Instead she looked down at her stout bare feet and wiggled her toes. The long current from mind to toe, that was miraculous to her. Lupe was twenty-four, large-boned and somewhat overweight. Her thick, curly, fine hair, beautiful facial bones, and large almond eyes had not helped her think of herself as pretty. She never took note of her attributes because Lupe did not bother herself with how she looked. She was always lost in books or lost in thinking. After all, she relished books and learning, she relished people and music. In fact, people to her were like music —feelings rising, falling, all fire. Fito she loved more than life itself. It was only then that she wished to be beautiful.

Cleopatra had been considered beautiful. Supposedly she had bean dark and fat, but men had loved her passionately. Beauty must have been judged by different standards during those times. She imagined a young queen on a barge surrounded by lovers.

There had been no lovers in Lupe's life. She heard the crescendo of rain outside her window. The smell of rain was an excitement of the blood. She breathed in the fragrance of wet earth. Lupe felt like Cleopatra, her pores drinking in the gladness of nature, at one with sky and earth.

Feeling like Cleopatra did not last. She did not have the beauty endowed to certain females meant to be loved by men. Fito had loved Belén all his life. She was the real Cleopatra of the barrio. Belén had promised halfheartedly to marry Fito when he came back from war, at his passionate insistence. But the impatient, restless Belén had found a new lover, a rich lover, and had left the impoverished confines of Smeltertown, never to be seen again. Fito had lost a leg in Nam, but worse than that, he had lost Belén.

Lupe felt grayness, a sunlessness. The air suddenly became oppressive. She didn't want to cry; she mustn't cry. She had cried out her gray loneliness for years. But imagination and the purple mountain behind Papá At's tiendita always saved her, filled her with a thankfulness. There were so many things to be thankful for. She had made it to the university. Every morning Fito would come over for breakfast. Then, there was her abuelita. She had been nurtured by the radiance of a loving grandmother. So, the gray clouds broke and the sun came through, and the days were full with work and learning and loving.

When she returned from work that afternoon she set about cleaning her bird cage. The canaries were her grandmother's but they were a pleasure in the midst of her plants. The back porch with its southern light was perfect for the profusion of plants Lupe had brought there to live with her.

She washed the supper dishes as she listened to her grand-mother's soft praying of the rosary. After Lupe had made prepara-tions for the night, she tucked her grandmother into bed, then brushed her hair. She sat listening to the rain amidst her plants and sleeping canaries. The rain sang in her veins. She brought out her guitar and sang to the coming night and the ways of rain gods. Deep in her being, she knew she could be Cleopatra to Fito.

*   *   *

Fito felt ridiculous. He was no preacher. The school cafeteria was full and all eyes were on him. They had come to listen to him in spite of the rainstorm. They had come to listen to his plan, but it was not really a plan. It was a plea. What was ever accomplished after a town meeting in Smeltertown? What could powerless people do? The town as one voice had demanded that electricity and water be sup-plied to the barrio. They had succeeded only because a clever politi-cian had used their plight and sided with the poor. He got good pub-licity and a better image. He hadn't really cared a hill of beans for the poor. Roads, a new school, all the desperate needs of the people had been made public by a champion. But who would champion their cause now? Who cared about the breakup of another poor bar-rio? It happened often: the building of the freeway, shopping center, or warehousing had pushed people aside, like Indians shoved onto reservations. Progress! It never changed, the use of the poor by the rich. But his plan . . . his plan . . .

There was a clap of thunder as he stood gathering his thoughts. His strong Mexican face was intense. He balanced himself on his crutches, standing as tall as he could. Fito began hesitantly.

"We are a people that go back, how many generations? We know our neighbors as we know ourselves. We are like a large fami-ly, a tribe. We have made a web like a spider, our lives linked to other lives, in a sameness, a warmth, the confidence of who we are. This is what makes me 'me' and you 'you.' "

The crowd was quiet, waiting for him to continue. Fito wiped one hand on his pants. He was perspiring and it was hard to hold onto the crutches with slippery hands.

He cleared his throat, continuing, "It's a crime, what the smelter bosses want to do. They will succeed by scattering the evidence of what they've done to us. The poison has killed many of us, though we were unaware of it. Many of our children have been poisoned. For years the bosses didn't care, until the environmental people pointed a finger and accused them. Now they want us out of this town, families moved to strange neighborhoods. Gringos move around a lot, but money makes it easier—and they really do not have the kind of ties with family and friends that we do. They can't treat the poor that way; relatives and friends are the wealth of the poor. We must not let them!"

A worker spoke from the back. "They're going to do what they want. They have the money."

Another man joined in. "Are you crazy? You think any of us can make them find a place for all of us to go together? Don't be a dreamer. They don't care what happens to us. They wouldn't put out the money for that."

"Not if we decide to leave together, like the Israelites left Egypt . . ." Fito felt the beginning of a new excitement.

Someone laughed. "Where would we go? Where is our Promised Land?"

Fito spoke haltingly, "The gesture of leaving together."

An angry voice protested, "A gesture? What in the hell will that do? The whole town leaving together with no place to go? Only fools would do that."

Yes, thought Fito, we'd be a joke. The reality of that had to be faced. But Fito gave reasons, a plan. "We would tell the newspapers, speak on television, let it be known we intend to leave together. Don't you see? The smelter bosses would look bad."

Murmurs rose, mostly negative. It wouldn't work; the ASARCO people could take the bad publicity. Such a thing had never been done before, a whole town refusing to be scattered to the winds of chance.

Fito had thought his plan majestic, grand, but, now, seeing the reaction of his neighbors, it seemed impractical, all in disarray. One more meeting had come to an end.

*   *   *

Miguel walked home with Sergio and Felipe after the meeting.

Miguel stared into the dark and felt a great respect for Fito. His plan was great. If only there were a place to go, if only the whole town had a green valley like the one El Indio Tolo had found so long ago.

"Got cigarettes," Felipe informed them. They made their way to the fire escape at the back of the school. That's where they always did their secret smoking. They sat on the stairs huddled together, smoking and flicking live ashes beyond the wet stairs. Miguel announced, "We could find it."

"Find what?" Fellpe asked.

"The green valley." Miguel knew his friends knew what he was talking about.

"Beyond El Hoyo?" Sergio echoed in disbelief.

Miguel was serious. "Yes. We gotta cross it and find the valley. The whole town can go there."

Felipe threw his stub as far as he could. "You're as bad as Fito. No one has ever crossed El Hoyo, and who says the green valley's there?"

"Gotallama." It was a truth to Miguel. "Papá At knows it's there."

Sergio was interested. "I've never seen El Hoyo."

Felipe quipped, "You try, you die."

Miguel had made up his mind. "I'm going. If you don't want to go, that's okay."

Felipe reminded, "We do everything together."

"That means you're going with me?"

"Sure, what the heck. You game, Sergio?"

"¡Que sí! maybe we'll find El Indio Tolo's bones."

Miguel closed the matter. "We go tomorrow morning, early. We have to take food; it's a long trip."

His friends did not back down. The sense of a new adventure had made them all of one mind.

*   *   *

"Fito!" Lupe hurried to catch up with the lonely figure on crutches. Fito turned and saw her in the moist, sweet dark. They walked in silence for a while. Fito was glad to have her company. Of all people, Lupe knew how he felt. Lupe, the one who waited in shadows. Why did he think of her in that way? She was so bright and imaginative, so full of life, but, still, all the years he had known her, she had been wrapped in an aloneness. But then, she was different from most of the girls in the barrio. She was different from Belén. Belén . . . the thought of her was still painful. The beautiful Belén was a closed chapter in his life. He glanced at the young woman beside him. Lupe has cared for me all my life, he thought, but I never bothered to see. The sense of her caring lessened his gloom.

"You know what keeps me going these days?"

She asked, not without shyness, "What keeps you going?"

"You, making me breakfast, singing at night."

"I don't sing to you," she protested halfheartedly.

"Don't you?" He smiled in the darkness.

Lupe spoke in soft earnestness. "I wish I could wipe all your bitterness away."

"You do." Fito reached out and found her hand.

"Your plan is a good plan . . ." She could not say any more.

Fito was reminded of the fact that he had made a fool of himself. But knowing Lupe, she would never think that. He reached out and placed her head on his shoulder. Yes, he was discovering something wonderful in his life.

Lupe began singing softly, the timbre of her voice sensuous and deep. "El amor es suspiro . . ."

"Did you compose that song for me?"

"Yes. When I get home, I shall take my guitar and sing. Open your window and listen, like you always do."

"The one I like is the one about a raindrop on a butterfly's wing." Yes, Lupe could make him dream again. She could make him new.

"Una perla temblorosa descansaba en una flor . . ." She sang the contentment in their togetherness all the way home.

*   *   *

Miguel's mother was waiting for him. As he sidestepped mud holes he caught sight of her standing at the door.

"Where were you?" She asked, smoothing his hair away from his face. "You're all wet."

He realized his clothes were clinging to his body. He kissed his mamá on her cheek. "At Fito's meeting."

"Your papá got home before you. Everybody's sleeping."

"I'm sorry."

He began to take his wet clothes off as he walked to the bedroom he shared with two younger brothers. "Night, mamá."

As he prepared for bed he could hear one of the familiar night sounds his mother made. She was washing pinto beans to soak overnight. She was always the last one to get to bed, waiting until everyone was safe at home. When he heard the squeak of the old rocking chair, he knew she was darning. Sometimes he heard the rhythmic murmurs of prayer.

Once in bed he felt the familiar warm feet of his brothers. He reached across and pulled three-year-old Tony's thumb from his mouth. Then he lay there, eyes wide open, thinking about the journey ahead. They would cross El Hoyo and find the green valley, or maybe a map leading to the place. Papá At had talked about a map given to El Indio Tolo by Gotallama.

They had to start early, before anyone asked questions. He'd take what food he could, then meet his friends at the end of the dry wash by the large sewer pipes at the edge of the arroyo. They would go around the giant shovels where ASARCO was excavating and follow the hill a mile beyond the arroyo. This would bring them to the foot of the purple mountain. Another climb, this one a rocky one, along a path that snaked upward, a long climb to the entrance of the cave, El Indio Tolo's cave. Here they would start the real journey to the recesses of the clifflike crevices deep in the cave. A couple of hours' walk would lead them to El Hoyo, the great hole with no bottom, the forever falling. The thought was sobering. They would find a way; they had to find a way to make Fito's plan possible, to save the barrio.

Miguel listened to the fierce falling rain and imagined the god Gotallama creating clouds and storms and silver water in caves. His heart began to race. Gotallama could be in that cave. All he created in crystal and stone would be before them. Something in him ran, ran, ran like a shimmering as his tired body gave in to sleep.

*   *   *

The Red Wind plays in the desert. He plays artist; he plays architect. He plays as men play, as all living things play. The Red Wind swims in space, dipping and turning, shouting, "See? See? How eternity stretches?"

Sometimes the Red Wind says good night to Gotallama and goes on his way. He has responsibilities for he must make way for river waters. Sometimes he makes a dune. Through time he takes a free hand to create the language of winds, to shape giant sculptures of sand, changing the form of the desert surface, all varied, all mysterious, all movement at rest. Days come when he crosses the path of Gotallama again.

One day he found Gotallama making calculations of change, complicated mathematics, but Gotallama winked at the Red Wind, saying, "Enough! Let us just accept the beauty and mystery of change, a journey in the universe, a journey for all things—dunes, hills, mountains, winds, stars, suns. Shall we dance?"

The Red Wind and Gotallama danced. They were motion, up, down, twist, turn, circle, run, carry, fly, walk, so gently in the sky. In allegro the Red Wind sang as moving water vapor, shifting earth particles, as energy of light.

After all, the desert is the Red Wind's gift. Water gives life where oceans are. But in the desert, the Red Wind shapes another kind of life.

When Gotallama calculates he comes up not with amounts, but with the why of things. If all is movement and change, everything must stay on its feet. Balance is the answer, dancing is the joy.

* * *

By the time people came, the land had been shaped by the Red Wind and Gotallama. It was a mural of prairies, caves, crevices, mountains, hills, and flowing rivers.

People built and gave Smeltertown a face. The ways of men left their mark; house-shacks, a wooden church, mortared smokestacks, bulldozed caves, giant blackened buildings housing machines, and gaping holes eaten by excavations. Amidst all these were the incidental buildings of civilized men to create a given order in life.

Smeltertown was a poor town inhabited by the workers of ASARCO. At a distance stood the two propitious mountains where long ago Cabeza de Vaca had ciphered the name of El Paso del Norte. After three centuries the migration of people through these mountains had patterned small towns all along the way. Once the river had abounded with deep waters, and the flash floods common to the area had carved the surrounding landscape. Now, because of men's misuse of the river and land, the town could no longer receive the natural drainage of floods.

Forty years earlier the natural course of the river had been distorted when the state built a dam and a flood retaining wall two feet above riverbank level to keep the high waters of perennial floods from inundating Smeltertown. Ironically, the riverbed was usually dry and the retaining wall sealed. But the hasty construction north of the town brought floodwaters and mud from eroding soft mountainsides eaten by big machinery. So the main street of the town, below the construction area, received the impact of mud and water swarming and filling the streets until they came to a stop opposite the retaining wall near the dry river.

Every time after a long, hard rain the streets became mud sponges. To stop the flooding waters, the men of the barrio improvised by digging ditches along a series of sand hills.

Along with the poverty, the people suffered the constancy of sandstorms black with ash from the smelter, poisoned air, and the threat of flash floods. Not three miles away on a high plateau was the city of the affluent with its twenty-two-story concrete buildings, scattered shopping centers, and well laid-out suburbs, with parks and easy access to the freeways, a land totally alien to the people of Smeltertown, except for the few who had made it to the university. They, too, suffered alienation because they were the poor among wealthy students. To the city fathers Smeltertown was an eyesore, an arroyo sometimes flooded by heavy rain where in some mud hut an anciano lay dead from pneumonia or black lung.

* * *

When Miguel woke up it was still raining. Outside his window he saw a series of charcos with swirling water. The smell of cooking oatmeal with brown sugar and cinnamon told him his mother was already in the kitchen. He heard distant thunder as he dressed hastily, putting on his one heavy sweater. His younger brothers were fast asleep. They always slept late on Saturdays. So did his father. As he put his shoes on, he looked out at the sunless day. Four days of constant rain. The thought made him uneasy. He went into the kitchen and put his arm around his mother's shoulders. "May I have some before I go?"

His mother filled a bowl. "And where are you going on a day like this? This is a day for staying home."

He never lied to his mother, so he told her the truth. "The guys and me, we're going up to El Indio Tolo's cave."

"You crazy?"

"May I go?" He was asking permission. He also knew that his mamá would let him do what made him happy, when his papá was not around.

"You boys know what you're doing? We're going to have another flood. Look outside."

It's not a lie; it's just a new idea, he told himself as he found a reason.

"We want to see how the town looks from up there."

"¡Qué bárbaros!" His indulgent mother smiled, shaking her head.

"Please, Mamá? We'll be safe. It's dry up there. Please?"

"I'm glad your father doesn't know. He has plenty for you to do."

"Mamá, I help him every Saturday. Please, let me this time."

Mamacita hesitated but a second. "Go on. You deserve to play this Saturday. Here, let me get some food for you to take. I know you boys. You'll get hungry before long."

When he finished his breakfast, he found a sack with apples, raisins, and bean burritos by the kitchen sink. His mother, who was sorting out the ironing, looked up and smiled. "You boys be careful and don't come home too late."

Miguel kissed the top of her head. "Bye, Mamá."

He felt a little guilty not having explained why they were going to the cave. But then, she would worry and might not let him go. It was better this way. He would explain when he came back. He went out in the hard rain, stopping under a tree. He made it to the dry wash and went under a rusty skeleton of a car. There was now a constant drizzle. He saw Felipe and Sergio, soaking wet and grinning, running toward him.

For a while they watched the water rush into the wash. It was like a small river now, and the ditches on the opposite side were full.

They began their climb, plowing through mud. There was still about a mile to the cave's entrance. The path was slippery, so the boys were careful to find sure footing on large protruding rocks. It was difficult to see very far ahead for clouds were swallowing the side of the hill. They looked down right over an area eaten by the smelter's excavators. The whole site was fast becoming sliding mud, mud that had a given path right into main street.

"Jeez!" Felipe exclaimed. "It's going to flood the town."

"Maybe we should go back." Sergio's voice was uneasy.

"No. What we're doing is important."

No one doubted anymore as they trudged up the hill. Miguel called out, "Who brought matches?"

Felipe reminded him, "You told me to, remember?" He touched the bulge in the pocket of his jacket.

They had now lost sight of the excavation and had come to the side of a mountain that seemed to be all rock and sagebrush. Their clothes were dripping wet when they reached a ledge where rock crushed upon rock in chaotic clusters. Under the ledge, the boys sat shivering, huddled together, teeth chattering. Felipe reached in his jacket and brought out a small tin box with matches.

"We can start a fire."

Miguel looked around. "What with? Everything's wet."

They sat down looking dejectedly out at gray-streaked clouds. Sergio was cleaning the mud from the seat of his pants as the other boys checked their canvas bags to see if their provisions were dry. Miguel encouraged, "It's just half a mile more to the cave. Come on, we can't just sit here."

The path beyond the ledge was steep, but the rain had become a drizzle, so they climbed slowly, finding sure footing with each step. They could see the mouth of the cave at a distance. Now the walk became mud, covering their shoes and ankles. Then came the smooth, grainy surface that led to the cave. A place to build a fire.

In the cave, they stamped out the wetness, then set about to look for dry brush. They found an old wooden crate, broke it, and piled the pieces with the sagebrush. Felipe set a match to the pile, and soon the flames looked good and inviting. Around the fire, their faces glowed.

Miguel began to strip, the boys following suit. Then they laid their clothes out to dry on a scooped rock close to the fire. They sat naked, looking silently into the fire, shadows dancing on their brown bodies. They were cavemen, silently wondering about mysteries. Gotallama was a mystery, but very real in Miguel's imagination. He was part of the shadows, the fire, the rain, and the long silence. "Gotallama's here."

Felipe looked thoughtfully into the fire, but Sergio broke the mystery with a practical statement. "I'm hungry."

They reached for their satchels rummaging through raisins, apples, sausages, oranges, candy, sardines, burritos, and pecans.

"Wow," declared Sergio as he reached for a sausage. While they ate Miguel cautioned, "We don't know how long it's going to take us, and this is all the food we got. We better save some."

They ate with relish. Nothing could taste better than food eaten in a cave. No one knew how long it would take to find the green valley. Felipe pulled out some soggy tortillas. "We better not waste these."

Sergio came up with an idea. "Let's roast them, like marshmallows." The thought was exhilarating. Three naked bodies looked for sticks, found them, then impaled mushy tortillas. They gathered round the fire. Some of the tortillas were too wet, falling right into the flames; others caught on fire, exciting the boys to whoops and hollers.

"Look, vatos," Felipe showed them. "Like this."

He took a tortilla and rolled it before he stuck it right in the center, holding it high over the flame, every so often bringing the stick down close to the fire. It wasn't bad. They expressed the spontaneous joy of savages. They were drunk with the special power that touches the unknown. Sergio looked around. "You really think Gotallama's here?"

There was no doubt in Miguel. Gotallama filled the cave with what was to be. "He's here."

"Where?" The question did not deny but evoked an acceptance of the god's presence.

"In the darkness, and up there." Miguel pointed to the fingers of light coming through the top layers of rock.

The boys stared at the slivers of light from the outside world, their imaginations reaching beyond. Sergio resisted weakly. "We're Christians, we don't believe in other gods. You're going to hell, Miguel."

"Who cares?" Miguel was too full of Gotallama.

Their naked senses had raced back to a beginning where light and fire were mysteries, a beginning where senses played and wove themselves into the imagination. Their bodies, warm and rosy, squatted closer to the fire in a primal pose. The silence was full of Gotallama, for the cave echoed centuries of rock language, formations beyond understanding. They stared and stared into the fire, and when the fire dwindled, they became aware of their nakedness and in childlike embarrassment began to shove, kick, and chase one another until there was a clap of thunder, followed by lightning. Outside the cave the rain fell harder than ever, and from the opening where slender light filtered from the heavens, the rain fell in elongated rushes all the way down to the floor of the cave. The boys rushed to the entrance. Felipe pointed to the distant excavation which seemed even farther due to the angle of the climb and the height of the cave. While they put their clothes back on, Sergio observed, "Mud's sliding fast. Looks like chocolate."

The boys looked down at the excavation which was about to collapse. Miguel knew it was time. "We better get started."

El Hoyo was a two-hour walk beyond the belly of the cave, a long, winding passage to the chasm, a bottomless pit of jagged darkness. No one had ever gone beyond the chasm. They started their walk, Miguel leading until the mouth of the cave was no longer visible. The passage had become high granite. Miguel knew they were walking into a deep, deep mystery. Under his feet, soft gravel broke like sugar cubes.

Out of the dusk came Sergio's doubting voice. "What if there's no map?"

Miguel reasured again, "Papá At says it's there."

No one ever doubted Papá At. The sound of whirring winds, funneled through rocks, whistled its own mystery. Miiguel called out, "Let's stop. I'm tired."

The wind sang a strange language as the boys sat down and listened to the lighthearted whizzing melting into stone. It was not a discomforting sound. Miguel took the wind, the tunneled silence, and the dark into himself.

"Wanna Hershey?" Sergio offered, passing out candy bars to reaching hands. When they finished eating, the boys continued their way, the wind following, a solvent dissonance, the music of stone and air. The narrow passage was getting wider and the crevices, one upon the other, were much higher now. Suddenly a path appeared, broken in two with slanting, curving rocks, a silent, moving thunder of ages past. The sky peeked through in patches. The rain had stopped. The area was now spacious. Light sifted through the high shafts of the rocks. To the right was El Caracol, a long opening that had to be scaled. The snaking funnel leading up could only hold one body at a time. Once they made it through El Caracol, they would come upon El Hoyo.

It was a time to linger, to lie down and look at the sky. This was the last time to look at open sky. Before them was a hazardous task.

The dark confines of El Caracol, as each boy found sure footing leading up, was narrow and uncomfortable, yet it had little of the danger that lay ahead once they reached El Hoyo.

Miguel looking up at the sky and felt Gotallama shimmering down, dancing a certainty, the certainty of the green valley. He stood to lead the way, again, into El Caracol. The believer in pagan gods reached upward, hands tensed against the walls of the hole, small particles of rock falling on his head. He looked down to avoid the falling debris. He could feel Felipe's breathing behind him.

After a long time, the climb seemed endless. Fear jelled, and desperation became the breathing process. Miguel began to wonder and imagine, to stop the feeling of aimlessness. The green valley, the green valley, where was it? In some strange way, imagining soothed the ache of the crouched position. A soft assurance grew as he thought of finding the map to the green valley. What would it be like? Papá At had told them that Gotallama, with flame and water, in time had carved the map on a flat stone left somewhere beyond El Hoyo for El Indio Tolo to find. He was sure it was still there, waiting for them to find. Miguel had no doubts.

Finally the sinuous climb became a torture. Miguel hunched down, squirming to position himself for the weight that now fell on his back and shoulders. The three boys burrowed slowly, laboring to reach the opening, burrowed through its sharp angles and sudden zigzags which made the tunnel seem endless. All at once it branched off. Miguel knew he had to make up his mind: should he go right or left? There was no hesitation. Something or someone told him to go right. He could hear the scraping sounds of Felipe and Sergio behind him, debris raining down, enough to make their eyes smart and fill their mouths with grit. Miguel noticed the space was widening now. He drew his knees up and pushed out, stretching full length. In the distance light gleamed through. They had reached the end of the entombing catacomb. Miguel gave a final push into an open chamber. Soon after, Felipe and Sergio, spent, reeling with fatigue, hauled themselves out to open ground.

They were in a large chamber with strange rock formations, evolution crushed and heaped at Gotallama's will.

They fell to the ground in utter exhaustion. It was a time to rest, a time to sleep, before finding El Hoyo.

                              *   *   *

Mamá Chita placed a bowl of hot cereal before Lupe, asking, "You're not going out in this rain, are you?"

"Mary Ellen's waiting," replied Lupe as she sprinkled sugar and poured milk into her cereal. It was a bad day all right, but Mary Ellen would be waiting at the university library where Lupe tutored her in chemistry on Saturdays.

Mary Ellen was Mexican, but her family had made it into the gringo world, a world of material things and self-aggrandizement. Her chemistry professor had assured Lupe that she could make it too. She was up for a scholarship to a first-rate university. Upon graduating, the professor had promised, she would have many job offers from industrial labs all over the country. But Lupe had no such plans. Her ambition was to be a teacher, to teach in the barrio where she had been born. She had always felt estranged from the American mainstream. She too quickly recognized the banalities and mediocrities of greed. She had known for some time that her true worth was inside herself. It was as simple as that. She wanted to stay in the barrio and make Fito happy.

This Saturday her abuelita sat facing her, drinking her morning coffee. She watched her grandmother stir sugar into her cup with thin, blue-veined hands. How sweet, how warm, was home. The day was gray, but her heart was bright. But the rhythm of contentment was shortlived. She heard a heavy thud against the wall of the kitchen and glanced up to see horror on her abuelita's face. La anciana was pointing to the window in disbelief. Lupe moved her head, focusing her eyes on what her abuelita was looking at. The window was thickly splattered with mud, and in the leaden ooze clung the sprawled figure of a giant scorpion. The size of it was unimaginable.

What was happening outside? She quickly went to the window and looked out beyond the horror of the dead scorpion. A mud river, with dead scorpions floating on its surface, was growing along Main Street. She immediately knew what had happened. The excavated hill had collapsed, and the floodwaters had taken with them the earth and its creatures, strewn like seeds, moving to and fro, sideways and forward, wildly dancing, dead.

Out on the street a murmurous tumult grew. Countless voices cried in terror, and there was a rush of women and children spouting from doorways. Where were the men? She remembered. They were all on high ground working to stay the possibility of a flood.

She knew she had to calm her abuelita, to get her out of the house to high ground.

Main Street was on low ground. It was the main artery for the coming flood, and the last flood had carried several houses away. She turned to her grandmother and put her arm around her. Fear quivered on la anciana's lips.

Lupe comforted, "We're going to be all right. We just have to go to higher ground, like before, remember?"

The old woman held to one thought, her eyes glazed over with disbelief. "A rain of scorpions. It's the end of the world."

"No, Abuelita, no. The rain brought down the mountain. The scorpions were inside. They're dead. I know they're horrible to look at, but they're harmless."

"Harmless?" La anciana was still shaken by the thought of scorpions. Lupe felt a growing repulsion. They would have to wade to higher ground through water filled with scorpions. But she knew she had to be calm and strong for Mamá Chita's sake. La anciana closed her eyes and began to pray while Lupe stared at the dead scorpion, still clinging to the window. For a second she felt as helpless as the creature. She looked toward the door. Mud was curling in slowly at the bottom. It was pressing hard. Now was the time to leave. She took her grandmother's hand and led her to the kitchen table. "Now listen carefully, Mamá Chita, you have to climb on my back."

La anciana shook her head vehemently. "No . . . no . . ."

"You have to, Mamá Chita."

La abuelita clutched Lupe's hand but did not protest when Lupe helped her climb up on the kitchen table. "Get on my back."

The grandmother did as she was told, putting her arms around Lupe's neck. Lupe, mastering a kind of calm, whispered, "Just pray, Abuelita, pray."

The old woman was heavy on her back, but Lupe made it to the door. When she opened it, the mud rushed in, snaking, in patches. La abuelita began to cry, gasping prayers in the air. Lupe instructed, "Close your eyes and just hold tight."

Mud and scorpions filled the doorway like heavy vomit. Mamá Chita's tight hold on Lupe's neck made breathing difficult.

There was large elm at the end of the street. She had to make it to the tree—fifty yards. Lupe stepped off the curb into the street, body taut to take the impact of her grandmother's weight. Don't let her fall, please God, don't let her fall, she prayed. Water was swirling up to her thighs, scorpions sweeping round and round. In cold despair, she felt mud spattering on her face, a dead scorpion sliding down her cheek and down her shoulder; then it was wiped away by rain. Lupe continued on her way, her vision narrowed to one spot, the elm. When she reached it, she leaned her weight against it to rest.

Her walled-in mind took note only of the surge and flux of dead scorpions around her, some clinging to her wet clothing. Even breathing had become pain as she made her way down Main Street, the mud rising past her waist. Wild thoughts arose. Are we to be drowned in mud and scorpions? Was there anyone around to help? A voice rose soft within her mind. "Keep going; you'll make it." One laborious step after another, pain screeching up the sides of her body because of the weight of la abuelita.

A lap of water hit her face and left a cold, dead scorpion on her lips. A scream formed, but gagged in her throat. She tried to wash the scorpion off by raising her shoulder up against the side of her face to brush it away. It did not cling, but fell into the mud. Not a sound from the grandmother. Poor Mamá Chita, thought Lupe, she must have fainted. The body on her back seemed limp and loose.

The rain started hard again, and she thankfully raised her face to the sky. The rain rinsed it clean. I must keep going, she told herself, I must keep going . . . going. But her breath was like a knife in her throat. She tried to take one more step, but her body could go no more. Scorpions clung to her in numbers now. She no longer cared. Her knees began to buckle. Then, she felt someone lift the weight of her grandmother off her back. There were two men by her side. Lupe fell to her knees, heading into a sea of dead, shriveled scorpions. The last thing she remembered was her grandmother's whimpering.

*   *   *

Miguel awakened to sunlight warm against his face. Light sifted into the chamber through gigantic jagged boulders that formed a steeple, high over Miguel's head. He sat up and looked around the chamber. There were puddles on the ground and the rocks glistened wetly. The patch of sky that was visible showed traces of blue among the clouds.

Words came to Miguel's mind, Papá At's words. "There is a stone guard before the entrance to El Hoyo, a sentinel of Gotallama's . . ." Miguel got on his feet and began to look at every rock formation. To the left was a recess. Miguel's eyes shone with recognition.

There it was, a stone guard, stern and solitary. His first impulse when he reached it was to touch it. It had been carved by the power of Gotallama, water and fire molding it through the centuries.

He went back to his sleeping friends and shook them awake. Miguel whispered excitedly, "I found the stone guard."

Soon the three of them stood before the sentinel. It was curiously made of three huge stones. There was no outline for feet. But the center rock had two side projections that looked like arm stumps, one of them raised upward. The top stone was rounded off like a face; above it, a canopy that resembled a helmet.

The boys inspected the mute sentinel that knew centuries without end. About four hundred yards away, they found a curved mount that resembled a narrow bridge. This was it. This was the beginning of a natural ledge to the entrance of El Hoyo.

"I'm hungry." Sergio's words reminded them that they hadn't eaten for some time. They set about opening dirty, dusty knapsacks and found most of the fruit, sausages, and tortillas squashed and stale. But it was good enough for eating. Every can was saved for a later time. The food tasted delicious to the famished boys. Later, Felipe came across trickles of rain water in crevices. It quenched their thirst.

Satisfied, they formed a circle and looked at each other. The sense of bigness was somewhat overwhelming. Felipe wondered, "You think Gotallama's a giant?"

The boys laughed nervously. Then Miguel remembered Papá At's words. "Gotallama's not a person. He just is, like water and fire that go on and on and on. That's why he's a god."

Sergio scowled. "He's only an Indian god."

"He's an earth god. He lives forever."

"What else does he do?"

"He made all this." Miguel's voice was deliberate like the timeless erosion around them. Here, everywhere, the solvent action of steam, gases, waves, and water ran silently through rock, creating a history, a being in granite, a making of eternity. The stone was mute, but all around the voice of Gotallama called out "Life!" in silent, moving thunder.

"You think Gotallama will help us cross El Hoyo?" Sergio looked to Miguel, doubting. "You said he would."

"He will." Otherwise, reasoned Miguel, why are we not afraid? Why do we feel as if all this is part of it? Though the journey was hard, and they had squeezed through narrow openings, the cave was not oppressive. He had no doubt that they would make it to the other side of El Hoyo. They would find Gotallama's crystal room, the room that was proof of earth gods. The crystal room had been a home to El Indio Tolo. It was the sometime home of the Red Wind. Miguel didn't actually know they would be safe crossing the dark span of the chasm, but every pore in his body, the part of his brain where mysteries hovered, his very heart, said Gotallama would be watching out for them. "I'll go first."

The three put away their provisions, and Felipe and Sergio followed Miguel cautiously to the ledge that began the crossing of El Hoyo. Miguel could hear his heart pounding as he looked down at the fathomless darkness. He gulped, then looked ahead, telling himself, "Don't look down."

The ledge arched across El Hoyo. Through its axis was a long, diminishing view of jagged rocks whose symmetry was broken by ripples of small crevices. They must be surefooted and brave if they were to cross the yawning mouth of darkness.

They were crossing the profound abyss. Miguel's eyes remained focused ahead, never looking down into the inky gulf. He walked ever so cautiously on the ledge, putting each foot down firmly, using his hands to grab protruding rocks for safety. First he reached out to find secure support, then he took a firm step, never looking down, never looking down. Felipe and Sergio followed Miguel, doing what he did and never looking down, never looking down.

Miguel lost his sense of time. There was only darkness staring wide. Each step was a tidal ebb in time. His narrowing mind of fear could not imagine the distant end, but it had to be there, just another step. This gave new energy to his will. Similarly, the shutters of his mind closed, refusing to accept the thought of falling, though there were depths upon depths. All concentration merged into each new step. Miguel felt the ever-mastering presence of Gotallama. Finally he saw ahead of him, in a duskiness, the end of the ledge leading to safe ground. He spoke easily and clearly. "I see the other side. We're safe!" His voice resounded, swirling in the precipice.

How long had it taken? They could not tell; an hour, a year. It had seemed endless. But it was now over. They could hardly believe they had made it. Relief shone on their faces. They were now standing on a wide stone platform, yellowish-gray in color. There was sky again, but it was no longer blue. It was dark, caught in reflections of starlight.

"It's night," Sergio observed.

Felipe was listening. "Hear? It's water hitting rocks."

"Raining again," Sergio sighed.

Felipe shook his head. "No, we would be getting wet."

They all listened. It sounded like a subterranean stream.

"It's in here somewhere," Felipe figured out. "We've been gone a long time. The town probably flooded. You think anyone missed us?"

Miguel felt a pang of guilt. His mamá probably had already missed him. But this was important.

"If it's night. Let's sleep." They agreed with Sergio.

The crossing had left them exhausted. Felipe and Sergio fell a-sleep in no time, but in spite of his fatigue, Miguel was wide awake. His imagination meandered. In the semidarkness he made out an arklike boulder sprawling wide. To the left were outlines of dark, opaque masses of rock formation that fed his imagination. There was a panther tearing a victim with its claws. The shadow of thin rock was strangled by smaller, jagged adversaries. And in the shadows turned into a shimmering by a low-flung light, he saw a shape move. Was it El Indio Tolo watching. Was it Gotallama? Thoughts of El Indio Tolo and Gotallama gave him a sense of peace. He wanted to understand the rock domain of the god, to read the substance of everything around him. But what did he know? He only felt what was true. His eyes were closing with fatigue as his lips formed the words "Gods play . . ."

*   *   *

Gotallama flowed in the sea called night. He had come from a place empty of stars. Someone had called out his name. It had come from a desert cave, his name spoken by the voice of a mortal boy, a boy with woven systems from his mother's womb. Gotallama had plunged through space to find the desert mountain and the boy. It was a mountain where he and the Red Wind had played before. Gotallama sighed. If only mortals would learn to play! If only they were nimble in simplicity. But systems led to other systems that did not reach beyond. Ignorance and arrogance made mortals blind. Rapacious beings who forgot how to play. But the boy knew.

Gotallama saw the young mortal who had called his name. Gotallama knew his kingdoms, caves patterend by millions of years into light and reflections of light, chaos playing, solidifying into stones to form an order. But mortals were more precious, more miraculous. If they only knew . . .

Gotallama laughed at the coming Dawn who sang to him the song of planets. The god called out, "Where's the Red Wind? I want to play."

*   *   *

In the morning, the boys listened to the sound of flowing water, very clear in the silence. Miguel was one with earth things. Miguel remembered the vision conjured by his mind the night before. He walked to the arklike boulder, looking at all its sides. Light was streaming in from small openings, but nothing big enough to pass through. The boys began a search for a way out, feeling the curves of the rock formations on all sides. Miguel seemed to remember a small cleft behind the arklike boulder. Maybe it was big enough to squeeze through.

He tried it, his face pressed against hard rock. The rock was not loose and grainy, but smooth and slippery. Small protruding edges dug into his body. His body fit through if he held his face up. The position made it hard to breathe. After a while he noticed that the higher he went, the wider the passageway became. He was certain it led somewhere. He made his way back and told Felipe and Sergio, "It leads to somewhere."

Felipe, who was the thinnest one, decided to go first. Miguel and Sergio watched him until he was out of sight, lost in the sandwiched rocks. They heard Felipe yell, "There's light up ahead." They heard him whistling along the way. Soon the whistling became a faint swirling noise. They they heard Felipe call out again, "I found it! The crystal room!"

Eagerly Miguel made his way through the narrow opening, Sergio following. He could hardly push himself along between stone walls. Miguel began to anticipate what was to come so he wouldn't feel the discomfort of the tight squeeze. The only sound was the scraping of their bodies against the rocks. Then all of a sudden they were no longer cramped in the narrow passage. They could fit much better. Miguel noticed the shade of rocks was flesh colored.

His feet were wet. He could look down and see small, scattered remnants of water making puddles in the recesses along the edge of the passageway. As the area became wider, limestone formations began. Floods of sunlight glowed on the rocks, perpendicular joints rising, red and white, one fitted on the other. Gotallama had left his magic, the toll of solvent action of steam, gases, waves, and water from an ancient ocean running silently through rock.

There were prisms of crystal, fedlspar, and black tourmaline forming geometric adventures of light. The feldspar shone in flesh-red and blue brilliance, as if highly polished by sunlight. The light streamed down into a million colors upon stalagmites jutting from the ground, petrified in a palm of granite. The crystal room. They walked out into the chamber. In the center, in a stream of rainbow light, was a pool, limpid and silent.

Miguel could do no more than look in utter wonder. Here Gota-llama had shaped eternity in stone. The stream of water fell over pastel rocks. It hurried over a bed of ledges and widened into a pool. The bottom of the pool was clear, covered by pink and cream gravel.

Bless Papá At and his dreams! This was the room where El Indio Tolo had found the map of the green valley. Sergio and Felipe were already drinking the clear water from the pool. It was time to lie down and look up at the light miles above, the soft light of early after-noon. To Miguel, the light was Gotallama. He felt the warmth of its glow. Felipe looked at the pool and pointed to a huge red stone shaped in tiers of small columns, holding smaller skeletal arms like a web. It was sitting in the middle of the pool. "There's something on that thing."

Miguel knew what it was. "The map."

The three of them plunged into water warmed by the sun. They pulled themselves up and sat on the maze of stone. In its center were three ceramic jars, orange in color. They were man-made, so some-one had put them there. Miguel's heart jumped. El Indio Tolo! Alongside the jars was a slab with prism colors, the size of a writing tablet. Miguel reached out and handed a jar to Sergio and another to Felipe. He took the third, then the three swam back to the edge of the pool and placed the jars carefully on the ground.

Miguel swam back and reached for the slab. He held it carefully as he made it back to where the boys were waiting. The three of them examined the flat stone. Miguel looked on one side. It was ab-solutely smooth. When he turned the slab over, he saw a single circle with an Indian word in the center. Miguel made out the letters. "K . . . e . . . a . . . r."

Sergio asked, "What does it mean?"

Miguel shook his head. Felipe took it from Miguel, trying to find something else on it. "Where's the map? This isn't it. We better look around some more."

Miguel stopped them. "No. This is the map."

Felipe scowled. "A circle and an Indian word? We don't even know what it means."

Miguel was certain. "I don't either! But it is the map. I feel it. It's the map."

Felipe looked at his friend incredulously. "Well, me and Sergio, we're not so sure. We didn't come all the way for just this."

The boys looked at Miguel as if he were to blame, then set out on another search of the crystal room. Their search was fruitless, but they did find beautiful, fragile crystal that looked valuable. Felipe and Sergio filled their pockets. Miguel sat holding the smooth stone on his lap. Once in a while he would look up at the streaming light, expecting an explanation from Gotallama.

Something inside told him he had the map in his hands. There was no need to look any further; still, a question turned over in his mind. Was the green valley just one word? How could one word lead them to the green valley?

He did not want to question. Somehow all would fall into place, and now he felt at peace in the sanctuary of light, within a song of images, images cast by the reflection of crystals and sun. The light seemed to sing, "Map of hope, map of love, map of peace." Miguel fell into a remoteness. He became a part of the light, of circles, of whirls that expanded, contracted, and sprang forward. It was a communion with Gotallama; it was Gotallama singing a vastness, a shimmering of stars growing beyond understanding. Gotallama flowed, charting the human heart, winding and branching and curving and threading, unendingly. Gotallama had all the answers to all mysteries. Miguel had none. It didn't matter. The human heart and light had merged. Both had hidden forms and powers, both were the vastness of Gotallama. Gotallama flowed into him.

"K . . . E . . . A . . . R." Miguel repeated the letters slowly, carefully, over and over, as he picked up pebbles and tossed them into the pool. He watched the pebbles strike the water, ripples disturbing the colored reflections of the sun.

Sergio was beside him, holding out an ebony stone veined with gold. "You think it's valuable?"

"It's beautiful."

Felipe and Sergio, tired of looking for treasures, sat down beside Miguel. Felipe looked around, still full of awe by what he saw. "Isn't it great? You think this is the green valley?"

Miguel shook his head. "No, but we have the map."

"I wanna go home." Sergio's words heralded a finality to the search.

"How do we get out of here?" Felipe wondered.

Miguel recalled Papá At's words. "El Indio Tolo walked with Gotallama in the crystal room, until he longed for earth and sky again, so he went up the stairway . . ."

"Where is it? We ain't seen nothing like a stairway in here. We've seen everything. I didn't see any stairway." Felipe was certain, and he was not about to look.

"Maybe it's a secret passage," Sergio suggested.

"It's somewhere." Miguel's vague reply was no assurance.

An excitement grew for a search in unlikely places, behind movable rocks or in hidden crevices. It became a total concentration, finding El Indio Tolo's stairway. Then, Sergio came across it, a rectangular boulder covering which led to a narrow opening running upward. It wasn't exactly a stairway, but it was letting in a lot of light.

With some difficulty the boys rolled away the boulder. Again the opening was narrow and cryptlike, so Felipe lay in it and pushed himself through to investigate where the tendrils of light were coming from. He had found the stairway.

The boys followed him into a continuous serpentine circling up and out. The sky was visible. They could actually push themselves up to a standing position, each following the circular dimensions of the hard basalt. There were enough holes to secure a footing.

The climbing took a long time. The light slowly vanished to become dusk. A little later Sergio saw a beam streaming down in narrow ribbons upon the rocks. It was the moon, a full moon.

Miguel held the slab inside his jacket, knowing that somehow it would reveal the secret of the green valley. They were climbing toward the outside world, the world of clean sheets, hot food, and family. Arms ached as the boys made their way up slowly, carefully. Miguel's eyes fell on rat holes clustered in breaks along the flat rocks and among scraps of green growth. He glanced up to see Sergio reaching the top. Soon all three were on a circular ledge close to the opening.

Rocks covered the opening, and threads of light falling from the cold moon filtered through. The smell of a cold wind dissipating the heat of the desert filled their senses. With effort, they lifted stone after stone. The first rock was the heaviest, after that, each one rolled back with ease.

One by one they climbed over the top, out into the middle of the desert. They were out of the cave—but where? The only things visible were miles of desert and a ridge of mountains looming in shadows at a distance. The opening was on the lower slope of a hill. They scrambled down, Felipe leading the way.

*   *   *

Gotallama is always there. In warm distances or shadowy beginnings. One sun, two suns, three suns . . . all suns know of Gotallama. The names of kings all fade in time, but Gotallama is always there. All that mortals know is but a sliver of light between rocks. Gotallama is pure light, continuing life, always incalculable, a pageant, formation of species, planets, stars moving, changing, disappearing. Gottallama sings, "You! Yes, you! You are, you're not, you were, and forever shall be!"

The Red Wind whispers in Gotallama's ear. "It will take mortals forever . . ."

Gotallama loops and soars, calling out, "Not even then!"

Then he sails down to play with the Red Wind.

*   *   *

Papá At captured thoughts in la tiendita. El Amigo de Los Pobres had been spared. The whole presidio along that street had been spared, for it was an incline set at a higher level from the rest of the basin. Above it was the street where the school and the church were located, then higher, the charcoal face of the smelter. The smelter workers were salvaging supplies that had not been ruined by mud.

News in the city of the mud slide full of scorpions had brought television cameras and news reporters to the town. The rain had stopped, and heavy equipment from the smelter was banking the thick mud full of scorpions. However, the massive part of the avalanche would take a longer time to clean up. People in the midst of cleaning up the damage and putting their lives back together were interviewed; the most anguished, the most tearful, were good subjects for a crew. But in spite of scorpions and the media, families sat at their supper tables, fatigued and desolate but thankful to go on with their lives.

When a local reporter discovered that several fathers were looking for their sons but could not find them, his nose for news told him he had something better than rain and scorpions. Three boys had disappeared and were nowhere to be found. Where were they? A woman had seen the boys climbing the hill behind the excavation, the one that had given way early Saturday morning. Were they buried under the avalanche?

Already city authorities were making plans to dig into the tons of mud that had collapsed on the spot where they thought the boys had been buried alive. It would be almost an impossible feat. Pumps were to suck Main Street free of mud.

Papá At carried a large box of dried red chiles over his shoulder into the storeroom. He set it down on a low wooden table. A darting pain knifed down his left shoulder. A touch of rheumatism. He rubbed his knuckles and went into the kitchen. His eyes sought to look at his purple mountain, but the window was streaked with mud. He sniffed the air. What was it? He recognized it. Wet, rotten timbers mixing smells with rain water in adobe jars. He like the pungent smell. He put water in the coffeepot and measured out one tablespoon of coffee. It was nice, to sit and drink a cup of coffee.

He sat at the table and traced the faded squares on the oilcloth, his mind working in silent speculation. The town mustn't believe the boys were dead. The boys were alive. Something told him they were safe. Was it Gotallama? The feeling of Gotallama was strong in the room. But it was true that Gotallama was the rain. He had come to kiss the desert. Gotallama knew where the boys were. Papá At stood up with some stiffness, took a wet rag, the one he had used to clean the table, and walked to the window. In a circular motion, he removed the dry mud just enough to see. He peered out toward a mountain hued purple by haze and sun. He visualized red ocotillo blossoms after rain. Then, there were cacti veined in purple. The desert was the most beautiful place in the world after rain.

Papá At had a feeling that the boys had gone into the cave. It was Miguel's way, to try to find the green valley at a time when the town

needed a place to go. And, of course, Felipe and Sergio went wherever Miguel went. They were looking for the map. A music floated in
the room-space, Gotallama.

The coffeepot was boiling. It broke Papá At's reverie long enough
for him to serve himself a cup of coffee. He sat down again to sort
out what he must do. The whole town had picked up on the hysteria:
the boys were dead. They were surely dead. Television had announced that in all probability the boys were buried in the avalanche.
After all, they were nowhere to be found. Papá At wanted to go up
to Miguel's father and Sergio's and Felipe's and reassure them that
the boys were alive, that they had gone into the cave to look for
Gotallama. But the fathers were a sober lot, God-fearing men who
would not believe him. They were practical, hard-working men who
had little time for mysteries. No one would believe—except the children of the town.

Papá At sipped his coffee and sighed. How soon people lose
their magic, the tie to things unknown, hovering to be understood. It
would do no good to tell the children. The pain in his shoulder was
gone. He smiled and went back to look at his mountain. The purple
and pinks palpitated. It was the play of the sun; it was Gotallama.
The boys would come back. He had no doubts.

When he finished his coffee, he took a basket and filled it with
oranges, jam, and fresh bread. It was for Mrs. Gómez. He was going
to cheer her up after the storm.

* * *

Everything was dear in the little house, the shabby, sagging,
faded couch, the old hooked rugs, the stuffed chair dreary with the
dirt of years. Lupe's eyes were full of rich memories. She glanced at
her abuelita busy scrubbing the skeletal, wobbly kitchen chairs with
torn plastic covers. Mamá Chita had come home sometimes with a
bargain shining in her eyes. She had bought the used set of chairs
with a table at the Good Will, and Don Estevan, who owned a scrap-
metal yard, had hauled them to their door for free. At that time the
brittle plastic covers had been in better condition.

Mamá Chita was cleaning and scrubbing with the energy of a
younger woman. Behind her were yellow chintz curtains, newly
starched and hung, billowing in the breeze. Lupe and Mamá Chita

had swept and mopped away dried and dismembered scorpions since dawn. There still clung the musty stench of wetness.

Later in the morning, Lupe started cleaning our her plant room. It was really a screened front porch where her variety of plants had breathed themselves to giant size. Southern light, water, plant food, and loving care had fondled her plants' luxuriant existence. She also liked to sing and play guitar for them at sunset to keep them happy. And they were. It was a lovely spot where Lupe could sit and think, or read and study. Lupe had cut away dead foliage and turned the soil while Mamá Chita cleaned out the birds' cages. The canaries and las palomas sang their contentment at dawn and continued in various tonalities during the day. Limón, Mamá Chita's pet canary, was sitting on her shoulder as the grandmother lined the cages with clean newspapers. Limón liked to perch on la abuelita's shoulder, for the ritual had special meaning to the bird and the grandmother. Lupe smiled, feeling that deep, contented love for la anciana. What could be lovelier or more deeply mysterious than a woman who had lived a lifetime outside herself, growing with each struggle, and loving life as a natural extension of her world? Yes, decided Lupe, I want to be like my grandmother someday. Memories swelled . . .

Mamá Chita talked to her God. How many times had Lupe heard the one-way conversation between two loving beings? When trouble came, Mamá Chita scolded, "You think, dear Lord, you should make it so hard on women? I know my great-grandmother and my grandmother and my mother believed women were made to suffer. I do not believe it, my Lord!"

The old woman had always waved away the uncertainties of life and rolled up her sleeves to look for salvation in hard work. That was her medicine for everything. The time Grandfather had disappeared into the mountains of Chihuahua for three years, supposedly to look for gold, Mamá Chita started her own business, a little tortillería. Lupe remembered at the age of six watching Mamá Chita knead her corn flour with palms and fingers dancing poetry, shaping the thin, neat tortillas, pile after pile. She would wrap them warm in towels. The mornings would start for Lupe with the slapping of tortillas and the sound of her abuelita singing "Las Golondrinas." On Sunday mornings the old woman would buy candles, and, with a young Lupe at her side, she would go into the church before Mass and both of them would make their offering, lighting candles with a prayer on their lips. Lupe had been so sure of God then, that warm knowing that he would take care of them. Mamá Chita's eyes still gleamed with the faith, but Lupe wondered where she herself had lost the fervor of those early years. A long time ago in church Mamá Chita had looked at her and confided, "Each vela that we light for the Virgin shapes our soul."

Yes, thought Lupe, watching her grandmother with Limón, her soul is shaped in a loveliness well solidified.

The sweetest memory of all was sitting on the floor by Mamá Chita's lap in the late afternoon, listening to Mamá Chita's stories. Lupe had wondered then, How does she know so many? And they were true. It had showed in the old woman's face.

Sitting in the old stuffed chair with Nube on her lap, la abuelita would lay a gentle hand on Lupe's head, every so often stroking her hair, and then begin another tale. Her face would come to life, her voice would rise and fall in the right places, her hands would dance a pattern in the air, and Lupe would be transported to another world. Whether it was El Niño Dios or duendes, they had always been real to Lupe. And I suppose, thought Lupe, they were real to the cat, for Nube would listen with half-closed eyes and purr.

Papá Julián had died when Lupe was thirteen. After the funeral Mamá Chita had dried the girl's tears and made her a cold glass of Kool-Aid to wash down her sadness. She had confided again, "He's still around, Lupita, in me, in you, in music, in the dawn and the setting sun. He just came full circle."

Lupe had not quite understood at thirteen, but now she knew too well what Mamá Chita meant.

Again Mamá Chita had rolled up her sleeves, to go on with life, para ganar el pan de cada día.

She did what she had to do. She had confronted the outside world, spending her energies cleaning rich women's houses. Once she had taken steps away from her kind, once she was among the ominous rich, she did what she did best, wielding broom and mop, spraying Pledge on fine furniture and vacuuming fine, thick carpets, all day long. She was taking care of strangers' children who could not speak her language and laundering tons of sweaty, soiled clothes worn by people who barely acknowledged her existence.

But she, like a Tibetan monk, gave little value to material things, and late in the afternoon she would come home to the red elm tree, to the purple mountain, to plants and birds, and to neighbors. Best of all, she would come home to the child she loved so well. Lupe would be waiting to run into her open arms, to smell the sweetness of her grandmother's love, to feel the warmth of her soul, and to hear the words drop from her abuelita's lips, "Gracias, Diosito, for the richness in our lives."

*   *   *

Lupe had fixed a chicken casserole for supper, and Mamá Chita had taken some next door for Fito's supper, then gone off to rosary services. Lupe no longer went with her. More and more, God was becoming an abstraction, a belief of the mind, so Lupe's faith was no longer intact. Perhaps she had read too much. But Mamá Chita's radiance was faith. God touched her shoulder each day and that gave la abuelita her sense of well-being.

After the supper dishes were done, Lupe showered and shampooed her hair. She wrapped her hair in a towel and put on a light wrap to sit in the flower room. She must not miss the sunset. She took her guitar just in case the sunset was too beautiful. At times like that she had to free the world with music. The sun was going down. It dusted the walls of houses pink and made the elm seem as if it were on fire.

Lupe looked out into the coming night. Her eyes fell on a dog sniffing the residue of scorpions lumped up against the edge of the sidewalk. Old Estevan, hauling a dismembered chair, stopped long enough to wish her a good evening. The sun was down and the brilliant hues of the sky filled the horizon. At a distance, tattered gray clouds hung between trees.

The moon rose full and orange as dusk overwhelmed the colors of the sky. Shadows danced between light and dark in the already moon-soaked porch. The breathing of her plants anointed the air. She closed her eyes, breathing deeply. The smell of tar mixed with the scents of honeysuckle and gardenias. Raising her arms, silver in the moonlight, she stretched. It was her favorite time.

Across in Fito's house, the bedroom light was on. Sitting down on an old cane chair, she untoweled her hair. After rubbing the long silky strands vigororously with the cloth, she sat back and closed her eyes again.

After a while she looked up thoughtfully to contemplate the pink horizon sinking on the turn of the earth. Yes, she must play. She began strumming ever so softly. A song rose to her throat, an old Indian melody, "All in a circle within me, the newborn child, the fallen tree . . ." Then she stopped to weave and stitch pieces of memory.

Lupe, the child among children, following her Pied Piper, Fito, to Papá At's where he bought nieve raspada for all of them. The taste of the sweet melting against her tongue, Fito's eyes, amber, illumed by the sun, Fito's confident laugh and his gentleness with children; pieces, little pieces, making the claim of love; and she, speechless as all children are when feeling shy, grieved in a silence even then.

There was the girl, Lupe, walking home from school, lingering against the red elm, Fito's arm brushing her cheek, his palm against the tree, his eyes, alive, liquid with a tenderness, confiding to her . . . so close, so close. She could not breath for love, but she could not tell him how he kindled her with his presence for what he confided was like a knife gashing her heart. He told her of his love for Belén, his consuming passion for the lovely Belén, the only existing universe for him. Always Belén, Belén, Belén. Lupe, silent, would wonder, How many times have I measured life in tears?

She had sat at parties with cold, listless hands in her lap, forgotten. Not being asked to dance—the little girl in her cried and wanted to vanish from the earth. And when she saw Fito holding Belén's slender body in his arms, Lupe would shrivel and fade until she could bear it no more; then she would run out into the night. The music mocked; the moonlight mocked; the blending of honeysuckle and love song filtering out into the street hurt, hurt so much. She would sob her loneliness, and when there were no more tears, there was comfort from the stillness. Only the tapping of her heels would echo sharply on cold cement as she walked home alone.

Lupe shook herself free of sad memories. She began to brush her hair, a dark silk cloud around her face. Then she picked up the guitar again. Music was a kind of solace. She really believed that music was a proof of some kind of heaven.

Belén was gone. Fito felt he was not whole because of his leg. Lupe wanted to make him feel whole. He was whole and beautiful, but there was no more Belén. Love me, Fito, she commanded fiercely in her mind. I know about the love that counts because I have passed through the fire of loneliness. That has made me whole. Now, let me make you whole . . .

In dreams, Fito was hers. How many times had he surfaced in her sleep? His touch, his smile were for her then. Strange, how her desire would flow. In her sleep, there was a symphony of minds, bodies, free, in a world before the world. She saw him, smelled him, touched him, heard him, a love dance, a starkness burning. Don't wake—dream on and on and on, night out of time. Don't wake. But she would awaken, grasping in the darkness for something gone, her mind tracing reasons, ways to dream again. At times night would become the living part of her, passions breathing the full-blown fragrance of his presence, sinews, skin, heartbeat.

This night her thoughts had run into the music. She looked up at the light in Fito's room. All things were in accord, the circle within, the circle without. Love? What did she know of love? The alphabet of love was undecipherable to her. Yet, the night was interlaced with dreams. She conjured them up again and again to give substance to her day. He had kissed her the night of the meeting. He no longer kept the picture of Belén on the nightstand by his bed.

Barefooted, hair loosened, holding the thin wrap around her body, she made her way to his door.

*   *   *

Fito had fallen asleep on the sofa of the living room. He dreamt. Memories running back to Nam. Images clicked, a dull blazing orange of machine gunfire, then long furrows along a road with the dead and maimed, winding, winding until, in sleep, he felt his body tense with some occulted fear. Then a whirlwind of orange, full of faces without eyes, heads severed from bodies. A parade of debris, splinters of wood, scum, grass, blood, all swirling into the orange. His mind folded cold. The memories lurched forward like a continuous scream; then, a jolt. The nightmare had shaken him into wakefulness.

The room was already dark. With the back of his arm, he wiped the sweat from his brow. His bones still felt the cold of terror. He told himself, The past is past, the past is past . . .

He stood up and shook himself free from remembering the war, the stumbling on a mine, the explosion that rattled the life out of him, then the hospital and the amputation that took part of his soul. No, he repeated, the past is past. I'm alive, and somehow I am more whole now than when I had two legs. And he knew why: Lupe.

The future was nothing but uncertainty. There would be no more Smeltertown; the barrio would be scattered to the winds. He shrugged. He would find a place to live in one of the Mexican barrios in the city. He would set up his repair shop somewhere. The important thing was, he intended to take Lupe and Mamá Chita with him, as one family. It seemed to him that it had always been like that anyway.

Dark on dark. Human beings could do such awful things. The business of the world, they called it. He was sure he could face anything with Lupe by his side.

Now he knew she had loved him all of her life. Lupe had always been there, in the shadows, hurting. He had been such an empty-headed fool. He had to lose a leg and the woman who had once been the love of his life before he could see. But had it been love with Belén? More the lust of youth, the blind physical groping of passion. He and Belén had argued, fumed, blamed, and made love, like plunderers. He wanted to tell Lupe that the fierce burden of Belén was gone. His heart was crystal now and truth between them was possible. Anything was possible with the bright and giving energy that was Lupe.

He noticed the light in his bedroom. Lupe was probably sitting on her porch as she usually did on evenings such as this. He went to the bedroom window and saw her sitting so still. Then she begin to brush her beautiful hair. This was the woman with whom he was going to spend the rest of his life.

He looked at the bed where he and Belén had made love so many times. But that passion had always puzzled him. Now he wanted Lupe, no one else. He heard her lovely voice singing. To him, of course. She had admitted it. She had so many talents, such capacity for love. It was time for their desire.

He saw her leave her porch and walk toward his gate. All the random pieces of his life came together in some distilled contentment as he went to open the door for her.

*   *   *

Sergio's stomach was growling. "When I get home I'm going to eat all the sugar doughnuts I want and a whole quart of milk."

"Shut up!" Felipe said as he chewed on a piece of mesquite.

Miguel hugged the map, very much aware of his gnawing stomach and dry mouth. Still, it was difficult thinking of food. His lips were brittle and cracked from thirst.

Felipe and Sergio were carrying the orange jars from the cave,

and Miguel carefully held the map under his shirt. It was night. The
best time to travel in the desert. Miguel had found the North Star.
The boys had figured that the path of the cave had been toward the
north. They had to set out the opposite way to head for home.

The North Star was clear and bright among the smaller stars,
solar stones of light. The tired travelers kept away from the density of
mountain in order to look for a road, or, if they were lucky, the highway. The black mesas soared out of the east in the moonlit night.
The sagebrush still smelled green after the long rain. The freeway
would be more discernible from a distance, stretches and stretches of
endless horizon. They walked all night, every so often huddling close
to the side of a hill or near heavy brush to keep warm. By dawn it
seemed as if they had walked forever.

"We better make time before it gets too hot," Miguel suggested,
peering off into the distance. He pointed toward the west to a long
strip of smooth ground.

Felipe knew what it was. "A cattle trail."

"That means the highway's not far off," concluded Sergio.

By late morning Miguel's body ached with fatigue. The boys' lips
were cracked and burning. Felipe spied some tall mesquite clustered
by large rocks. It offered the best shade. Now they had to wait for the
unmerciful sun to give way. They fell asleep out of pure exhaustion.
But not for long. Miguel felt something run up his leg. It was a lizard
making its way up to his chest. Miguel watched it sit placidly on the
slab under his shirt. Carefully he cupped his right hand and swooped
down on the lizard. Instinct took over. "They got water. Look,
there's another one!"

Felipe caught it, refusing to accept the fact that it had liquid. Out
of hazy desperation, Miguel bit bravely into his lizard. He tasted a
slight wetness, bitter, smelling of ants. Felipe could not bit into his.
"I'd rather die of thirst." The taste of ants went up to Miguel's nose,
gagging him with acrid sharpness; but, he had wanted wetness.
"Cacti have water."

Sergio was already hitting a spiny cholla and was able to yank a
piece off, spines cutting the palm of his hand. The boys ate the pulp,
which was wet and juicy. The cholla was a godsend to the three
boys. They rested under a jojoba bush until the early afternoon, doz-
ing off in the still redness of the sun. When the sun went down, they
scrambled to their feet and walked for about an hour, when suddenly
Sergio doubled over and fell to the ground.

Miguel, still torpid and in a heat-haze, looked down at his fallen friend. "You okay?"

Sergio nodded, but he just lay there, lifeless in the sun. Miguel sat by Sergio's side, wanting to just stay and let the sun swallow him up. Still he managed to say, "Gotta get away from the sun. Can you get up?"

Sergio moved his head, his body curled up on the ground. Felipe had gone on ahead to look for the highway, doggedly walking toward what looked like water ahead. Miguel pushed Sergio's hair away from his face and wondered if he should give up like Sergio. Then he looked up to see Felipe coming back, zigzagging and waving.

"The highway! Over there!" Felipe called excitedly.

Miguel was already helping Sergio to his feet. Sergio staggered to a standing position, leaning heavily on Miguel. They walked shakily ahead, Felipe leading. Before long they saw the long scar of highway at a distance. Relief gave them new energy. They walked a little faster until they reached the long stretch of desert road. Now they would wait for a passing car, forgetting the harsh sun and their fatigue.

"It's the old highway," Felipe said without much hope. "Cars use the freeway now. No one's going to pick us up."

Hope began to wane. Sergio put his head between his legs. Miguel felt as if he were burning alive. Felipe set off walking along the road trying to spot a car. After a while Miguel shook Sergio into wakefulness. "We better go with Felipe. Walking is better."

They walked for what seemed an interminable time. All was silence. It was getting cooler now. Suddenly Felipe spotted a truck coming from the north. Again exhaustion disappeared. Felipe was already waving for the driver to stop. In a cloud of dust, the truck came to a halt. It was a vegetable truck. The driver stared at them in disbelief, three bedraggled boys in the middle of the desert. "Where you kids come from?"

Miguel pointed to a great distance away. "From a cave up there."

The man scratched his head. "Where you from?"

"Smeltertown."

A mystery began to unravel in the man's face. "You weren't buried alive . . ."

"What?" Miguel did not understand.

Felipe perked up with interest. "What do you mean, buried alive?"

"The whole town thinks you're dead," the man explained, staring at them curiously. "You went into the cave before the mud slide?"

Miguel stopped him. "Start from the beginning . . ."

The man informed them. "The town flooded. There was a mud slide. A hill fell . . ."

Sergio rasped, "A hill fell?"

"Yeah, full of scorpions."

"Anybody hurt?" Miguel's voice was full of concern.

"You three were supposed to have been killed in the mud slide. I passed by there yesterday and saw the whole thing. You boys are supposed to be dead."

Thirst prompted Miguel. "You have anything to drink?"

"Jug on the front seat."

Sergio opened the side door without asking and found the jug with water. He drank and passed it on to Miguel. The water was the most delicious Miguel had ever tasted. He passed the jug to Felipe who drank the last of it. The man grinned. "Now you had my water, you want something to eat? Jump in and help yourself."

The back of the truck was covered with baskets of vegetables, mostly turnips and potatoes. The boys helped themselves while the driver, still incredulous, offered, "I guess I'll take you home. Imagine, I'm bringing in the dead. Ha!"

They were soon on the way home. Miguel called out, "How far to Smeltertown?"

"It's twelve miles to the state line."

"We're not in Texas?" Felipe found it hard to believe.

"New Mexico."

The boys were silent after that. Miguel was feeling guilt. Sergio warned ominously, "We're going to get it."

Felipe and Miguel looked at each other, then stared out at the swirls of dust on the road. Miguel touched the slab under his shirt. "We got the map. It was worth it, the whole thing."

Miguel's memory swelled with thoughts of the crystal room and the miracles of nature inside mountains. Felipe also agreed. "I'd do it again. It was something special."

The truck rattled on southward with the three boys sitting on baskets full of turnips and potatoes.

*   *   *

"You remember your Padre Nuestro?" Fito asked jokingly as they made their way down the hill path leading to the church. Papá At smiled and looked about him at another day. He felt the warmth of the sun and the piercing blue of the sky. The words of the Padre Nuestro came to mind. Santificado sea tu nombre—the face of the earth. Dame el pan de cada día—the face of men. Maybe that was the big problem. Mexicans in Smeltertown asked for little of men and of God—el pan de cada día. Papá At breathed deeply, thinking, A time had been when all men had asked for just that—el pan de cada día. Now it was a sin, a disaster, a crime against mankind, to ask for little. His people who had roamed the hills so long ago asked for little —food, shelter, and the force to multiply. It was the first place of man in nature . . .

"What are you thinking?" Fito always respected Papá At's silences, for they went deep to find some truth. Papá At looked out toward the ASARCO plant, concluding, "Men ask for too much these days."

"Is that wrong?"

"Too much and too little are each bad."

They were circling Main Street at a higher level on their way to the special mass. The pumps and the giant shovels operated by city people had worked for three days cleaning up Main Street. They filled an old arroyo with a sea of mud and dead scorpions. Fito and Papá At walked leisurely, enjoying the greenness left by the rain. Main Street looked empty; the buildings were like giant clusters of mud frozen in time and space. The pumps and shovels lay silent like sleeping prehistoric animals. They would dig another day for the bodies of the boys.

"You don't think they're dead, do you?" Fito glanced at Papá At from the corner of his eye.

"No. They're not dead." Papá At said it so firmly and with such conviction that Fito could not help but believe.

Papá At pointed to a small mount above the path. It was a conspicuous show of life. Thorn plants and brittle bushes, bearing live roots, flourished. Papá At made his way up to a grassy area and sat down. Fito followed with some effort, for it was a task managing the climb on crutches. Papá At was absorbing a single creamy blossom on a saguaro. Such beauty was the true food of being. Papá At asked, "How's Lupe?"

"Happy. We're getting married."

Papá At nodded his approval. "She is what you need."

"I know. The anger is gone; at least, the wrong kind of anger. If I can't change things, I have to make the best with what I have."

Papá At smiled. "That's not asking for too much or too little."

Fito continued, "We found a house yesterday in east El Paso. It's green there. Valverde."

Papá At looked intently at Fito. "Green valley. It means green valley."

Fito laughed. "It's not your green valley. It's not Gotallama's green valley."

Papá At was silent. Then he got up, moving toward a cluster of cacti and green sagebrush that glinted in the sun.

"Where are you going?" Fito asked.

"You wait. I'll bring you something special."

Papá At knew exactly where to look, for it had become a ritual for him. After a heavy rain, in autumn and in spring, one would bloom, only one, always in the same ground. There it was! A mariposa lily, just one. He pulled it from the dark, moist soil and made his way back to Fito. He offered it to his friend, who recognized it. "A mariposa. They last about a day. They're good luck."

Papá At watched Fito handle it ever so gently. Fito asked, "For the Virgin Mary in church?"

"No. Give it to Lupe."

Fito's face lighted up. "You had to think of it. Look how beautiful and rare it is."

Papá At's eyes twinkled. "Just like Lupe."

The sound of the church bell reminded them it was time to go. They made their way down to Main Street and headed for El Sagrado Corazón de Jesús. Papá At never went to church anymore. Like every generation in Smeltertown, he had been part of the church as a child. It had been the Great Security. Then, one day, the Great Security was no longer the church but the mountains, wind, and rain. The land whispered its secrets to him and people shook their heads. He had reverted to pagan beliefs. But he was greatly loved, so people overlooked what they considered his failing.

Faith had an undisputed foundation for the other people in the town. They accepted the kind authority of Father Santiago. Heaven and hell existed, in white and black. Their God had the passions of a man, and they had been created in his image. That thought was immediate in Papá At's mind. Maybe, maybe, he wondered, that was the beginning of asking for too much. That had been the beginning of a lost journey. The church bell tolled again.

The church was already full. Papá At and Fito sat in a back pew. Papá At looked at the proud face of an old world, all inspiration leading to heaven. Funny! The plaster saints stood in humanly poses with expressions of inert rapture, grief, and wonder, their eyes looking only to heaven. These days, the thought that all reward was in heaven made Papá At uncomfortable and sad. He knew better. The reward of life was in the living of it. But all these people wanted more; not knowing why, they wanted more.

The people came to church, some men with liquor on their breath, some with stomachaches, lovers holding hands, children fidgeting, and the women always with the perpetual hope wrapped in suffering and tears, wanting more. They came, not realizing that it was they who brought God into the church.

The mothers of the lost boys were sitting together as if gathering comfort. They wore the black of mourning. The mass began.

All of them must be reminded of the Sacrifice. Why, wondered Papá At, wasn't it natural for humans to sin? Sin was no more than blind groping. All living creatures did that, in their search for light. There was no such thing as sin, only the littleness of human beings, a littleness reflected grandly in the cycle of creation. Jesus himself had journeyed away from temples and priests to find and live among people who did not ask for too much.

The dance of prayer began: standing, kneeling, sitting, the soft prayers blown through teeth. Father Santiago faced the altar calling upon the heart of man to repeat his unworthiness. Papá At felt a sorrow. Would they ever understand that human beings were worthy? If only they learned not to ask for too little or too much! He bowed his head, but not in contrition. He bowed it with the weight of sadness.

"Kyrie Eleison." Yes, that was like the greenness of the earth; it always came around. The bounty of grace and nourishment.

Father Santiago read an epistle, then a gospel. After that the whole congregation, as one, recited the Creed. Papá At was silent. He simply did not remember. Father Santiago was offering the Divine Gift of Body and Blood, Holy! Holy! Holy!

From the Sanctus to the Pater Noster, the experience was swift and ephemeral, like the life of the mariposa lily.

> Through Him
> And with Him
> And in Him

Papá At glanced up to see Gotallama streaming down through stained glass windows. People were warm and alive: the earth was warm and alive.

> Through Him
> And with Him
> And in Him

Things as they are. Take the scorpions, for instance. They were a piece of life, ugly, awkward creatures, vile to the touch, looking ominously fatal. Still, an accident in evolution, a deliberate accident of chance, for chance was the great order human beings still had to learn and understand. What had brought scorpions into existence? An explosive disturbance of chemicals? Of organic combinations? A touch of the sun and the season of water had brought them into existence. No different than human beings. Scorpions dig deep, to turn the soil, to give it breath, perhaps offering a chance to something like the mariposa lily. All parts of a whole.

In Smeltertown a sea of dead scorpions were something else now. They were withered bits of black, dismembered and lost in dried mud. A new peace for them, a new change . . .

*   *   *

"Scorpions?" Miguel's voice was incredulous. The driver had parked the car near the slope where Papá At had found the mariposa lily. It was the edge of Main Street. There were warning signs posted by the city department. To the right was the fallen hill, a huge bleak lump that looked like a sleeping dinosaur. The truck driver informed the boys, "That's where you're supposed to be buried."

All eyes were on the fallen hill. Miguel remembered the morning they had seen the beginning of the mud slide. He felt a pang of guilt. His mother, his father thought him dead. How had he done this to them? He saw the same thought on Felipe's and Sergio's faces. The church bell tolled.

It's not a day for death, thought Miguel looking at a sky without a single cloud. The air was lucent, like glass, but the earth was fast drying into cracking creases. The town seemed empty.

Sergio asked, "Where's everybody?"

The driver pointed toward the church. "Over there. They're having a mass for you boys. I heard it on the radio."

The boys looked at each other uncomfortably. Miguel decided, "We better go there."

The boys hurried toward the church, followed by the truck driver. Felipe tried to sound hopeful. "Nah, it's not a funeral mass. They haven't dug us up yet."

When they reached the church, Miguel hugged the slab under his shirt. The priest was giving communion. Miguel and the others waited until it was over, then Miguel swallowed hard and led the way into the church. As they made their way down the aisle, Miguel could hear whispers of surprise. The whispers mounted to a large hum until Sergio's mother stood and opened her arms. "¡Hijo mío!"

Sergio ran into his mother's arms and both began to cry unashamedly. The men in the congregation looked stern and unforgiving, eyeing the boys for some explanation. Father Santiago looked from one bedraggled boy to the other. Miguel ran to his mamacita who put her arms around him, squeezing as if to never let go. He looked up to see Felipe trying to wipe his mother's tears away.

Before their fathers reached them, the boys made it to the front of the church. They were a strange sight, dirty and unkempt. They were both a deliverance from God and an intrusion upon God. The people, faces full of astonishment and puzzlement, waited in silence for them to explain.

Miguel felt ashamed for the worry they had caused and embarrassed because it was difficult to explain a dream to practical people.

But he did began, and when he spoke Sergio and Felipe stood tall and firm on some strange truth. "We're sorry we gave you a hard time. Is this mass for us?"

The congregation only waited for his explanation. Miguel cleared his throat. "We went to El Indio Tolo's cave to look for the map of the green valley, so we could give it to all of you. When they make us go, leave Smeltertown, we would have a place to be together. It's important to stay together . . . " He swallowed, then announced, "We found the map."

Miguel took the flat stone from inside his shirt and held it up for everybody to see. There was a growing murmuring of disbelief. Miguel's voice was an excitement now. "We went beyond El Hoyo and found the crystal room made by Gotallama. And there we found the map, Gotallama's map. Maybe El Indio Tolo wrote what's on it. There's one word, but we don't know what it means . . .!"

The boys talked about a pagan god in the midst of a Christian congregation. They had brought the pagan god into the church. But to the boys, there were many ways of reconciling gods. Miguel continued, "There's only one word written here. Papá At will know what it means."

The mass had ended. The boys talked of Gotallama as Indians used to talk of communion with the earth. Gotallama was real to the boys but not to the people, not anymore. The harsh toil that consumed their lives had closed their hearts to old beliefs. Their faith now belonged to a suffering God, not to free gods that played.

*   *   *

The Red Wind watched the rain boil away. The Red Wind asked Gotallama, "Is there a green valley?" Gotallama laughed and echoed, "Is there a green valley?"

Gotallama circled a mountain, a purple mountain. The Red Wind fell into the arms of an orange sky.

Gotallama and the Red Wind played and sang, the ripples of their voices calling, "Hey, you! Yes, you! You were, you are, you shall be—for ever and ever!"

*   *   *

Unbelievers, the people of the town were unbelievers. Everywhere the boys went, they were scolded soundly for being irresponsible, for believing in the impossible. But people would sigh and shrug. "They're just boys. What do they know?"

The boys' parents did not punish them, for after all, their boys had been given back to them by some miracle. Prayers had gone up to heaven. The boys were not under the fallen hill.

Most of the people did not believe in the nonsense of a green valley. Yet, somewhere deep, deep in ancient instincts, something was felt, a tremor of their own earth, their own organic being.

The whole town had been scrubbing for weeks. Some had invested in fresh paint although they knew that soon they would have to leave Smeltertown for all time. Still, all things were, life went on, day by day.

Miguel, Felipe, and Sergio were varnishing tables at Pepe's Bar. Champurrado was supervising the job. "Keep the brush wet—a little more on the left. Is there really a crystal room?" he asked, his mind on the wonder in the world.

"Yes," said Felipe, eyeing with pride the table he had just finished painting. "You wouldn't believe how beautiful it was. Stones like jewels, the water clear like crystal."

"¡Hijo!" Champurrado exclaimed. "Why didn't you invite me?"

"You're too old," Sergio said, dipping his brush in varnish.

Champurrado's thoughts were still with the boys' adventure. "You sure that's the map? In Roman letters? Gotallama can't write."

"Papá At thinks El Indio Tolo wrote the word. He learned the white man's language in a mission school," Miguel explained, cleaning his hands with a rag. He overheard Manolo, the salesman, talking to a stranger at the bar. "The town could make some money. Put up a sign by the highway in big letters. A rain of scorpions in Smeltertown."

The stranger shook his head. "Who wants to see dead scorpions? And anyway, it didn't really rain scorpions."

Manolo, always looking for gimmicks, visualized an amusement park, all kinds of momentos to sell. You could make people believe anything, buy anything. "When the people go, when the whole town is evacuated, imagine—a ghost town, the town of scorpions, with a restaurant. You know, sidetrack tourists going across the border to Mexico . . ."

Miguel never liked to hear Manolo's scams. He motioned to Felipe and Sergio, letting them know it was time to go. They were going to Papá At's. While he waited for Felipe and Sergio to wash their hands, Miguel suggested to Champurrado, "Wanna go with us?"

"Where to?"

"Papá AT's. He's going to explain the map."

Champurrado thought about it, then looked around the bar. "I better not. The place will be full soon and Pepe needs help."

The boys were silent on their way to Papá At's. Miguel knew how his friends felt. Their adventure would be put away, and nobody really cared about the map except Papá At. Miguel remembered the excitement in the old man's eyes when he had handled the map.

When they got to the store, it was full of children and a few ancianos who had come to listen. To a few, the story of pagan gods was still a truth. Papá At greeted the boys with a smile. He had been sifting flour. He wiped his hands on his apron and took the map from under the counter.

All gathered around to listen as he sat on a stool and fingered the word on the slab, a mystery glistening in his eyes. Miguel felt the same mystery running in his veins.

"What does it mean, Papá At?"

"K . . . E . . . A . . . R. It's an Indian word."

"What does it mean?" Miguel's excitement caught in his throat. All ears were listening.

Papá At's voice was almost holy. "It means 'you.' "

Everyone looked at one another in disappointment. But Miguel knew there was more. He looked at Papá At, his eyes bright, eager.

Papá At smiled reassuringly. "It is wisdom beyond years."

Miguel began excitedly, "A code—a symbol?"

Papá At had placed all the things they had brought back from the cave on a table for everyone to see, the orange jars, small mounts of lovely crystals and stones. They were not valuable moneywise, but la gente coming into the store would wonder at the beauty made by light and time. The water in the cave created a language of forces. Maybe they would feel the shape of beauty inside themselves, centuries discovered inside the heart.

Papá At went to the table and held up one of the stones. "This was water long ago. Light made it stone."

Miguel defined it. "Gotallama." Papá At handed the stone to Felipe to pass around. Feeling it was part of the mystery. When it was in Miguel's hand he looked up at Papá At, asking, almost demanding, "The word, Papá At, what does it say?"

"A fire," explained Papá At.

The children chorused, "The Stone?"

Miguel echoed, "The Word?"

"Both." It was said without finality.

Light, water, stone, fire, people, a composition. Papá At continued, "What made the crystals made you."

"That's no explanation." Felipe scowled with disappointment. Then, the affirmation from Papá At. "We are the green valley." Miguel understood now. "I am the green valley."

His voice was so solemn everybody laughed. Papá At continued, "When El Indio Tolo found the cave, he had done many things in his life, bad and good. But always he remembered the part he played in the universe. It was a message in his blood. In the cave, he left the world behind and found a simple clarity called peace. He had journeyed, looking for a place to belong, a place of peace. He found it inside himself. He was the green valley."

Miguel had always believed they had found the map. Papá At was right, with the wisdom beyond years to feel whole, to be a part of the earth, to believe in mysteries—for human beings could not know everything—to understand that every breathing being was a miracle, a green valley.

It was all good and clear to Miguel.

*   *   *

A rain of scorpions was a clumsy thing. It was a humor, a play of change. The rain of scorpions had been to some an extravaganza, to some a horror, to some an omen, to some a lie. And there were many who knew nothing of a rain of scorpions. One thing was sure: gods play in full circle. The Red Wind and Gotallama, sitting on the purple mountain, looked down at the boys who had gone to a cave to find a part of themselves. There would be time to share the green valley in journeys to come.

Bibliography of Works By and About Estela Portillo Trambley

Patricia Hopkins

This bibliography includes print materials by and about Estela Portillo Trambley. Materials are subdivided by genre. Items in Sections A and B are alphabetized by title. Items in Sections C, D, and E are alphabetized by author when the author's name is available; otherwise, they are alphabetized by title.

I. Works by Portillo Trambley

A. Books

1. *Rain of Scorpions and Other Writings.* Berkeley: Tonatiuh International, 1975.
2. *Sor Juana and Other Plays.* Ypsilanti, MI: Bilingual Press/Editorial Bilingüe, 1983.

Besides the title play, this collection includes *Puente Negro, Autumn Gold,* and *Blacklight.*

3. *Trini.* Binghamton, NY: Bilingual Press/Editorial Bilingüe, 1986.

B. Short Fiction, Plays, Essays, and Poems

4. "After Hierarchy." *El Grito* 7.1 (Sept. 1973): 84.
5. "The Apple Trees." *El Grito* 5.3 (Spring 1972): 42-54.
6. "The Burning." *The Third Woman: Minority Women Writers of the United States.* Ed. Dexter Fisher. Boston: Houghton Mifflin, 1980. 349-355.
7. *The Day of the Swallows. El Grito* 4.3 (Spring 1971): 4-47.

Rpt. in *El Espejo—The Mirror, Selected Chicano Literature.* Eds. Octavio Ignacio Romano-V. and Herminio Ríos-C. Berkeley: Quinto Sol Publications, 1972. 149-193.

Rpt. in *We Are Chicanos: An Anthology of Mexican-American Literature.* Ed. Philip D. Ortego. New York: Washington Square Press, 1973. 224-271.

Rpt. in *Contemporary Chicano Theatre.* Ed. Roberto Garza. Notre Dame, IN: University of Notre Dame Press, 1976. 205-245.

8. Excerpt from *Morality Play. Chicanas en la literatura y el arte.* Special issue of *El Grito* 7.1 (Sept. 1973): 7-21.
9. "If It Weren't for the Honeysuckle." *Grito del Sol* 1.2 (April-June 1976): 79-91. [Rpt. from *Rain of Scorpions and Other Writings.*]
10. Introduction to *Chicanas en la literatura y el arte.* Special issue of *El Grito* 7.1 (Sept. 1973): 5-6.

11. "La Jonfontayn." *A Decade of Hispanic Literature: An Anniversary Antholo-gy.* Special issue of *Revista Chicano-Riqueña* 10.1-2 (invierno-primavera 1982): 241-250.

12. "The Paris Gown." *El Grito* 6.4 (Summer 1973): 9-19.

13. "Pay the Criers." *The Third Woman: Minority Women Writers of the United States.* Ed. Dexter Fisher. Boston: Houghton Mifflin, 1980. 361-376. [Rpt. from *Rain of Scorpions and Other Writings.*]

Also in *The Ethnic American Woman: Problems, Protests, Lifestyles.* Ed. Edith Blicksilver. Dubuque, Iowa: Kendall Hunt, 1978 (expanded). 380-393. [Rpt. from *Rain of Scorpions and Other Writings.*]

14. "Recast." *Grito del sol* 1.1 (Jan.-March 1976): 63-72. [Rpt. from *Rain of Scorpions and Other Writings.*]

15. *Sun Images. Nuevos Pasos: Chicano and Puerto Rican Drama* Eds. Nicolás Kanellos and Jorge A. Huerta. Special issue of *Revista Chicano-Riqueña* 7.1 (invierno 1979): 19-42.

II. Works About Portillo Trambley

C. Critical and Biographical Articles and Papers

16. Castellano, Olivia. "Of Clarity and the Moon—A Study of Two Women in Re-bellion." *De Colores: Journal of Emerging Raza Philosophies* 3.3 (1977): 25-30.

17. Castro, Ginette. "Memorie ethnique et religion dans *Rain of Scorpions.*" *Le Facteur religieux en Amerique du Nord.* Eds. Jean Beranger, Pierre Guillaume. Religion et Memorie ethnique au Canada et aux Etats-Unis, 7. Talence: Centre de Recherches Amér. Anglophone, Maison des Sciences de l'Homme d'Aquitaine, 1986. 307-324.

18. "The Chicana in Chicano Literature." *Chicano Literature: A Reference Guide.* Eds. Julio A. Martínez and Francisco A. Lomelí. Westport, CT: The Greenwood Press, 1985. 97-107.

19. Dewey, Janice. "Doña Josefa: Bloodpulse of Transition and Change." *Breaking Boundaries: Latina Writings and Critical Readings.* Eds. Asunción Horno-Delgado, Eliana Ortega, Nina M. Scott, Nancy Saporta Sternbach. Amherst: University of Massachusetts Press, 1989.

20. Fisher, Jerilyn Beth. "From Under the Yoke of Race and Sex: Black and Chicano Women's Fiction of the Seventies." *Minority Voices* 2.2 (Fall 1978): 1-12.

21. Garza, Roberto. Introduction to *The Day of the Swallows. Contemporary Chicano Theatre.* Ed. Roberto Garza. Notre Dame, IN: U. of Notre Dame Press, 1976. 205-206.

22. González, Laverne. "Portillo Trambley, Estela." *Chicano Literature: A Reference Guide.* Eds. Julio A. Martínez and Francisco A. Lomelí. Westport, CT: Greenwood Press, 1985. 316-322.

23. Herms, Dieter. "Chicano and Nuyorican Literature—Elements of a Democratic and Socialist Culture in the U.S. of A.?" *European Perspectives on Hispanic Literature of the United States.* Ed. Geneviève Fabre. Houston, TX: Arte Público Press, 1988. 118-129.

24. Herrera-Sobek, María. "La unidad del hombre y el cosmos: Reafirmación del

proceso vital en Estela Portillo Trambley." *La Palabra* 4/5.1-2 (primavera-otoño 1982/3): 127-141.

25. _____. "The Politics of Rape: Sexual Transgression in Chicana Fiction." *Chicana Creativity and Criticism: Charting New Frontiers in American Literature*. Eds. María Herrera-Sobek and Helena María Viramontes. Special issue of *The Americas Review* 15.3-4 (Fall-Winter 1987): 171-181.

26. Huerta, Jorge A. "Where Are Our Chicano Playwrights?" *Revista Chicano-Riqueña* 3.4 (otoño 1975): 32-42.

27. _____, and Nicolás Kanellos. Introduction to *Sun Images*. *Revista Chicano-Riqueña* 7.1 (invierno 1979): 19-20.

28. [Kernahan, Galal.] "Una Isla de Pobreza." *Tiempo/Hispano-americano* 74.1922 (5 marzo 1979): 14-15.

29. Lattin, Patricia Hopkins and Vernon E. "Power and Freedom in the Stories of Estela Portillo Trambley." *Critique* 21.1 (Fall 1979): 93-101.

Revised from paper presented at the Midwest Modern Language Association, Minneapolis, Nov. 1978.

30. Lattin, Vernon E. "The City in Contemporary Chicano Fiction." *Studies in American Fiction* 6.1 (Spring 1978): 93-100.

31. Lewis, Marvin. Introduction to "The Paris Gown." *El Grito* 6.4 (Summer 1973): 9.

32. Lomelí, Francisco A. "Chicana Novelists in the Process of Creating Fictive Voices." *Beyond Stereotypes: The Critical Analysis of Chicana Literature*. Ed. María Herrera-Sobek. Binghamton, NY: Bilingual Press/Editorial Bilingüe, 1985. 29-46.

33. Martínez, Eliud. "Personal Vision in the Short Stories of Estela Portillo Trambley." *Beyond Stereotypes: The Critical Analysis of Chicana Literature*. Ed. María Herrera-Sobek. Binghamton, NY: Bilingual Press/Editorial Bilingüe, 1985. 71-90.

34. Ordóñez, Elizabeth J. "Narrative Texts by Ethnic Women: Rereading the Past, Reshaping the Future." *MELUS* 9.3 (Winter 1982): 19-28.

35. Parotti, Phillip. "Nature and Symbol in Estela Portillo's 'The Paris Gown.' " *Studies in Short Fiction* 24.4 (Fall 1987): 417-424.

36. "Portillo Portrays Culture." *Para la Gente* (Austin, Texas) 1.6 (Dec. 1977-Jan. 1978): 7.

37. Ramírez, Arthur. "Estela Portillo: The Dialectic of Oppression and Liberation." *Revista Chicano-Riqueña* 8.3 (verano 1980), 106-114.

38. Rebolledo, Tey Diana. "Abuelitas: Mythology and Integration in Chicana Literature." *Woman of Her Word: Hispanic Women Write*. Ed. Evangelina Vigil. Special issue of *Revista Chicano-Riqueña* 11.3-4 (1983): 148-158.

39. _____. "Tradition and Mythology: Signatures of Landscape in Chicana Literature." *The Desert is No Lady*. Eds. Vera Norwood and Janice Monk. New Haven: Yale Univ. Press, 1987. 96-124.

40. _____. "Walking the Thin Line: Humor in Chicana Literature." *Beyond Stereotypes: The Critical Analysis of Chicana Literature*. Ed. María Herrera-Sobek. Binghamton, NY: Bilingual Press/Editorial Bilingüe, 1985. 91-107.

41. Rocard, Marcienne. "The Chicana: A Marginal Woman." *European Perspectives on Hispanic Literature of the United States*. Ed. Geneviève Fabre. Houston: Arte Público Press, 1988. 130-139.

42. _____. "The Remembering Voice in Chicana Literature." *The Americas* 14.2 (Summer 1986): 150-159.

43. Rodríguez, Alfonso. "Tragic Vision in Estela Portillo's *The Day of the Swallows.*" *De Colores: Journal of Chicano Expression and Thought* 5.1-2 (1980): 152-158.
Revised from paper presented at the Midwest Modern Language Association, Minneapolis, Nov. 1978.

44. Salazar-Parr, Carmen. "Estela Portillo-Trambley: Chicano Liberationist." Paper presented at Philological Association of the Pacific Coast, Seattle, Nov. 1978.

45. _____. "*La Chicana* in Literature." *Chicano Studies: A Multidisciplinary Approach.* Eds. Eugene E. García, Francisco A. Lomelí, and Isidro D. Ortiz. New York: Teachers College Press, 1984. 120-134.

46. _____. "Surrealism in the Work of Estela Portillo." *MELUS* 7.4 (Winter 1980), 85-92.

47. _____, and Genevieve M. Ramírez. "The Female Hero in Chicano Literature." *Beyond Stereotypes: The Critical Analysis of Chicana Literature.* Ed. María Herrera-Sobek. Binghamton, NY: Bilingual Press/Editorial Bilingüe, 1985. 47-60.

48. Salinas, Judy. "The Image of Woman in Chicano Literature." *Revista Chicano-Riqueña* 4.4 (otoño 1976): 139-148.
Revised as "The Role of Women in Chicano Literature." *The Identification and Analysis of Chicano Literature.* Ed. Francisco Jiménez. New York: Bilingual Press/Editorial Bilingüe, 1979. 191-240.

49. Schiavone, Sister James David. "Distinct Voices in the Chicano Short Story: Anaya's Outreach, Portillo Trambley's Outcry, Rosaura Sánchez's Outrage." *The Americas* 16.2 (Summer 1988): 68-81.

50. Tatum, Charles M. *Chicano Literature.* Twayne's United States Authors Ser. 433. Ed. Warren French. Boston: Twayne, 1982. 75-76, 91, 97-100.

51. "Trambley, Estela Portillo." *Contemporary Authors.* Ed. Frances Carol Locher. Detroit: Gale Research, 1979. 77-80: 552-553.

52. Vallejos, Tomás. "Estela Portillo Trambley's Fictive Search for Paradise." *Frontiers: A Journal of Women's Studies* 5.2 (Summer 1980): 54-58.
Rpt. in *Contemporary Chicano Fiction: A Critical Survey.* Ed. Vernon E. Lattin. Binghamton: Bilingual Press/Editorial Bilingüe, 1986. 269-277.

53. Vargas, Margarita. "Lo apolíneo y lo dionisíaco hacia una semiótica en *Sor Juana* y *The Day of the Swallows* de Estela Portillo Trambley." *Gestos: Teoría y Práctica del Teatro Hispánico* 5.9 (abril 1990): 91-98.

D. Dissertations

54. Fisher, Jerilyn Beth. "The Minority Woman's Voice: A Cultural Study of Black and Chicana Fiction." *DAI* 39.3A (1978): 1565.

55. Vallejos, Thomas. "Mestizaje: The Transformations of Ancient Indian Religious Thought in Contemporary Chicano Fiction." *DAI* 41.4A (1980): 1602.

E. Reviews, Interviews, and Bibliographic Annotations

56. Bader, Eleanor J. "Alive and Well and Living en la Frontera." [Review of *Trini.*] *Belles Lettres* 3 (May 1988): 13.

57. Bruce-Novoa, [Juan]. "Estela Portillo." *Chicano Authors: Inquiry by Interview.* Austin: University of Texas Press, 1980. 163-181.

58. Eger, Ernestina. *A Bibliography of Criticism of Contemporary Chicano Literature.* Berkeley: University of California, 1982. 50-51.

59. Gutiérrez-Jamail, Margo. *"Trini." Books of the Southwest* 362 (Jan. 1988): 17.

60. Huerta, Jorge A. "From Quetzalcoatl to Honest Sancho: A Review Article of *Contemporary Chicano Theatre." Revista Chicano-Riqueña* 5.3 (verano 1977): 32-49.

61. _____. Review of *Day of the Swallows. TENAZ Talks Teatro* (Cal. State Univ., L.A.) 2.2 (Spring 1979): 6.

62. Kempf, Andrea Caron. Review of *Rain of Scorpions and Other Writings. Library Journal* 102.1 (1 Jan. 1977): 128.

63. Kimble, Ed. "Original Play Set in Barrio." *El Paso Times* 25 May 1977.

64. [Laird, Linda.] Review of *Rain of Scorpions and Other Writings. Books of the Southwest* 225 (Aug. 1977): 6.

65. Lattin, Vernon. Review of *Rain of Scorpions and Other Writings. NAIES Newsletter* 2.2 (Jan. 1977): 20-22.

66. Lewis, Marvin A. Review of *Rain of Scorpions and Other Writings. Revista Chicano-Riqueña* 5.3 (verano 1977): 51-53.

67. Lomelí, Francisco A. and Donald W. Urioste. *Chicano Perspectives in Literature: A Critical and Annotated Bibliography.* Albuquerque, NM: Pajarito Publications, 1976. 54-55.

68. Mael, Phyllis. Review of *Day of the Swallows. Frontiers: A Journal of Women Studies* 5.2 (Summer 1980): 54-58.

69. "Portillo Trambley, Estela." *Chicano Scholars and Writers: A Bio-bibliographical Directory.* Ed. Julio A. Martínez. Metuchen, NJ: The Scarecrow Press, 1979. 389.

70. Ramírez, Elizabeth C. Review of *Sor Juana and Other Plays. Latin American Theatre Review* 17.2 (Spring 1984): 103-104.

71. "Rayaprofile." *RAYAS* 5 (Sept.-Oct. 1978): 3.

72. Review of *Rain of Scorpions and Other Writings. Choice* 13.12 (Feb. 1977): 1600.

73. Valdés, Ricardo. Review of *Rain of Scorpions and Other Writings* by Estela Portillo Trambley and *Below the Summit* by José Torres-Metzgar. *Latin American Literary Review* 5.10 (Spring-Summer 1977): 156-162.

74. Vowell, Faye Nell. "A *MELUS* Interview: Estela Portillo Trambley." *MELUS* 9.4 (Winter II 1982): 59-66.